Teatime Trouble

A SHELL ISLE MYSTERY

Tonya Penrose

This is a work of fiction. Names, characters, places, and incidents are products of the author's imagination or are used fictitiously and are not to be construed as real. Any resemblance to actual events, locations, organizations, or persons, living or dead, is entirely coincidental.

World Castle Publishing, LLC
Pensacola, Florida
Copyright © 2025 Tonya Penrose
Hardback ISBN: 9798296381811
Paperback ISBN: 9798891264533
eBook ISBN: 9798891264540
Second Edition World Castle Publishing, LLC, September 22, 2025
http://www.worldcastlepublishing.com

Cover: Cover Designs by Karen
Editor: Lindsay

For Lindsay. My sincere thanks for swooping in to edit this book. Page and Betsy said they owe you one. You might need to worry.

Books By Tonya Penrose

The Shell Isle Mystery Series
Baubles to Die For
Red, White, and Boom
Murder by Numbers
Teatime Troubles

Old Mountain Cassie: The Three Lessons
A Secret Gift
Welcome to Charm
Venetian Rhapsody

CHAPTER 1

Page hung up the phone and turned to her cousin. "You've really outdone yourself this time, Betsy Ross."

"Aw, thanks for the compliment." Betsy tossed her head, trying to loosen a damp curl on her forehead. She let the wooden spoon take another turn in the mixing bowl. Honey Bees Shop's marble kitchen counter lay covered in a heavy dousing of flour. Ingredients for banana bread were lined up like soldiers. "Aunt Tilly always said I had a gift for doing the exceptional."

Page's eyes narrowed. "It wasn't meant as a compliment, and I don't ever remember Aunt Tilly saying—oh, never mind. Do you know who just called?"

"Of course, I know." Betsy laughed. "I was standing right here. You were talking to Alice, the new owner of Three Fables Inn. Isn't it nifty how she's attracting small groups for long weekends?"

"Real nifty. To continue—"

Betsy jumped in. "Maybe Three Fables' reputation for being a smidge haunted is only known here in Shell Isle. Or maybe some guests are into ghosts." Betsy sprinkled pecans into the mixture.

Page handed her cousin a loaf pan. "As I was attempting to say—"

"Get this. Alice shared that she'd experienced another unsettling moment last evening while in the attic rummaging." Betsy leaned toward Page and whispered, "She saw a shadow." Betsy swallowed. "She said it moved."

Going along with her cousin's attempt at distraction, Page replied, "Isn't the inn like two hundred years old? It should have all kinds of creepy shadows and sounds, not to mention stories or fables." Page grabbed a dish towel to wipe down the counter. "You're very messy, Betsy. To get back to the subject of —"

"I keep meaning to ask Alice the origin of the inn's name. Three Fables. Most curious."

Page sighed and bit Betsy's bait again. "I heard the name came from the original owner, who wrote the book *The Three Fables*. Now about Alice's call —"

"Despite the woo-woo doings, Ina Funk and I had a delightful lunch there earlier." Betsy poured the batter into the pan and turned back to Page. "The lunch menu special is fire poblano peppers in the most amazing sauce." Betsy closed the oven door and set the timer.

"Enough about the woo-woo and your latest love affair with a hot pepper. I want to know what Alice meant about having our final head count by five o'clock." Page moved closer and lifted a spatula from the canister. She waved it toward her cousin. "My answer, if you please?"

Betsy stepped back, grinning. "Now, Page, I can explain. You'll be over the moon with what I've done to enhance our shop's coffers. I acted on what you preach all the time."

"Which is? Enlighten me." Page didn't bother to hide the sarcasm from her cousin.

"I acted carpe diem. I seized the moment for our Honey Bees Shop's greater good," explained Betsy.

Page frowned, letting the worry take hold. "Spill the whole story and start at the beginning for a change."

Plopping down on the green metal stool, Betsy grabbed her hand fan and set it in motion. "These hot flashes need to end before I turn grey."

"I may turn grey waiting for an explanation. I'm listening but maintaining a big dose of skepticism because this is you up to something. I know it. Betsy, tell me why we care about a head count?"

Betsy released a groan. "My surprise isn't going how I planned at all. And this hot flash misery won't leave me for five minutes of peace."

"Enough about your flashes. Stop stalling. Maybe I should call Alice and have her—"

"You don't need to call Alice. I was building up for my ta-da." Betsy lifted a toffee cookie from the cooling rack.

"You can eat that later." Page grabbed the cookie and placed it back on the rack.

Betsy's eyes sparkled. "I've outdone myself by scoring our first catering job, and it's at Three Fables. Get a load of my latest Best Betsy."

"What in all that's holy is a Best Betsy? That's a new one. My worry just amped higher."

Betsy waved her hand dismissively. "Hush yourself. A Best Betsy means I've done the exceptional like Aunt Tilly always said."

"Stop channeling our Aunt Tilly and tell me what you've got us doing at Three Fables." Page felt exasperation rushing through her mind to drain her emotionally.

"On Saturday afternoon, we'll serve high tea to a small group of bestselling authors from England." Betsy folded her fan but kept her satisfied expression.

"You can't be serious. Saturday, as in tomorrow?"

Betsy bobbed her head and tried again for the cookie.

Page snagged it and took a bite. "Honestly, Betsy, you live to give me a migraine. We're supposed to discuss things regarding running Honey Bees."

"And we usually do, but this was one of those moments to strike while the griddle is hot."

Page made a sound. "It's 'strike while the iron is hot.' We can't do this job. There isn't enough time to prepare."

"Yes, we can. This catering gig will be a smashing success, and we will mingle with writers. Alice said they were arriving this afternoon. I wonder what they write. Very pip-pip books." Betsy activated her British accent.

"Has it slipped your mind that we don't know a lick about what makes for high tea and all the fancy cakes and sandwiches these tea aficionados will expect?"

Betsy pointed to her laptop. "I'm sure whatever we need to know is there waiting for a search. Besides, I dated this chef from Brighton years ago, and I picked up some tricks of the trade from him. I think his name was Rhys. No, that's not right. It was Rory. Boy, did he ever have this annoying habit of using a pendulum to decide what to eat. Do you know—"

Page lifted her hand. "Please spare me one of your past dating sagas. At fifty-something, I don't know how there's a man left out there you haven't gone out with once." Page finished the cookie and eyed her cousin.

"I'm ignoring that remark. We're the same age and have the same birthday. You were fortunate to find a great fellow and marry once. My great fellow has yet to show." Betsy's voice held sadness.

"You're right. I was fortunate." Page nodded. "To return to the subject at hand."

"Look, I've got it all sorted in my head. That's another British way of speaking. I wish I had hailed from Oxford. I'd be ever so clever." Betsy paused for effect.

"You're clever enough. I can't believe—"

"Listen. We'll come in super early tomorrow morning and prep. The hoity-toity tea isn't until four o'clock. Relax.

Ina's agreed to help."

"Having Ina in the kitchen supervising gives me some comfort. Still, we don't know what accompanies a proper English tea, although I've always yearned to attend one."

Betsy reached for a notepad and pen. "It's no big deal. First, we'll make sure the crusts get trimmed from the bread. Then we create lovely little triangle sandwiches and dress them with what we wouldn't eat, like butter and cucumber slices. Maybe a dash of hot sauce would jazz them up." Betsy's tone turned to cajole as she jotted a grocery list for Ina. "Simple as a crumpet."

A flicker of impatience shone in Page's eyes. "So simple. Nothing to it, except we can't possibly pull this off in less than twenty-four hours. I've always admired the British and their excellent manners. And that's how I know we can't possibly rise to this occasion. We lack their tea etiquette."

"We can and we will. Have faith. I'm sure Ina can guide us on proper tea brewing. She's always got a cup of something in her hand. Come on, Page, it's sandwiches and baby cakes. We put the hot water in a fancy floral kettle, toss in the teabags, and voila."

Page lifted her hands. "See? We're already in trouble. Even I know it's a fancy China teapot that serves the tea. The kettle is the tool you boil the water in."

"Right," said Betsy, stretching out the word and nodding. "I got confused momentarily because Brits always talk about putting the kettle on. I love to watch any and all of their television mystery series. I've noticed the tea kettle gets activated a lot. Did you ever see the show—"

"Are you done?" Page moved toward the kitchen door.

"Not yet." Betsy took the mixing bowls to the sink for a wash. "I've picked up some really good sleuthing tricks watching these shows, should we have the misfortune of getting another case. I'm so pleased we've had six blissful months without one of your inklings."

"All true." Page adjusted her yellow apron. "Don't jinx us by talking about my inklings. Listen, I need to get back to the sales floor and —"

"We always end up in the thick of some sinister doings, with Detective Tanner delivering non-stop lectures. I hate his lectures about us being snoops. Don't you, Page?"

"Enough of your deflecting jabber, Betsy. It's not working on me." Page paused. "I hear the customer's bell jingling. We'll continue this catering discussion later."

"You go take care of them. I need to mix another praline cake. Ina should return any minute, and I don't want her fussing about the batter becoming too thick." Betsy's arms motioned at her cousin. "Skedaddle."

As Page stopped to straighten a display of honey body lotions, the surprise of an inkling washed over her. "Betsy Ross, you called this to us," Page muttered. The flushing sensation passed, but not the knowledge that a tragedy would soon befall someone.

CHAPTER 2

Betsy emerged from the bakery's kitchen wearing her signature yellow Honey Bees apron over a bright floral muumuu. She sashayed over to Page. "The table of new honey-whipped body butter jars looks so nice. You have a real knack for merchandising. I told Ina the other day that our shop has an eclectic vibe that customers love. And it's all thanks to your talents that extend everywhere but the baking side. It's okay because that's where I shine."

"Puffing me with praise won't work." Page chose to keep silent about the fact that Ina's baking skills allowed Betsy to shine. "You're still in charge of this shindig at Three Fables. Our new partnership rule is that whoever agrees to a catering job runs it. That makes me the helper bee." Page stood back, eyeing the stack of jars. Her hand adjusted the embossed sign describing the cream's benefits.

"Fine. I shall rise to the task and accept your new rule." Betsy lifted her once-pronounced chin. "You'll be pleased to hear that Ina and I finished planning the menu. She's buzzed to the market to purchase Darelene tea and the rest of the fixings."

A laugh escaped Page. "It's Darjeeling tea."

"Right." Betsy studied Page's expression. "I can tell that you're still chapped at me for agreeing to the catering job." She handed Page two jars to add to the stack.

"I'm still chapped because it's added stress to our already busy Saturday. Plus, I hate rising before the birds chirp to prepare for this tea party." Page hung a satin ribbon with a tiny, gold spoon around a jar.

"That's why I've brought a peace offering." Betsy gave an impish smile. "Take the rest of Friday afternoon off. I'll handle our customers while Ina bakes the tea cakes." Betsy reached for the empty lotion box. "Go home, put on your favorite turquoise bathing suit, and get to the beach. It's April and warm enough for lounging and wading."

Page turned to face her cousin. "Basking in the sun does sound nice. Know what? I'm going to say yes and thank you." She'd avoided telling Betsy about her latest inkling. No point in awakening her cousin's fretting.

"Hey, don't forget to try out the new beach chair with the storage pockets for snacks." Betsy's mouth turned up at the corners. "Am I forgiven?"

"Almost." Page grabbed her straw handbag and headed toward the shop's entrance. "Color me gone." She heard Betsy's footsteps and turned around. "What? You have more to say?" teased Page.

"I always have more to say." Betsy's smile creased her face. "Tell you what. To guarantee I get out of Page Purgatory, I'll swing by after closing Honey Bees and make us a nice dinner."

Page panicked at the thought of eating one of Betsy's spiced-up meals. "You don't need to fix dinner, though it's a nice offer."

"I do need to cook for us. I'm going to the market anyway to buy more ingredients for the finger sandwiches. I'll grab the fixings." Betsy bobbed her head. "I know. I'll make my famous Sure-Fire Tacos."

Page touched her stomach, recalling how many antacids it took to put out the flames in her digestive system from Betsy's last taco recipe. "Please, don't worry about dinner. I've got a frozen pizza."

"No frozen anything for you. It's Friday. Taco Night at Hibiscus Cottage. The cooking oracle—that's me—has declared it."

Page pulled her last ace card and hoped for the best. "What about Andre? I thought you two went out on Friday and Monday nights since he's off duty."

"Yeah, that's our usual, but your hunk of burning love, Detective Tanner, asked him to work tonight and take off a different day. That leaves me free to cook for us. We can use the time together to research the proper way to serve this fancy tea."

"Well, I suppose—"

"My cupcake timers are chiming, and Ina's banging on the back door."

"Okay, okay. I'll see you later for dinner," agreed Page, thinking her free afternoon came at a high price.

Betsy shouted back. "Don't eat anything to spoil your appetite."

Page stepped outside and inhaled the salt air. In anticipation of the meal, she popped a tummy-settling peppermint into her mouth and crossed the street to her vintage British SUV. Shell Isle defined a sublime life, except when the inklings alerted that her sleuthing gifts were needed…like right then.

***

As Page drove home, her eyes reflected on Shell Isle's ever-changing vibe. The beach town had a knack for attracting its share of interesting and colorful residents. Boredom never described life at Shell. Betsy's and her decision to make their move permanent had proven wise. They'd succeeded in finding their niche by opening Honey Bees. With their kids grown and scattered around the world, both found peace when it mattered most.

Page still experienced periods of missing her husband, Jeff, and their shared life. His passing cut a hole in her heart. The idea of marrying again held no appeal. Betsy's story was different. Relocating to the beach allowed her to reset and move past her last failed marriage. Shell Isle served as their healing elixir, and most every day, the sun rose and brought them doses of joy.

In the short time they'd called Shell Isle their home, Page's inklings had delivered three murder cases for her and Betsy to solve. The calling to use her unique gifts wasn't optional. It had never been. She knew from years of experience that the first inkling signaled that a dark state of mind was stirring in someone. All she could do now was wait and see if the harmful thoughts shifted to actions.

Page parked in the cottage's driveway. Her aqua eyes glanced next door at Detective Steve Tanner's bungalow. Laughter bubbled out of her, seeing Barnacle gnawing on the red dinghy Steve had been working to restore. The spaniel lived up to his name almost daily. As for his owner, Page had succumbed to the attraction but maintained her strict emotional boundaries. She vowed that casual fun with the detective fit her lifestyle, and "no strings" was her mantra.

Steve exited the screen door carrying his yellow surfboard. His well-defined muscles flexed as he hoisted the board over his head. Page sighed and stepped out of her vehicle. "He and that stealthy black Navy Seal wetsuit will be my undoing one of these days." Page waved and escaped inside her cottage before he could saunter her way. A dire need to locate one of Betsy's flowered hand fans and down a glass of iced lemonade came calling.

***

Toting her lounge chair and bag down to the beach, Page noted the fluffy clouds hung like cotton candy, decorating the azure-blue sky. The sun competed for attention by sending warmth to those enjoying being by the water. The afternoon held promise.

Page kicked off her sandals and tucked them into her bag. She squished her toes in the warm sand as she walked. Freedom wore many faces, even if it was only going barefoot on a spring day. Page stopped to watch a sandcastle come to life under two young boys' hands. "That's quite a moat you're building."

The towhead was the first to answer. "We're filling it with water to make sure it's...."

"To make sure it's protecting the castle," finished the other freckle-faced boy.

"It looks plenty strong to me. See you guys later." Page waved at their mom and, out of habit, continued to Betsy's favorite spot. The lifeguard stand stood empty for another week until the season officially opened. Page chuckled, recalling her cousin's constant flirting with whomever had the misfortune to get assigned lifeguard chair number eleven.

Her own misbehaving eyes searched for Steve amongst the surfers. His yellow board was easy to spot, bobbing over the ocean swells. At least she didn't need to worry about him motioning her to swim out. He knew the chilly water temperature would keep her away.

Page grabbed a bag of chips, a ginger ale, and a gardening magazine from her tote, then settled into her chair. She listened to the sounds of the waves announcing their arrival on shore. Pelicans splashed down for a tasty fish, providing the background noise as minutes ebbed away.

"Hey, there." Steve adjusted his surfboard under his arm.

Page glanced up, using her hand to block the sun. "Hey, yourself, surfer dude." The coal-colored hair and steel-grey eyes gave him an irresistible rakish look. Page swallowed, thinking no early fiftyish man should look so hot. Tall, dark, and too handsome described the ex-Navy Seal and FBI agent who'd traded the high-octane world of crime-busting for a quieter lifestyle at Shell Isle. Page ignored her mind's chatter and found a few words to offer. "Despite the water temperature, you've got nicely formed waves out there today."

Steve squinted at the ocean. "Yeah, but the current worked me over." He parked the surfboard and swiped away the water cascading down his tanned forehead. "I gotta ask. How did you manage the afternoon off from Honey Bees?"

"Easy. Betsy is in the doghouse with me. She agreed to have Honey Bees cater an afternoon tea party at Three Fables Inn without first discussing it with me. Setting me free to enjoy my beach chair was her attempt at doing penance and courting my forgiveness." Page's mouth turned up at the corners.

"Did it work?" Steve peeked into Page's tote. "Do you have a soda to share?"

Page handed him a root beer. "Yeah, I can't stay mad at her long, and she knows it." Adjusting the straw hat to shade her face, Page watched as Steve drained half the can.

"I forgot how much I like root beer. Thanks." He paused to take another sip. "At least Betsy's finally moved into her renovated bungalow. You've got the cottage to yourself now."

"That I do, except for your pal Barnacle paying me daily visits and bringing his latest excavated bone."

"I'm sorry. Believe me, I've given Barn lectures on this matter, but he persists with his daily mission. Blame it on Betsy. She encouraged him while living there with you." Steve wiped his hair with a beach towel.

Page recalled feeling amused when Betsy had assigned

Barnacle a seat at their table. "I love your pooch. He's always welcome sans the bone."

"And me? Am I always welcome?" Steve's expression turned to teasing.

"Hmm, I'd say most times." Page watched as he placed his towel and waterproof-encased cell phone at the foot of her chair.

"Do you mind me resting here for a spell?" Steve lifted Page's legs so he could sit.

Page shook her head, failing to ignore his touch. She grabbed her ginger ale and took a cooling sip. "I noticed some jellies on the beach. 'Tis the stinging season."

"My wetsuit does a good job of protecting me from jellyfish. However, the two nurse sharks visiting out there sent me paddling to shore." Steve waved to a surfer as he passed by.

Page gulped. "Two sharks? Tell me you aren't going back out to surf."

"I haven't decided. The waves need to look more enticing." Steve poked inside Page's tote. "Chips? May I?"

The flush of another inkling came to her. *No, not again this soon.* Steve's voice called her back.

"Hello? Me? Chips? Yes? No?" Steve waved his hand. "Where are you? Hang on. I know that look."

Page pulled a face. "Whatever are you going on about? I have many looks. Eat the chips."

Steve's brows drew together. "This look I recognize. Tell me I'm wrong. You haven't gotten one of your tinklings. Have you?" He popped a chip into his mouth. His eyes stayed locked on Page.

"For the zillionth time, they're inklings and not tinklings. I swear you say that to get a rise out of me, Detective Tanner." Page buried her face in the magazine before feeling it tugged away from her hands.

"Page?" Steve held the magazine hostage. "Listen, if you've had an inkling that something is going to happen here at Shell, I need to know. We've developed an understanding of working together. I expect you to deliver by being forthcoming with those intuitions. You succeeded in making believers out of Detective Koch and me, but we need transparency. Let's try this again. Did you get an inkling?"

"Okay, fine." Page released a loud huff. "I hate it when you read me. It's so annoying."

"Duly noted. Do continue."

"I received one this afternoon. A slight one—ever so slight." Page's fingers signaled small. "And maybe another now, but mild. Nothing's happening...yet."

Steve groaned. "Shell Isle was enjoying a quiet winter and early spring until you went and got an—"

"An inkling. But maybe nothing will come of it. Maybe—"

"Keep your maybes. After working on three murder cases that you and Betsy snooped your way into solving, I'm worried. Something's going down soon." Steve stood and grabbed his board.

Page knew her words had robbed them both of a carefree afternoon. "Where are you headed?"

"Back to the waves. At least those I can understand and predict. Would you keep a watch on my phone and towel?"

"For a price, Detective Tanner." Page blinked at him, determined to restore the lighthearted mood they'd always enjoyed.

Steve tossed the empty root beer can into the nearby receptacle and returned. "Okay, I'll bite your bait. What's the price?"

"You come to my cottage at six for Betsy's Sure-Fire

Tacos. I need help disposing of them. And bring Barnacle. He's developed an iron constitution from eating her offerings."

Steve groaned. "My poor dog and I must suffer Betsy's culinary debacles to spend time with you. That's asking a lot, Sherlocka."

The nickname bestowed by the detective had been activated. It signaled he was taking the new inklings seriously. "Surely you agree my delightful dinner repartee trumps your worry over Betsy's flammable tacos. Do you want me guarding your phone and favorite towel or not?"

Steve rubbed his chin, pretending to consider. "Well, I did trade on-call nights with Andre so I could go cheer for my buddy at this evening's Shell Isle Sailing Regatta. Say you'll accompany me, and Barn and I will act as the taco disposers."

Page shoved her hand toward Steve. "Deal. When can we escape taco hell for fun?"

"Excellent. We'll flee hell at 1900 hours." Grabbing his surfboard, Steve moved toward the beach.

"I don't need your retired Navy Seal time. I need it in my time!" shouted Page, realizing he didn't hear her. She'd have to look up 1900 hours on her cell phone. Her pulse gave a little jump thinking about sailing with him on Carpe Diem. Maybe now that the weather was warming, she'd finagle another sailing invite. The thought caused happiness to awaken her traitorous hormones.

Page reached for her phone and deciphered the 1900 hours as seven p.m. Her fingers punched in Betsy's number. "Hi, Bets. I hope you don't mind, but I invited Steve and Barnacle for tacos. I wanted to let you know before you stopped at the market."

"No problem." Betsy's voice sounded pleased. "I know how much Steve enjoys my culinary gifts. And since I moved into my place, he and Barnacle are undoubtedly in a constant state of longing."

Page choked on her drink. Only her cousin could spin such insane cooking yarns.

"Are you okay? You'd better have your bottom in the beach chair." Betsy's tone booked seriousness.

Giving one last cough, Page replied, "I'm fine. The liquid went down the wrong way. I'm in the lounger with a gardening magazine."

"Hey, is our cute lifeguard—"

"No, Betsy. Next week, the guards return, and you'll have your ogling eyes activated." Page looked skyward. "And one more thing. Steve and I must leave a little before seven to attend a sailing regatta."

"That works. It slipped my mind that the Mermaids are bowling tonight. Ina reminded me before she left. I'm closing up a tad early. All the special orders have been picked up."

"So, okay. See you in a little while. Count on me making our salad tonight."

"Nope. My menu's all planned. Just make sure you're hungry." Betsy hung up.

Page sat plotting how to survive dinner until the words of a younger couple parked under a nearby umbrella caught her attention. Another inkling arrived—it was time to pay attention.

CHAPTER 3

Hearing the couple say the name Three Fables Inn and the way anger colored their words had Page lean back in her chair to hear more. Out of the corner of her eye, she saw the young woman arranging her lounger to capture more of the sun's warmth. The fellow sitting next to her was fiddling with his phone.

"James, please stop playing the game and listen to me." She positioned herself in the chair. "I get so tired of competing with your screen."

"You're so bossy, Mara. Okay, fine." He tucked the phone in the chair's pocket. "Convince me you've got us on track."

"I'm telling you, Three Fables is the inn. I know I'm right. Don't you dare say a word about what happened at the last stop."

Her hair color rivaled Betsy's recipe for 'Beets Alive,' a dish that Page had suffered through the previous week. The curly mop was secured in a topknot by a large clip. Square sunglasses hid her eyes, but not the bright-orange lipstick. The beach coverup print was loud enough to attract sharks to shore. Just stealing a glance her way threatened a migraine.

"Are you listening to me? Stop watching the bikinis."

James gave a disgusted groan. "What makes you so sure it's Three Fables? How about the B&B up the coast listed as Three Keys?" James's voice grew louder, competing with the waves.

Page took stock of his size when he stood. One word

described the red-faced guy's body frame: lanky. Page stole another glance at his face, bare of sunglasses but not of anger. Both young people appeared to be in their early twenties.

"No, the job ad was at Shell Isle," replied Mara. "It's either the Three Fables Inn or The Mint and Buckle B&B, but I'm telling you it's the Fables place."

James paced around their chairs. "You messed up everything when you lost the report. We can't risk the repercussions by asking for a copy."

"Nothing is messed up. I didn't lose the report. I misplaced it because you never clean out the car." Mara waved her hand dismissively. "Look, I only got a chance to read the first paragraph before you insisted that we stop for hamburgers at that disgusting diner. At least I remember she's running an inn at Shell Isle and has posted two job openings. It's made things easy. It's the Mint or Fables. And I say it's the latter." Mara reapplied the bright lip gloss and made smacking sounds.

"Okay, we'll play it your way. So, what's our plan? Just show up saying we're here to apply for the front desk and housekeeping jobs?" James's expression looked resigned.

"Yep. And we'll make sure to confirm her name. After that, it's as simple as eating apple pie. I'm telling you, if we succeed at this assignment, we'll soon be back having all the bread we need. We only need to play our parts super chill." Mara patted the empty beach chair. "Settle down. We'll head over to the inn once you get it together."

"I've always got it together. It's you—oh, forget it. Let's do this now." James tossed his towel over his shoulder and folded the chair. "Besides, Shell Isle isn't my kind of beach. I've got my eyes on another place once we get what's promised." His face wore a bored expression.

"Okay, Mister Beach Snob. You'd better land this job. I

won't clean rooms while you sit at some tiki bar downing rum swizzles." Mara handed James her chair to carry and brushed the sand off her purple sandals. Unable to maintain balance and strap them on, she tucked the pair into a plastic bag.

Page watched as the two trudged toward the beach access ramp. She wondered why they insisted on working at Three Fables and what that missing report was about. They lacked maturity and definitely needed the money. Should she interfere with Alice's innkeeping by saying something? What would she even say? *Maybe I'm reading too much into their exchange, but the inkling had to mean something.* Page opened her magazine, releasing a heavy sigh. The answer waited in the future. She suspected her peaceful life would become topsy-turvy again soon.

***

"Here I am at last." Betsy deposited the grocery bags on the kitchen island and exhaled loudly. Her eyes surveyed the pots and pans inside the cabinet. "Lucky for us, I've cooked many a meal in this kitchen while I waited for the perfect bungalow to call my name."

Page emptied the contents of the first grocery bag and felt anxious thoughts flush heat to her cheeks. What role would marmalade and radicchio play in a taco? "Yeah, lucky ducky me."

Betsy cut her eyes over to Page. "Do I detect sarcasm?"

"Never," joked Page. She lifted a plastic bag containing something curious. "What's—"

"Don't touch that without protection." Betsy grabbed the sack away. "It's a special treat for our taco night. Since Steve asked to dine with us, I wanted to jazz things up."

Page watched as Betsy used a clean dishcloth to free the chilies.

Lifting one by the stem to admire it, Betsy explained,

"This is a ghost pepper. Bet you've never tasted one."

Panic set in, seeing Betsy's hand dangling the igniter. "Um, no. You know very well that I've never taken to hot peppers—"

"Until I introduced you to so many delightful chilies. You liked the Grim Reaper Salad I made for us. Remember?" Betsy turned on the faucet and deposited both peppers in the colander.

"I remember that particular pepper." Page recalled she and Steve had chewed antacids for a week. "What can I do to help?"

Betsy pulled out the salad ingredients. "Here you go. Make us a lovely salad to go with the special dressing I'm preparing. It's a new Bets recipe. I call it—"

"No, don't tell me. You should announce it at the dinner table." Page reached for the colander and rinsed the lettuce. At least she could enjoy the expression on Steve's face when he faced whatever bowls and platters made it to the table. Finishing the salad, she placed it on the table, awaiting the toss of the mystery dressing. "Done. What else can I do?"

Betsy dumped the remaining taco ingredients into a skillet and turned the burner on high. "Disappear to the porch. You know I like to have my big reveal. Wait. There's Steve's knock. Tend to him while I tend these Sure-Fire Tacos." Betsy licked the spoon from the pot she'd stirred. "Not quite right. Needs more fire and maybe anchovies to salty it up."

Page made a face as she opened the door. "No anchovies. Hey, Steve. Hiya, Barnacle." Page reached down to rub the dog's velvety ears. "Come on in, guys. Betsy wants us seated at the porch table for her serving event."

Steve entered, bringing his grin and dog. "Something smells…hot." He craned his neck at the cooktop as he passed by the kitchen. "Hi, Betsy. Please, go light on the fire for me. I have to work tomorrow."

"Very funny. You're an ex-Navy Seal. You can eat rattlesnakes and tree bark if you have to." Betsy waved a spatula. "My little extra zest is tame compared to what you've ingested in the wild."

"Sure, but none of it was ever doused with enough hot pepper sauce to ignite an—"

"Stop it, you two. Come on, Tanner. I'll pour you a cool, refreshing iced tea." Page tugged on his sleeve. "Maybe you can tell me about the regatta we're attending."

"Sure. You'll soon see some impressive sailboats. We'll make it a brief visit, as these things can last until late. Enough said there." Steve leaned in and whispered as they entered the porch. "Did Betsy ruin the tea with some flavoring like her pineapple-chocolate syrup again?"

Page shook her head. "Nope. I made the tea."

Steve and Page took their seats and stared at the liquid in the pitcher.

Barnacle sat in the empty chair and whimpered, noting his owner's worried face.

"Sorry, I guess she sneaked in whatever makes tea blue. This addition doesn't bode well for dinner. I'll slip back into the kitchen and get extra napkins to stash food." Page rose.

"And count on me treating us to a frozen coffee with extra whipped cream after we pretend to eat whatever hellfire is brewing in those pots." Steve looked over at the beefy bone on Barnacle's metal plate. "Trade ya, buddy."

"Hey, maybe the Fates will pity us, and the tacos will turn out edible. We must cling to hope at all costs." Page's eyes sparked. Steve Tanner's magnetism kept proving irresistible. She enjoyed their banter, among other things.

"So far, these Fates have been MIA for us. But okay, I'll

cling along with you."

Page spied Betsy bringing a platter of tacos and her proud smile. "Battle stations." She could only hope it applied to tacos and not more inklings.

CHAPTER 4

The Perk Coffee Shop kept later hours on Fridays and Saturdays. While the espresso machines hissed, the trio of musicians let their smooth jazz flow. A quiet group tucked in the corner played bridge. A young couple studied a jigsaw puzzle and sipped their frozen-coffee confections. The patrons seemed uncharacteristically subdued to Page as she and Steve waited for their turn to order.

"The regatta was the perfect outing. Thanks for inviting me. It makes me miss sailing." Page adjusted her handbag strap.

"We'll get out on the water soon. I promise." Steve pulled Page in for a quick hug. "Coffee is a great finisher since the tacos turned out to be a pleasant edible surprise." Steve cut a sideways smirk at Page. "And best of all, you're buying."

"Yeah, and I want a closer look at the coin you tossed." Page studied the menu for a moment before turning to the barista. "I'd like a frozen Love Ya A Latte. And what's your pleasure, Detective Tanner?"

Steve's eyes gleamed in merriment. "Ah, the barista doesn't need to hear my answer. You shouldn't taunt a detective."

Page smacked his arm. "Enough. Decide on your coffee."

Turning to the young woman, Steve read the selection board. "Let's keep it easy. Double the order."

"Here's the money. I'll go claim a couple of chairs for us." Page waved to Mickey, carrying a tray of beverages and muffins to the bridge players. He'd proven a loyal friend, supplier of Honey Bees nectar of the gods, and the best town gossip two sleuths could hope to have at their sides.

Page paused, considering where to sit. A nudge to sit near the group of six at a large table had her move in that direction. Choosing two wingback chairs upholstered in orange plaid, Page settled on the one closest to the chattering. Her curiosity made her tune into their dialogue.

A rail-thin brunette woman who appeared forty years old, but likely owned fifty, was speaking. Her charming British accent made the letter U sound like *ooo* rather than *uh*. That clued Page that she probably hailed from Yorkshire. She exuded an air of authority. Page noticed that the other three women and two men showed disinterest in what was being said.

"I thought since we're tucked in at Three Fables and enjoyed a light supper, it would be nice to share a pot of tea at Shell Isle's local coffee house to round out the evening."

On cue, Mickey's tray delivered a floral teapot, matching cups, and a plate of cookies. His offer to pour was rejected by the one leading the conversation. Mickey bestowed a wink to Page and returned to the bar.

Pretending to act engrossed in her phone screen allowed Page to eavesdrop without drawing their attention. They had to be the same British authors attending Saturday's tea party. Page watched the cheery-faced leader pour the steaming brew into waiting cups. She loved listening to their accents and envied their writing gifts.

"To press on, as your editor, I think we should have a nice sharing. I'd like each of you to tell the others what projects you've been involved in since we last gathered. Shall we? Evelyn, let's start with you." The editor blew into her cup before taking a dainty sip.

"Me, Fiona? I don't wish to go first. I know how everyone always reacts when I share my book sale numbers and grand successes. We all know I'm the topper." Evelyn reached for a cookie.

"Why must you always delight in flaunting your standing amongst us? How you achieve those numbers is questionable at best. Giveaways and hocus pocus sales numbers are what I think." The wearer of a flamboyant hat and strings of colorful beads stirred cream into her tea. Her frizzy, bleached-blond hair failed to touch her fuchsia jacket's collar. The deep lines edged around her mouth showed that bitterness had been a long companion and gave her age away.

"Ruby, do hush your ridiculous prattle." Evelyn narrowed her eyes at the editor. "Fiona, really, this is all quite tiresome. Can you hurry this soiree along? I'm knackered from the time change and prefer my room." Cherry-red manicured nails stroked a sizeable, pear-shaped diamond pendant resting against her too slender neck. The author's dark auburn hair was swept into a bun so tight a hurricane wouldn't budge it.

"I'm bored myself sitting here in this subpar, coffee-smelling enterprise," said the man wearing a red-checkered bow tie.

A smirk found the second man's expression. "Count me as one in agreement with Evelyn and Chaucer."

"Would you stop referring to me as a Chaucer? My name, as you well know, is Chester. I find you an annoying person, and when I get annoyed, my temper —"

"All right, Leo, Chester, and everyone. That's enough. I don't appreciate, nor will I tolerate, your lack of cooperation this weekend. I expect congeniality amongst the lot of you. Notice that wasn't a request but a non-negotiable. Now, let's enjoy our tea and try this again." Fiona lifted the porcelain cup.

Steve appeared from behind, startling Page. "Your frozen frappe, Sherlocka. Sorry it took so long. I had to wait for them to find coconut milk to make ours."

"Thanks." Page took a sip through her straw. "So good. I see you got an extra helping of whipped cream."

"I need fortifying. I'm on duty all weekend, and now on point with you getting a tink—inkling." Steve's hand swirled the frozen coffee around with his straw. His eyes locked on a quiet Page, who in turn was locked on the noisy group at the next table. "Page?"

"Shh, in a sec." Page scooted her chair back. "I need to hear this."

The fourth woman's voice was subdued. Even her attire reflected timidness. Unattractive glasses magnified small eyes set on a face that others would describe as ordinary. It was as if a paintbrush chose only beige to sculpt a countenance. No makeup was applied to enhance her features. She wore a nondescript, tan jumper, which succeeded at looking unflattering. "As Evelyn's assistant, I'd be happy to discuss what projects she has in the works. With permission to speak, one story is particularly enticing. It involves a hunky male who's a bestselling author and—"

"Quiet." Evelyn's face flushed in anger. "Grace, I'll thank you to mind your place. You're here to serve my needs and have no voice until I say." Evelyn turned back to Fiona. "I'm quite spent with this charade."

The editor touched Evelyn's arm. Her expression appeared defeated. "I only wanted you all to take a moment to celebrate each other's work."

"Celebrate without me. I'm returning to the inn and calling it a night. I can only hope the unsettling tapping noise coming from behind my suite's wall will not interrupt my slumber. I detest staying in older inns with an unsavory history and plumbing needing attention."

Fiona's voice rose. "Three Fables has an excellent rating."

"Not with me. Come, Grace. Summon us a ride." Evelyn rose and walked toward The Perk's entrance with a meek Grace trailing behind, carrying both of their handbags.

Page noted that everyone's attention turned to their teacups. The silence seemed revered.

"They sound like a cheery group." Steve set his coffee down and studied Page. "I've got a question. Why the interest in eavesdropping on this bickering bunch from across the pond?"

Page twisted in her chair to face Steve. "Since you asked, I have two reasons. First, we're serving them a proper English afternoon tea tomorrow at Three Fables Inn. And now I know what awaits us." Page used the straw to taste the whipped cream while deciding how to deliver the second reason.

"I'm waiting for what I expect will ruin our little coffee date." Steve's grey eyes narrowed on Page.

"You want me to keep you informed." Page inhaled. "So here you go, Detective Tanner. I got another inkling that relates to the ones at the table. And before you get all riled, let's wait and see how things play out." Page stole a glance and saw the group preparing to leave.

"Well, isn't that the best news all night?" Steve shoved his cup away. "And there's nothing I can do as a detective until something bad happens. You know, feeling powerless isn't something I relish. Just swell. You are portending another murder at our quiet little beach town."

Page lifted her hand. "Perhaps. All we can do is wait and see if the inklings continue."

"Maybe those intuits won't make an encore."

"There you go. Hold to that maybe statement." Page chose not to explain that once the inklings activated, they rarely stopped coming until she'd solved the case.

CHAPTER 5

Page took her glass of juice to the porch. She'd risen earlier than usual to help prepare for the tea party. A hectic morning awaited. Clearing her mind of thoughts, Page gazed at the scene outside. Low tide had sprinkled treasures along the beach. A cloudless sky was colored an unusual shade of indigo and violet as the sun's rays peeped over the horizon. She always paid attention to dawn's face once her inklings awakened. It could forecast the day ahead.

Inhaling the salt-kissed air didn't help soothe her worry as Page glanced at her watch. "Gosh, it's happened again! Time sped up on me. I'm late." Rushing inside, she grabbed her tote and keys. For the moment, her outer world remained harmonious. She'd keep silent a bit longer before alerting Betsy that their sleuthing gifts would soon be needed.

***

Honey Bees's kitchen buzzed with Betsy and Ina surrounded by mixing bowls and baking pans. The ovens had their second batch of scrumptious scones and muffins baking. Light classical music played in the background, keeping the mood upbeat.

A breathless Page entered. "I've got the donut and scone trays filled out front and ready for the customers when we open. What can I do to help back here?"

"See if you can find the cake decorating box. The strawberry frosting is ready to sit atop these demure sponge cake squares." Betsy held up the platter with pride. "My first contribution to our la-di-da tea trolley."

"Here's the decorating box. It was behind the bag of flour." Page reached for a lemon-colored apron embroidered with the Honey Bees logo and tied it around her petite waist. She clipped her blond hair up in a modified ponytail. Peering into the bowl to which Betsy was giving her attention, Page nodded. "What tea trolley? We don't own such a—"

"Over there." Ina pointed with a hand covered in flour.

Page's eyes followed the direction. "Oh, my stars and garters. That's one festooned tea trolley. How did it appear in our kitchen, all decked out in fresh flowers? And are those satin ribbons?"

Betsy's face lit up. "Yes, ma'am. You can credit me with the contribution. Our cart acquisition proved most advantageous. One of the Mermaids in my bowling league hosts a monthly Mahjong group. She mentioned using a fancy serving cart when she was here placing last week's order for lavender-honey cupcakes. Remember, Page?"

"Sorry, no." Page moved closer and bent down, touching the many adornments. "So, you borrowed the cart from her?"

"She did," said Ina, jumping in. "I loaded it last night in my husband's truck. We brought it to Betsy's bungalow. And you finish the telling, Bets."

Betsy puffed up like a hen ready to strut. "Yes. I stayed up late weaving all these lovely flowers from my garden around the wrought iron. I sprayed them with my secret preservative to keep them fresh. Ina brought it here in the truck this morning." Betsy paused, surveying her creation. "It's now a trolley worthy of an English tea party."

Page's mouth hung open, taking in the cart's wild color theme. It looked like a psychedelic creation from the sixties. Words stayed inside Page's mouth while her mind scrambled for how to tone down its sure-to-be memorable first impression on the guests. Betsy read her silence as a happy surprise.

"See here." Betsy's fingers straightened the ribbons' tangles. "I let the purple and orange ribbons stream down from the handle. I still have the red and chartreuse ones to add later, but baking comes first."

"She's something, our Betsy. Right, Page?" Ina hugged the trolley's decorator.

"Very something indeed." Page nodded. "Um, Bets, don't we need to leave room for all the luscious bakery items that will ride on the trolley?" Page peered closer. "Are those honeybees tied on wire springs, waving our business cards?"

"Yes, ma'am. I was wondering when you'd notice that special touch. There's a baker's dozen of them."

"I'm noticing now." Page gulped, seeing two framed photos of her and Betsy on the bottom shelf. "Maybe we should consider removing these photos of us opening Honey Bees. And the ones of us on the beach could stay behind." Page reached for two.

Betsy's hand stopped the act. "It's free advertising while the group partakes of the delectables on the trolley. They'll be reminded who created their lovely tea party. Ina, we need a photo of you, too."

Page felt the first migraine pang. "Betsy, I think we might want to make minor adjustments to our advertising."

Betsy moved their photos to the cart's side shelf. "There. No further adjustments are needed to perfection. Besides, as Aunt Tilly taught us, we must always look our best."

Ina sent a wink Page's way and shoved two pans into the oven.

"You're right. Our tea trolley will be the talk of Shell Isle by sundown." Page sighed. After growing up with Betsy and their mothers being twin sisters, Page knew when she'd been Betsy bested. The psychedelic, migraine-inducing tea trolley would debut at Three Fables Inn in a few hours.

Before opening the shop, Page frosted and sprinkled enough cakes and tarts to compete in Shell Isle's annual Fourth of July decorating contest. She smiled, remembering Betsy had signed up for the blue-ribbon salsa competition happening next month. After sampling countless versions of her cousin's salsa entry, Page felt pity for the judges of the Foodies Fête. Hopefully, they were wise enough to have water, antacids, and a trash can follow them to Betsy's booth.

Ina came alongside Page and whispered. "Don't worry. I'm managing everything, including the hideous, decked-out tea cart. And with any luck, certain things might blow off while riding to the inn in my husband's truck."

"From your mouth to the tea trolley god's best ear. You're wonderful, Ina Funk. I need to tell you that daily."

Ina chuckled. "I shall make it a point to remind you."

Page glanced at the tray. "Those triangle sandwiches are a work of art. Thank you for saying yes to save us."

"Of course. You and Betsy have brought the fun back into my humdrum golden years. So, don't worry. I've got things under control back here." Ina placed the finished sandwich tray inside the refrigerator.

Page went to greet their morning customers. Surprise washed over her face when she saw who was waiting outside Honey Bees's door. "Welcome, Detectives Koch and Tanner. What an unexpected treat to have you two as my first customers. Our fresh baked blueberry scones are straight from the oven." Page stood aside as the two men entered.

"Scones? I'm a cop. I want doughnuts and strong coffee," said Koch.

"Grumpy, aren't we? Okay, cake donuts for you." Page

shot Steve a knowing smile and scooted behind the order counter.

Steve peered into the display case. "Ignore him. He lost the coin toss and is buying."

"You and that coin. Hey, Koch, you might want to put your detective eyes on this guy's coin. I've yet to win." Page passed him the donut. "On the house."

"Thanks, Snoop."

Page ignored the nickname. "You're welcome."

Koch took a bite and nodded approval. "And for the record, I'm not grumpy. I'm hungry."

"I can tell." Page watched as he devoured the donut.

"And I'm worried." Koch dropped the napkin in the wastebasket. "Steve told me you're getting those blasted feelings again." He turned to Steve. "What are they?"

"Tinklings." Steve pulled back to avoid Page's smack to his arm. "I mean inklings."

"Those." Kock nodded and accepted the cup of coffee. "This on the house too?"

"Sure is; enjoy." Page handed Steve his beverage. "Listen, don't worry about my inklings. Maybe the one thinking dark thoughts will change their mind and behave. Free will exists."

Koch motioned for Steve to choose something from the case. "Whatever all that means, I'm still going to worry. Steve, get that fancy fritter you like. We've got a meeting in ten minutes."

Steve held up three fingers to Page, watching her bag his favorite apple fritters made with extra cinnamon. "Thanks, Page." He reached for his credit card.

"My treat for you, too." Page waved the card away. "But next time we toss a coin. I'm supplying the nickel. Understood?"

"You're not good at losing. This I know." Amusement glinted in Steve's eyes. "Have I told you lately that I dig it when you're sassy?"

"I heard that, Tanner. No hanky-panky out there," hollered Betsy from the hallway. "Go find some baddies to arrest."

"I'm leaving, Duenna Betsy. You two stay out of mischief." Steve turned his eyes on Page. "I'm serious."

"I know." Page glanced at Koch waiting at the door before turning back to Steve. "Be safe out there, Detective. I want to go sailing soon on Carpe Diem."

"Hey, want to kiss me bye?" Steve leaned across the counter, presenting his cheek.

Betsy appeared with a plate of cookies destined for the glass-domed dish. "Enough, Detective Dreamboat. I'm busy and don't care to monitor your hormones' bad behavior in our place of business. Take your hot lips and be gone." Betsy's arm made shooing motions.

Both women watched smiling as Shell Isle's most capable detectives made their leave.

"I feel safe knowing those two are watching over our beach town. Here, taste this new recipe." Betsy handed Page a cookie. "Tell me if the Spicer Cookie belongs on the tea cart."

Taking a bite, Page released a cough and covered her mouth. "What?" She coughed again and felt her eyes water. "What kind of cookie is this?"

"You've got the weakest constitution of anyone I know. I must work harder to get your taste buds to evolve." Betsy poured Page a cup of water and watched her drink down its contents.

"Those are lit matches disguised as cookies." Page laid the remaining cookie on a napkin.

"Very funny. It's the cayenne waking up your sluggish

taster. I think Spicer Cookie is the perfect name."

"Whatever you call them, they can't go to tea. They should be used on suspects to get confessions." Grabbing the feather duster, Page went to tidy a display of honey jars.

"You know, that's not a half-bad idea. I could increase the pepper a skosh." Betsy tilted her head, pondering. "I'm needed in the kitchen. Mustn't tarry."

Page watched her cousin mumbling to herself about teaspoons and cups as she sauntered away. Tossing the cookie into the trash, Page crossed her fingers that it wouldn't start a fire.

The bell jingled, announcing a winded Alice hurrying to greet Page. Her salt-and-pepper hair was swept into a French twist. An unlined face, devoid of makeup except for a rosy shade of lipstick, denied Alice's fifty-six years of age. The lavender cotton dress complemented Shell's easygoing lifestyle.

"Good morning, Alice. This is an unexpected treat," said Page.

"I need your help fast. I've got a group of fussy authors who requested I serve scones for breakfast. Can you fix me up with a baker's dozen?"

Page nodded. "I witnessed those fussy authors last night at The Perk. You have my sympathy." Page went behind the bakery counter. "Blueberry scones, okay?"

"Perfect. Thanks." Alice released a loud exhale. "The guest service bell has rung more in the last few hours than in the month of April. I left them accusing each other of walking the halls at two a.m., causing the floors to creak. All six maintained they were in their rooms and awakened by heavy footsteps. No one owned up to the annoyance."

A frown settled on Page's face. "So, who was the culprit delivering the creaking?"

Alice looked around before responding. "It's the same mischievous two who've been visiting since I purchased Three Fables. Of course, I've yet to see them."

Page gulped. "You mean the ghosts I've heard about? I didn't believe the talk, but you're telling me—"

"I'm telling you, I think something paranormal is happening at my inn. At least I don't pick up on the spirits being malevolent. And I don't think of them as ghosts so much."

"Well, that part is good, right?" offered Page, trying to hide her reaction to the innkeeper's words.

Alice looked thoughtful. "It is. I've read that some spirits can cause all manner of troubles. Mine seem more like pranksters and only with particularly demanding guests." Alice shrugged. "I know. It's all too weird. I'm still trying to adjust and accept this explanation for the curious goings-on."

"I don't know what to say. I'm not versed in these matters." Page reached for a cardboard box and placed the scones inside. "I gather you're not afraid to remain as the innkeeper."

"No, I'm not afraid at all. I love Three Fables and its colorful history. It's odd because I feel like I was tapped to own it. Hopefully, these two unseen guests of mine and I will find a way to coexist." Alice silenced her cell phone that had begun to ring. "That was the washer repairman saying he fixed my latest woe."

Page smiled sympathetically and dressed the box of scones in a yellow cord. "You certainly seem resilient in dealing with the inn's peculiar occurrences."

Alice paused. "Thank you, Page. I don't know any other way. My main focus is ensuring my employees and guests experience quiet enjoyment while at the inn. That leads me to thank you for saving the day." Alice's expression shifted to relief.

"You're most welcome. I have an idea. How about I add a jar of our Calming Chamomile Honey? That might help reset everyone." Page grabbed one from the shelf and passed it to Alice. Want to sample?"

"Right now, I'd like to drink the jar. Throw in two more to save my nerves." Alice passed her credit card.

"Hang on a sec while I put everything in one bag," said Page. "So, do you have full occupancy at the inn?"

Alice smiled and nodded. "I do. One special guest arrived last evening to surprise Steve Tanner. She booked a reservation a month ago and swore me to secrecy. I believe she's on her way to the police station now."

Page handed off the bag. "Can you hint at who this mystery woman is?" Page ignored the slight pangs of jealousy, wondering if Steve had a past girlfriend looking to rekindle something.

Alice glanced around before whispering, "She's his Aunt Chatty, also known as Chandelle Tanner. When Steve was a kid, he couldn't pronounce her name, so Chatty she became and definitely lives up to it." Alice smiled at her words. "She's quite lovely and lively. I'm sure you'll meet her soon."

"I'll insist on it. I like her already." Page took a white cloth and wiped the counter. "I can't wait to see how Steve plans to entertain his aunt."

Alice smiled with a certain wistfulness. "You know, I've met him a couple of times around town. The detective strikes me as quite resourceful and quite handsome, too. And Chatty is nice as can be. She's already become fast friends with my two new employees."

Page placed a donut on a napkin and handed it to Alice. "This one is maple nut. My treat. So, you succeeded in finding additional help? That's good news."

"Yes." Alice took a bite. "This donut is delicious. Actually, it's quite mellowing to my mood."

"Enjoy. I'll make sure to tell Ina and Betsy." Page felt pleased that the donut's recipe had a calming influence on Alice. "I hope the new hires do a good job for you."

"They're already proving themselves to be hard workers. James and Mara came to apply for the housekeeping and front desk jobs yesterday. They were godsends, especially with a full inn. Three Fables now has the staff it needs to thrive."

"I'm glad you've got the help, considering the demanding guests staying at the inn. What do you know about Mara and James?" Page hesitated to tell Alice she'd overheard them talking on the beach. She'd wait and see how her friend responded.

"Let's see." Alice took another bite before answering. "They are brother and sister, and wanted to escape the Nantucket cold and try beach life down south. They needed jobs to stay at Shell Isle, so I offered each room, meals, and a modest hourly wage. I've given them a month to impress me. Normally, I'd ask for references first, but I was desperate yesterday when I saw the authors would be a handful. Mara promised to provide references to vouch for their character."

"James and Mara sound ideal in many ways. Still, checking out new employees is always a good idea." Page felt relieved hearing Alice would confirm their references. "Can I help with anything else?"

"No, I'm set, thanks to Honey Bees. I look forward to seeing you and Betsy in a couple of hours." Alice walked toward the door and turned back. "Do prepare dear Betsy for this quarrelsome bunch. Thanks for the donut. I feel…more myself again." Alice gave a saucy wave and closed the door, humming.

Page frowned as she recalled the authors' interactions at The Perk. The inkling warning of looming trouble was somehow tied to them. She'd stay vigilant and wait for guidance.

CHAPTER 6

"I've got another cooler to retrieve from your vehicle. Would you unpack this one first? It's the finger sandwiches." Betsy's cheeks flushed the color of strawberries and testified to her labor. "Is it hot in the inn's kitchen, or is it just me?"

Page came alongside and scooted the trays forward. "It's you. I told you to slow down emptying the cargo area." Page grabbed a dish towel and waved it in her cousin's face. "Everything is humming along. Don't worry."

"Easy for you to say. You're not the one in charge of this tea party." Betsy popped the tab on a can of sparkling water and leaned against the counter. "And where is Ina with my trolley? The last time I saw her, she and Daisy had loaded it on her husband's truck." Betsy swallowed another gulp. "Are we good leaving Daisy to run Honey Bees? Fan faster."

"You're zinging me with questions. We don't need to feel concerned about Daisy. She's worked with us since we opened our doors. Besides, Ina is going back to the shop once she delivers the tea cart. Keep sipping. I'll head outside to see if Ina's here and grab the other cooler." Page handed Betsy the towel.

The afternoon sun seemed to glorify Three Fables Inn's gardens. Page waved and walked toward the truck sputtering to a stop on the curved driveway.

Ina hopped out, wearing the widest smile her face could manage. She motioned for Page to come her way.

"Glad you made it. I left Betsy in the kitchen with her worry genes running at mach speed." Page followed Ina around to the trunk's bed.

"Don't tell on me. I took Surfside Avenue because the breeze is rather robust coming off the ocean today. Problem solved. Take a gander." Ina waved her hand at the trolley.

"You genius. That's one smart breeze choosing to blow off our springy business cards and photos." Page covered her mouth, laughing.

"Notice how the red and chartreuse ribbons couldn't handle the wind either. Maybe embarrassment won't accompany you when the cart makes its grand entrance at teatime." Ina pushed the trolley toward the tailgate. "Quick, give me a hand. Here comes Betsy. I gotta skedaddle before she has her hissy fit about the missing embellishments."

Page assisted Ina in unloading the cart. "Done. Thanks a bunch for finding that breeze. Hurry. I see Betsy's picked up her pace."

Ina jumped in the driver's seat and hollered out the window before driving away. "Don't worry about Honey Bees. Daisy and I will handle everything!"

Page retrieved the cooler from her SUV and pushed the cart toward Betsy with her free hand. Now she must explain the unpredictability of wind in an open-bed pickup truck.

"What happened to my exquisite trolley?" Betsy peered down at the updated version. "Where are our business cards attached to the bees on springs? Where are my other ribbons? This won't do." Taking stock, Betsy set her hands in motion as Page continued the forward movement.

"Betsy, the cart is perfect. No one will notice the few things missing. Ina said a gust of wind found the cart while driving here. Stop wringing your hands and help me maneuver this thing into the kitchen." Page turned her head to hide her grin, watching Betsy's face register what else wasn't trolleying along.

"Our photos are gone. Some strangers along the roadside will find us and wonder—"

"It's okay. There isn't time for more fretting. We've got an uppity tea to serve in twenty minutes. Hold the door. Coming through." Page rolled the cart up the ramp into the kitchen.

Alice appeared. "What a—colorful trolley. It's so—festive." Her eyes seemed transfixed.

"You should have seen it before the wind de-flowered and de-ribboned it." Betsy released a heavy sigh.

Alice's expression changed to confusion. "At any rate, the group upstairs is enjoying what the editor calls 'singular reflective meditation'. They know when tea is being served, so I expect they'll mosey downstairs in the next little bit."

"Thanks for letting us know." Page handed Betsy a small dish of strawberry bonbons. "We're almost ready."

"Excellent. On a happy note, I did detect a measure of enthusiasm over this special treat." Alice pointed to a platter. "Do you need my help?"

"No, but thanks for the offer. Betsy has everything planned perfectly. We've made a special sampling plate for you to enjoy." Page straightened the flowers and ribbons.

Betsy passed the innkeeper her dish. "Enjoy. Hopefully, you'll invite us back to cater."

"How thoughtful. Now that I have James and Mara here, I can slip away and savor each bite." Alice moved toward the swinging doors.

Page handed Alice a napkin. "Do try the finger sandwiches with bacon, cream cheese, and chives."

Betsy lifted her hand. "Wait a sec, Alice. By any chance, do your flower gardens have pansies?"

Alice turned back, wearing a smile. "I have a bed of pansies and the roses are blooming, too. Why?"

"We'd like to pick some edible flowers to place around the tea cakes. They need a punch of color." Betsy pointed to the cakes arranged on a white doily. "Too plain."

"Gosh, I never considered serving flowers," said Alice. "Hmm, pansies are edible flowers?"

"They certainly are. I became very informed on this subject." Betsy lifted her chin. "I'm what our Aunt Tilly called a college of knowledge."

"Aunt Tilly said you should aspire to *become* a college of knowledge," corrected Page.

"And so, I aspired and became. Ignore my cousin. Page is still bitter that I was our aunt's favorite."

Page choked on the water, allowing her cousin to have her moment.

Betsy shot her cousin a look before placing the last serving dish and matching cups on the trolley beside the daisy teapot. "Anyway, Page and I learned what flowers were safe to consume when working our second murder case at Shell Isle. Too bad the girl guiding us ended up—"

Page jumped in. "Never mind that part, Bets. Can you direct us to the pansies and roses, Alice?"

"Of course. Head out the back door and turn right. You'll need to weave around the tall perimeter hedge to the edible garden. To the right, you'll see an iron gate where the perennial gardens thrive. Enter and you'll see two bronze statues of the husband and wife who built Three Fables almost two hundred years ago. Please take a moment to admire the artistry."

"We shall make a point to visit the statue gardens," replied Page. "We both adore flowers."

"Most especially hibiscus," chirped Betsy.

Alice took another look at the cart. "It's all so colorful, ladies. So very colorful. Thank you for creating a formal

English tea for my guests. I'll pop back and let you know when everyone has arrived."

"I'll put the kettle on when we return from posy picking," Betsy said. "I finally get to make the kettle talk like they do on the British mysteries. Page Wright? Are you listening?" Betsy turned away to search for something.

The inkling flashed through Page's body, leaving her stunned by its intensity. She gripped the kitchen counter for support, waiting for the sensation to pass. "I'm listening. Let's go find these flowers," answered Page, trying to hide what had happened.

"Here's our wee baskets for the flowers," Betsy engaged her Irish brogue. "Do you fancy the white or the tan one?"

"White. Thanks." Page draped it over her forearm. "We'd better hurry." The reason would soon become evident.

"Lead the way. You know how bad I am with directions." Betsy closed the door behind them. "It's a glorious afternoon. I almost hate being indoors."

"Me, too. I had no idea the inn's property was so extensive." Page listened as Betsy hummed a tune without a melody.

Both cousins continued walking in companionable silence, taking in the beautiful landscaping and bubbling fountains. The grounds appeared manicured at first glance, but upon closer observation, a gardener's eye would see that more care was needed for the property.

Betsy's voice broke their quiet. "Lavender. My gosh, I see a planting of it over there. You go on, and I'll catch up. I must have some to replace the flowers missing from the trolley."

Page pulled a face, thinking the tea cart would soon look like it belonged to a vendor selling flowers. "All right. I see the seven-foot hedge up ahead. I'll pick the pansies after

I peek at the statues." A familiar nudge of urgency touched her back.

Hurrying to the gate, Page lifted the latch and entered. The tall box hedge wrapped around the perimeter of the gardens and acted as a protector. A willow tree offered shade to a wrought-iron bench that usually invited visitors to pause and enjoy nature's beauty. Two five-foot-tall bronze statues were supposed to flank the far corners as if the original owners were overseeing the comings and goings. Only not today. Page took in the scene and gasped. A toppled statue lay next to a lifeless body draped over the bench.

CHAPTER 7

Page glanced around. Seeing no one, she approached the body she recognized as Evelyn Potts. The inkling's warning had proved valid once again. Her fingers checked for a pulse and found none. Quickly studying the scene, she noted the statue's base showed a crack, as if age had been unkind to its support. Was this a tragic accident? If it had been anyone else's face staring up at her, Page might have considered that a plausible explanation. But this was someone who courted others' dislike. A deliberate act to end Evelyn's life couldn't be easily dismissed. The inklings had brought her here. Page knew that her next step was to discover whose hand toppled the statue.

Evelyn had angered the wrong person. Bending down again, Page glimpsed a plain shirt button resting in the author's half-opened hand. And in the other hand, Evelyn clutched her cell phone. Page snapped a few quick photos of the upsetting scene and tucked her phone away.

"Page? Are you inside the garden?" Betsy's voice came from behind the hedge. "I've got scads of lavender to restore the trolley. Halloo, Page?"

"I'm in here. Go around."

Betsy appeared at the gate. "Oh no! What's happened?" Her fingers lifted the latch.

"Don't come inside. There's been a terrible—call Steve. Now!" Page's eyes scanned the area once more. All she saw were the sprinklers awakening outside the garden gate. The sound of a screen door slamming off in the distance offered no answers. Page walked toward her cousin. "Call."

"Right. I'm dialing Steve." Betsy's voice quivered. "Who is it, and is she—?"

"One of the authors." Page stepped outside the gate. "She's dead. And I'm pretty sure someone caused this tragedy."

Betsy shook her head with vigor. "No, you don't think that. Please don't think that. I know what it means to my peace and serenity. I feel horrible for the poor woman, but Page, you can't involve us in—Hi, Steve; it's Betsy. We're at Three Fables Inn, and Page has something important to tell you while I go have a big cry." Betsy shoved the phone at her cousin. "Your story to deliver. My tea party to go and cancel." Betsy sniffed loudly and hurried to find Alice.

"What's Betsy going on about now? She lives for drama in food and everything else in her orbit." Steve's voice sounded exasperated.

"Listen to me, Detective Tanner. I've found one of the authors we saw at The Perk last night. She's dead in the enclosed gardens, and it's not pretty. Her head is—just get here with your team."

"I knew it. Those inklings. I'm running out the door now and will dispatch who we need." Steve's words were coming in spurts. "Are you okay? I'm sorry, Page. I should have asked that first."

"I'm fine, or I wouldn't be talking to you right now."

"Do you feel safe remaining at the scene? I don't want someone to corrupt evidence."

"After my involvement in three murder cases with you, I know the protocol. I haven't seen anyone around, so I'll stay put until you arrive. I'm sure Betsy's gone to tell Alice." Page lifted the latch on the gate and stepped back inside.

"That's fine. Keep talking to me. Fortunately, Three

Fables is nearby. I'll be there before you know it." Steve spoke to the dispatcher, giving instructions.

Page glanced at the statue of the man. A look to compare the bases wouldn't pose a problem. Minutes passed while she listened to Steve speak to the medical examiner's office.

"Page? I'm back. You've gone silent on me. Don't you dare start snooping at my scene."

Her hand stroked the bronze statue of the man who once owned Three Fables. "Something doesn't add up. Why is one statue's base in good condition and—"

"Don't start adding up things that are police business. Step away from the statues. Stand under a tree and tell me about the tea soiree."

"We never had a chance to serve tea or have the trolley make its embarrassing debut. No one will sample our delicious cakes and sandwiches. Instead…" Page felt her throat tighten as the reality of what had transpired hit her full force. Tears pooled in her aqua eyes. She plopped down on the grass as she caught sight of Steve running like an Olympian toward her. Betsy and Alice followed behind.

Steve stooped down beside Page. His fingers lightly caressed her cheek and wiped away a stray tear. "Hey, I'm here. And I'm sorry your catering job ended in this way. Would you like to go with Betsy and Alice back inside the inn while I coordinate the investigation?"

Page looked over her shoulder and saw Alice and Betsy waiting outside the gate. Concern and shock registered on their faces. "No. I need to stay here and help you. Maybe I can offer something." Page stood and signaled her cousin and Alice to return to the inn.

"If you're sure. I hear the vehicles arriving." Steve led them toward the bench and Evelyn. "The medical examiner will give us a preliminary overview of what happened. Until then, I'd like to know your thoughts, Sherlocka. You were led here for a reason."

Hearing Steve's nickname for her helped lighten the moment as they gazed down. "It's Evelyn from last night at The Perk. She was the one who was all huffy. You can see how she's holding a cell phone with streaks of blood. I assume your IT guy can unlock it and see if it offers any answers?"

"He can try, but the phone will need to visit the state's lab. What else?" Steve's eyes narrowed as he took in the statue beside the damaged bench. Bending down, he pointed to the blood already drying on the bronze figure's leg. "Looks like this part made direct contact with Evelyn's head."

"Seems so." Page gave a quick nod and looked away. "Two things stand out for me. One, the statue's concrete base has a sizable crack, and the bolt holding it in place is missing. Having water get inside could compromise the structural integrity and create a safety hazard if someone pushed on it."

"You're right." Steve snapped a photo with his phone.

Page continued, "If Evelyn did the pushing, wouldn't it fall away from her? I doubt she'd pull it toward herself."

"I'd come to the same conclusion. We'll see what the M.E. says. What else?" Steve stepped back, taking in the scene around them.

"The other statue's base looks fine. Come and see." Page walked Steve over and pointed.

"Hmm, that's strange, assuming they're the same age. Perhaps Alice had this one repaired?" Steve typed on his tablet. "I'll ask her. What else? I see the team coming across the yard now."

"Let's go back to the body. That's the second thing I want to point out."

"Okay, point." Steve gazed at Evelyn and waited.

"Look closely. You can see a shirt button in her left

hand. And that's a clue most curious, Detective Tanner. Her clothes don't have buttons that match this one."

With a gloved hand, Steve pulled a small evidence bag from his pocket and scooped the white button into it. "It could easily belong to a man's or a woman's garment. I doubt the deceased would sit on a bench, clasping a button like it was a rosary. I suspect Evelyn pulled it off the person involved in this — maybe in a struggle."

Page felt the tightness return to her throat as emotions tried to surface. She forced her words out. "After overhearing Evelyn interact harshly with the others, I agree. We're looking at a deliberate or possibly an accidental act resulting in her death."

"I concur with your assessment." Steve waved to Detective Koch.

Page gave a little groan seeing the detective approach. "Just my luck. He's working today."

An amused expression passed across Steve's face. "Listen, the crew is coming in now. Would you mind waiting at the inn? Find Betsy. Have her make you a cup of plain tea. Tell her I ordered none of her special concoctions to touch your lips."

"A cup of tea is exactly what I need. Thanks. I'll see you in a bit." Page took a step. Steve grabbed her hand.

"Are you really okay? This scene is even tough for me to witness." Emotion flickered in his eyes.

"I will be." Page heard her voice crack. "Eventually." She turned, walking toward the other detective.

Koch had his words waiting. "Here I am again, finding Shell Isle's biggest snoop at a scene of —"

"Of another tragedy. Yes. And you'd do well this time to try and solve this case before me, Detective Koch." Page found her gumption and awarded Koch's typical taunts with a barb. She liked the man, but their banter was the last thing she needed. What she needed was a moment to accept the inklings had delivered her another case. And judging by what she already knew, this one was shaping into a doozy.

CHAPTER 8

Page searched for Betsy and Alice and found them on the covered porch keeping two wooden rockers company. "Are you trying to rock away this horrible death?"

"If only we could," responded Alice. "I don't know which way to turn. What should I do? It's all so awful." Alice released a sob.

Betsy reached over and patted Alice's hand. "There now. We'll see you through this. Won't we, Page?"

"Of course, we want to help in any way we can. What's needed right now is calming tea. Shall I get us cups from the trolley?" Page moved toward the double doors leading into the inn's parlor.

"No tea trolley treasures for us. The group is busy partaking as we speak. They insisted on having the cart brought in despite our imparting the sad news about Evelyn Potts." Alice dabbed her cheeks with a tissue.

Betsy's eyes locked on Page. "Get a load of this. No one, and I mean no one, seemed upset hearing about Evelyn. Teatime mattered more. We left them all oohing and aahing over our cakes and sandwiches. Can you imagine?"

"Didn't anyone want details about Evelyn's death?" asked Page, knowing that answer mattered.

"Alice volunteered that she'd been found beside a fallen statue in the garden. We heard a couple of tuts, and her assistant sniffed a bit. Then, it was, 'Please, someone pass the cake platter around.'" Betsy shook her head.

"Mara, could you come out for a moment?" Alice

motioned to her housekeeper, who was dusting an antique table just inside the open door.

Page recognized the young woman from the beach. She purposely dropped her sunglasses over her eyes in case Mara somehow recalled seeing her.

"Yes? Did you need something?" Mara wore a bored expression.

"Would you be a dear and bring us a pitcher of lemonade and glasses?" asked Alice.

"Certainly." Mara disappeared inside.

"She's proving most adept, which I so desperately need now more than ever. I trust that beverage is acceptable, ladies?" Alice waited.

"A tall, iced lemonade sounds even better than tea," answered Page. "Thank you."

"Fine by me." Betsy activated her hand fan with a loud sigh. "These miserable hot flashes don't discriminate on when they hit. In my next life, I'm coming back as a man if there's no draft. These feet don't march." Betsy lifted both legs and gazed at her sandaled feet.

The three women exchanged brief smiles before questions of what was facing them came calling.

"Anytime now, I suppose you and I get to suffer Detective Koch's wrath and twisted sense of humor?" Betsy glanced toward the garden and saw Evelyn's body being taken away. "Don't look. They're moving her."

"Yes, I expect we'll all have to be questioned." Page sat up straighter in the chair.

"Surely not me. I don't know the woman," said Mara, appearing with a tray carrying the pitcher and six matching glasses. "I brought extra glasses, should you have visitors."

Alice accepted her glass with a nod of thanks. "I wouldn't think my three staff would offer any help on this matter."

"Everyone will be interviewed. And Koch would question your cat if you had one. That's how they operate. Nice that you brought us cookies." Betsy smiled at Mara and reached for the single fudgy one. "I do love chocolate."

Alice rejected the cookie plate. "But surely an accident doesn't necessitate such in-depth involvement. Thank you, Mara. Please continue with your tasks."

Page decided to enlighten Alice and set the wheels in motion for what was indeed minutes away. "I'm sorry to have to tell you this, but I believe Evelyn Potts's death came from another's hand."

"What? How's this possible, and at my inn? And here I thought things couldn't get worse for me and Three Fables." Alice pulled her tissue from the box sitting on the wicker table. "Who would do such a thing?"

"Someone not very nice," chimed in Betsy. "I can't believe it either."

Alice gasped. "That means the person who did this is staying at Three Fables. Am I right, Page?" Her expression shifted to fear.

"That's likely true, and you can expect Detective Tanner to have instructions for everyone to follow. He'll probably assign an officer to ease worry and protect the crime scene."

Alice leaned forward. "Detective Tanner? Gracious, I completely forgot that his aunt is a guest here. Right now, she's off shopping for less formal attire. He'll no doubt have concerns about her staying at the inn."

"Page is correct. Steve has his methods. It's better to wait for things to unfold. Like our Aunt Tilly used to tell us, 'Don't borrow trouble.'"

"Steve will make sure Aunt Chatty is safe." Page stole a peek at her watch, already dreading the inquiry process.

"Please excuse me for a moment. I need to tell Mara to dust the library." Alice slipped inside the double doors.

Betsy set her glass on the table and released an exasperated sigh. "This is beyond dreadful on all counts. Your inklings have done it again. They've put us right back in the sleuthing business when all I wanted was to spend my days at Honey Bees and bake lovely delectables with Ina."

"I know, Bets. Shh, here comes Alice."

"Hand me a tissue while I decide if I'm throwing a hissy fit or getting into one of my snits."

"You'd better decide fast. Shell Isle's three finest are headed our way, too. And that includes your new beau, Andre." Page rose from the rocker.

"Page, did you say Andre's here? I look hideous. Check me out fast. Is my face tomato red from this hot flash? No, don't answer." Betsy pulled an ice cube from her lemonade glass and ran it around her cheeks.

Alice claimed her rocker, watching Betsy's actions. Her expression softened. "I must meet this Andre who causes you to smear a sticky lemonade ice cube on your face."

Page chuckled, appreciating their lighthearted shift, even if for a moment. "Our Betsy is quite besotted by this French Canadian."

"Would you two hush? Here they are now." Betsy tossed the ice cube over her shoulder into the grass. "Hi, Andre and Detective Dreamboat." Betsy caught Page's frown at her nickname for the detective. "Pardon the slip. I meant Detective Tanner."

Both men climbed the porch steps wearing solemn faces. Andre nodded to Betsy while Steve chose his spot to address the women. Koch stayed back speaking to an officer.

"I'm sorry we're meeting under these circumstances. I can now provide you with my official update on this case.

Shell Isle's medical examiner is confident Evelyn Potts died from the statue fracturing her skull and crushing her chest. We believe that it was likely pushed from its structurally unsound base." Steve paused.

"This is horrible." Alice reached for a tissue.

Steve nodded. "So, those are the facts. Now we begin the challenging task of discovering who did the act. I'd appreciate hearing if you noticed anything. And as part of the investigative process, I want to know your movements this afternoon. It's a formality." Steve pulled a chair to sit.

"Excuse me, Detective Tanner, would you like me to gather the guests and staff for your questioning?" Andre paused at the double doors leading inside the inn.

"See to it. But make sure the employees are separated from the guests." Steve offered a curt nod and watched Andre disappear.

Alice raised her hand like a student in a classroom.

"Yes?" asked Steve, not hiding his amusement.

"Your Aunt Chatty should arrive back any moment. She went shopping. Must you include that sweet woman in this most unfortunate affair?"

Steve rose quickly. "Do you have any other guests staying here unrelated to the British group, or is my aunt the only one?"

"Thankfully, just her. The inn is fully booked," replied Alice.

"And you have three employees who have rooms here as well, correct?" asked Steve, heading for the doors.

"Correct." Alice twisted her tissue. "This seems like a bad dream."

"Ladies, I'll be right back. I need to let Andre know about my aunt."

"I'm starving. I wonder if I could slip in and check out

the trolley? Maybe they left something for us?" Betsy started to rise, but glimpsed an older woman off in the distance stepping out of a taxi, carrying shopping bags. "Is that Chatty?"

"Oh, yes. I must go to her." Alice hurried down the steps. "Chatty, let me help. Judging by the bags, your shopping was a success. Please join us for lemonade."

"It certainly was. I'm parched and would love some refreshment." Chatty's twinkling blue eyes took in Page and Betsy as she chose a white, wicker swivel chair.

Alice poured the liquid into a glass and passed it to Chatty while making introductions.

"So, you're the Page my nephew likes inviting aboard his sailboat. I've been looking forward to meeting you."

"I'm always a willing first mate if it means sailing on Carpe Diem. And it's nice to discover Steve has an aunt." Page hoped she passed muster.

Chatty offered a friendly smile. She drank from her glass and gave a lip smack. "This lemonade is delicious. Do I detect a dash of cherry juice?"

"My secret is out." Alice forced a smile. "Chatty, I must tell you something positively dreadful that happened here this afternoon." Alice sniffed. "Pardon me. One of the guests has been —"

"Alice, let me explain for you." Page turned to Steve's aunt. "I discovered one of the guests, Evelyn Potts, in the garden a little while ago. The bronze statue from the gated garden had fallen on her." Page paused, allowing her words to register. "And even more tragic, the police feel confident someone pushed it."

"How frightful." Chatty's eyes darted toward the door and back to Page.

"It's horrible to have something like this happen at Three Fables and to a guest. Steve and the other officers arrived and began the investigation. He went inside to ensure you were kept separate from the writing group." Page swirled the liquid in her glass, lost in thought.

"I'm sure he'll soon find me here." Chatty tapped her chin in thought. "You know, I spoke to Evelyn earlier today. I was in the library choosing a mystery to read when I heard loud voices in the hall. I wonder..."

Betsy jumped in. "What do you wonder? It could prove important."

Chatty placed her drink on the table, glanced around, and lowered her voice. "I don't want anyone to hear me. When I was in the library, I heard one of the gentlemen who exhibits an affection for bow ties tell Evelyn that if he could resurrect one of the murderers from her books, he'd have them kill her on the spot. I believe his name is Chester something." Chatty reached again for her lemonade. "It's quite disturbing to have overheard that exchange now that the woman is dead."

"Did you hear them say anything else?" asked Page.

"Evelyn said something like he didn't possess an ounce of gumption to even dress like a real man, much less kill her." Chatty took a pause. "I remember she laughed. The sound of it was troubling. It wasn't the kind of laugh one would want to be directed at their person. The sound had a darkness to it."

"What else did Evelyn say to Chester?" encouraged Betsy.

"She told him if he didn't make the payment, she'd tell everyone of his deceit. That's when Evelyn entered the library and saw me. I pretended to be engrossed in reading, but it didn't work. She knew I couldn't help but have overheard the exchange."

"You said Evelyn spoke to you." Mentally, Page put Chester in first place on her suspect board.

"Oh, we had a most unpleasant exchange. Evelyn told

me I'd best forget everything I'd heard, or I might find my stay unpleasant. I assured her that I had no interest in meddling in her affairs. And then, I hurried out of the library."

Betsy nodded. "You were very wise to do that."

"I thought so, too, but I was wrong. I ventured to the veranda to calm my nerves. Unfortunately, someone followed me."

"Chester?" Page and Betsy said in unison.

Chatty bobbed her head, causing her hair to release from the antique, cloisonne barrette. "It seems Chester found a smidge of gumption and decided to try it on me. He advised me quite vehemently to consider finding another inn to stay at post haste."

Alice's expression shifted to anger. "The nerve. I must speak to this man. I won't have a guest—"

"Hang on. We need to let Chatty finish her story." Page sent an encouraging smile toward Steve's aunt.

Chatty clasped her hands in her lap. "I have one more thing to share from these two upsetting encounters. What troubled me most was when Chester looked me straight in the eye and said, 'There are spirits present that wish to cause harm. Take your leave while you can, madam, and speak nothing of what you've observed.'"

CHAPTER 9

"Those words sound like they belong in another century." Page swallowed more worry.

Betsy activated her fan. "Is he warning you about ghostly spirits or living ones at the inn?"

"I haven't a clue," said Chatty. "I can tell you I refuse to let some man with a tacky bow tie and tomato-red suspenders run me off."

"I find Betsy's question interesting and yet perplexing." Alice's lips drew a fine line. "Chatty, your support is appreciated, but I want you safe."

Page gathered her thoughts before replying. "In time, we'll have the answers. For now, we must observe the others."

Color receded from Alice's face. "I fear Three Fables' reputation will soon become besmirched with talk such as Chester's, especially after the tragedy this afternoon. What shall I do? I'm already in dire need of funds for upkeep, and now this." Tears streamed down Alice's cheeks.

Betsy reached for the innkeeper's hand. "Don't worry about any of that now. We're here to support you."

"That's right. You can count on Betsy and me. Everything will work out somehow. I know it," said Page.

"You must listen to your friends. And please see me as a new friend." Chatty's face brightened. "There now, Alice. We must soldier on. Excuse me for a moment. I need a breath of air."

Steve appeared in the doorway. "Apologies, we had one of the authors who was unwilling to cooperate. He's now enjoying Koch's company."

"Was it Chester?" asked Page.

"How did you know?" Steve looked puzzled.

"He'll soon wish he'd behaved and minded his Ps and Qs," responded Betsy. "We know some things about your Chester."

"And I want to hear about those things pronto." Steve caught sight of his aunt standing at the far end of the porch. "Aunt Chatty, I'm glad you're back. Please come join us."

"Of course." Chatty returned to her chair and made a fuss getting situated before turning her gaze to her nephew. "I have something to share regarding my interactions with Evelyn and Chester."

"You have my full attention." Steve sat next to his aunt.

"I believe I know who took Evelyn's life."

Steve's head shot up. "By all means, tell us. The sooner we close this case, the sooner Alice can return to running her inn."

The three women listened while Chatty retold her encounters with Evelyn and Chester. She'd omitted his final words.

"You're right. Chester's menacing exchange casts him as the likely one involved." Steve stood and paced the porch.

Betsy tapped Chatty's knee. "Aren't you going to tell Dreamboat — I mean Steve — about Chester's veiled threat?"

Page frowned at Betsy for the embarrassing nickname reference before turning to Chatty. "You need to tell Steve."

"All right, but I refuse to leave this inn." Chatty repeated Chester's words to her nephew.

"Hearing this means you're staying at my bungalow," declared Steve.

"I'm remaining here with Alice, where I'm comfortable. Your bungalow lacks a proper guest room. I promise that I won't interact with the guests. I can be your eyes and ears."

Steve's hands brushed through his black hair. "I don't need another snoop. I've got two sitting next to you that I can't control. After their involvement in another case, I may decide to sail away on Carpe Diem."

Page laughed. "You're not leaving Shell Isle. Your surfboard owns you. Besides, Betsy and I are assets. Listen, Steve, I sense it's safe for Chatty to remain at the inn. She's a keen observer. You need that if you want to wrap this case fast."

"Thank you, Page. I do intend to make contributions. You'll have an officer on the premises. I have no concerns." Chatty tilted her chin. "It's settled. What else do you want from us ladies?"

"Okay, I'll go along for the moment." Steve turned his attention to the other three women. "Did any of you notice anything or anyone suspicious before or after Page found Evelyn Potts?"

Betsy shook her head. "The only ones I interacted with since we arrived are Alice and Chatty. Wait. I did thank Mara for the cookies."

"Duly noted, Ms. Ross." Steve typed notes into his tablet.

Page lifted her finger. "Give me a sec." She glanced at her cell phone, reading Ina's text that she'd closed Honey Bees after an uneventful afternoon. Page turned her attention to Steve. "To answer your question, I was busy in the kitchen with Betsy preparing for the tea until we went outside to pick flowers. The only thing I heard after I found Evelyn was a door slam at the inn. I doubt that had any significance."

"Probably not. Anything else you want to add?" asked Steve.

Page tucked her cell phone back into her bag. "Just

that you were with me last night at The Perk. You listened to the group's conversation. Some of them aren't exactly bosom buddies. I feel certain that Evelyn Potts isn't—make that wasn't—liked. I can understand why, too. My question is, who most wanted her out of their way? There lies our motive. Then it's a matter of who had the opportunity to use the means—in this case, the statue."

"Agreed," said Steve. "Alice? What have you observed that might prove valuable? Take a moment and reflect."

Alice let the porch rocker take her back in time to ponder. "I can't recall anything meaningful except that some of the guests lack polite manners. Other than a quick check with the guests to confirm the teatime and then Page and Betsy in the kitchen, I spent the afternoon in my office catching up on the daunting number of bills. James was working the front desk and saw me enter the office." Alice paused her words. "I keep guest interactions to a minimum. They're here to relax and enjoy Shell Isle. Of course, with your aunt, I confess to breaking my rule." Alice smiled over at Chatty. "You're a pure delight, my new friend."

"You are too kind," replied Chatty. "If we're done here, I want to retire to my room for a rest before dinner."

"For now, yes. Let me know if you think of or see anything concerning." Steve turned to Page. A half smile appeared on his face. "Care to barter with me, Sherlocka?"

The detective's dimples were her downfall. Page sighed and felt the annoying flutters. "Depends. Let me hear it first."

Alice and Chatty disappeared inside while Betsy rose from her rocker and parked her hands on her generous hips.

"Stay put, Bets. This involves you." Steve's focus returned to Page. "I will allow you to do what you do best, which is to eavesdrop on my interview with the writing group and the three employees."

"I'm waiting for the catch." Page glanced at Betsy's sour expression. She knew their sleuthing caps were back on their heads.

"You may listen and offer inklings and intuitions, whatever you call them, if you agree to Betsy staying at Hibiscus until the case is solved. And before you throw up flak, my reasons are sound. The murderer knows you're involved because you found the body. And likely by now has heard of your reputation for meddling."

"Again with the meddling talk?" Betsy huffed. "Listen, buster, who solved three murder cases for you? We did. Me and Page. I'm having a flash and forgot the rest of what I wanted to say." Betsy looked at Page. "I think staying at Hibiscus is a dandy idea. For once, I like what came out of Detective Dreamboat's mouth."

"Would you stop with the Dreamboat? We're really good friends with possibilities. Tell her, Steve." Page lifted both hands and released a heavy sigh.

Steve's laugh rang out. "We're really good friends with all kinds of possibilities. And for the record, I like hearing Page thinks me a dreamboat."

"Enough of this malarkey, although gosh knows we could all use a dose of humor." Page stood. "I agree to the barter. Let's go do this."

"Excellent. Betsy, sit tight. I'll have Andre take you home to pack." Steve motioned to an officer. "Find Andre."

"We'll have fun tonight. It'll be like old days." Betsy clapped her hands.

"Betsy, you only moved out of Hibiscus two months ago." Page waved to Andre as he approached.

"It sure seems longer. I guess I've been lonely." Betsy looked wistful. "Steve, can you have one of your guys drop the tea trolley off at Honey Bees on Monday, unless you want to keep it for fingerprints or something?"

"Possibly." Steve silenced his cell phone ringing.

Betsy tapped her forehead with her bright purple fan. "Hey, here's an idea. How about the four of us grab dinner later at the Crab Shak?"

"Sounds good to me. Tonight's special is the Clam Po Boy," said Andre. He motioned for Betsy to proceed with him down the steps.

Steve patted his washboard stomach. "I'm in for the clams if I can get these interviews done and the crime scene secured. You two go, and I'll text you later to confirm."

Page sniffed, pretending disdain. "No one bothered to ask me if I was good with the plan."

"Apologies, my lady. Would you do me the great honor of dining with me this evening?" Steve did a bow.

"Does that mean you're buying?" quipped Page. "If yes, I'm your clam-digging date."

"Affirmative. Now, let's go rattle some suspects."

A pair of watchful eyes withdrew from the library's window, seeing Page and Steve move toward the French doors.

CHAPTER 10

The group sat corralled in the library with Koch's sour expression staring them down. No one spoke, but their unhappiness at being summoned to discuss Evelyn's death hung in the air.

Page sensed it as she entered the room. The five seated would soon learn they now carried the label of suspects.

Taking in the library's décor, Page thought it spoke of days long past when an evening invited a leatherbound book in one hand and a glass of sherry in the other. Walnut-paneled walls with a ceiling tiled in vintage tin created an old-world feel, as if the original owners wished to maintain certain decorum and lifestyle of the day.

Steve motioned Page toward a cream-colored, upholstered Victorian chair tucked in a corner. She sat admiring the Tiffany lamp on a table next to her, careful to avoid eye contact with anyone. She'd wait for Steve to explain her presence.

"All right, everyone, let me introduce myself properly. I'm Detective Tanner, and Detective Koch has been your host for the last few minutes. The woman sitting near the door is a police consultant whom we often rely upon to assist during investigations. I understand you've been Mirandized and know your rights. Is that correct?"

Steve was rewarded with nods and 'yes's.

"Excellent. Just so you know, Ms. Potts's body has been taken for an autopsy. We believe her death happened sometime between one and three o'clock today. We're treating Evelyn's death as a murder unless the final report says otherwise." Steve sat on the edge of the massive, carved mahogany desk. His eyes traveled slowly around the room, gauging reactions before he accepted the police tablet from Koch and typed something.

Page knew her role was to observe and pay attention to any insights that came. Steve would signal her if he needed more. She watched Koch move toward the door. It was a stance he always took when an interview might turn unfriendly. Page swallowed her apprehension and waited for Steve to continue. She ignored Chester's glare directed her way.

"Okay, I'd like to ask each of you to tell me where you were between one and three." Turning his gaze on Fiona, "Let's begin with you." Steve looked questioningly at Detective Koch.

"Her name is Fiona Salt. She's their editor," supplied Koch.

"You may call me Fiona." Her eyes looked directly at Steve.

"Thank you, Fiona. I understand you organized this writer's retreat. I regret that your visit to Shell Isle has resulted in the death of one of your authors. Now, if you wouldn't mind answering my question."

Fiona cleared her throat. "I spent the afternoon catching up on email correspondence in my room. I came down for tea and heard what happened to our Evelyn."

Steve moved toward Fiona and met her gaze. "Can anyone corroborate that you were in the room?"

Fiona glanced around at the others, who shook their heads. "Sorry. It seems not."

Page grabbed a small notebook and pen from her tote bag. She noted that if further investigation of Fiona's alibi was needed, Steve could check her laptop for the time emails were sent. Page knew he'd probably thought of it, but she didn't take anything for granted.

Steve turned to Leo. "You're up next. Can you tell me your whereabouts Mr. —"

"Leo Birdwhistle." The author scowled at Chester, who was making bird calls. "Shut up, Chaucer. Your surname is an embarrassment to speak, but it suits you."

Page bit her lip to keep from laughing, anticipating hearing Chester's intro. Steve's ability to maintain a solemn face was award-worthy.

"Please answer. I want to conclude these interviews and move on with my investigation." Steve leaned against the desk.

"I took a relaxing bath and had a quick kip until teatime. And no, I don't have any witnesses for these acts."

"What in dang blazes is a kip?" asked Koch from across the room.

"It's a British word for a nap or sleep," supplied Fiona.

Koch shrugged. "New one for me. Apologies, Detective Tanner; please continue."

"Thank you, Mr. Birdwhistle." Steve moved to stand in front of the second woman. "Would you mind telling me your full name and where you were between one and three o'clock this afternoon?"

Grace's eyes darted to Page as if needing a sympathetic face. "I'm Grace Culpepper, and a personal assistant to Evelyn. I was busy typing Evelyn's last three chapters." Grace brushed a teardrop from her cheek and wiped her hand on her unremarkable tan skirt. "You see, Evelyn didn't type."

Steve nodded. "I understand."

"I like to keep up with my work. I do a good job. Evelyn likes to tell me that often. I—"

"I'm sure, but can anyone vouch that you were working upstairs?" asked Steve.

"I can. My room is next to Grace's. I could hear her chattering away. The walls are thinner than tissue paper at this inn," answered Leo. "It was quite bothersome to my kip."

"So, you're telling me you didn't sleep during the hours in question?" Steve's focus shifted to Leo.

Chester did an encore of a bird chirping and was rewarded with a glower from Leo.

"Of course, I slept. I'm simply telling you that Grace's incessant talking awakened me. I assume she was conversing with herself." Leo pulled on his mustache and affected a bored pose.

"Grace? Were you talking to yourself or someone in the room?" asked Steve.

"Myself. It's a bad habit. You see, I talk to the characters when I'm typing." Grace lowered her voice as if the following words were exposing her naivete. "Evelyn's characters are quite liberated and do unspeakable things."

Raised eyebrows from the other two women followed Leo's loud guffaws.

Hearing his reaction, Grace seemed to shrink into her chair.

Page knew Steve's kind nature felt some compassion toward Grace, but his detective's heart ruled in this situation. He'd grab control soon enough.

"I have the picture, Grace. Thank you." Steve walked around the library's perimeter, giving Page a wink before he returned to the five. "You know what I find curious? So far, no one has said they visited another. Don't you all like each other?"

Chester leaned back in his chair. "I'd say your keen observation and questions deserve an answer. Personally speaking, I find the lot a bunch of tossers."

"Do ya now?" Ruby came to life sitting on the red velvet loveseat next to Fiona. "You need to shut your gob. We're all tired of you lording over us."

Steve held up his hands. "Enough of your gobs and tossers. Has it failed to register that I'm running this interview session because each of you is under suspicion?" Steve's jaw clenched. "Now, no one interrupts or interjects without me giving permission. Am I making myself understood?" Not waiting for answers, Steve turned his attention to Chester. "Okay, introduce yourself and tell me where you were this afternoon."

Chester straightened his bow tie. "I'm Chester Tickle, a paranormal mystery author of some fame."

Page covered her mouth. The description "full of himself" defined Chester Tickle. Still, he was the one who issued a cloaked threat to Chatty and Evelyn. Hearing his answers carried weight with Page since he was the primary suspect.

"I told you his last name was a doozy," chirped Leo Birdwhistle.

Steve bent down to get eye level on Leo's face. "One more comment, and I'll extend you a special invitation to the police station."

Leo's eyes narrowed at the words. "I'm done."

"Mr. Tickle, would you be so kind as to answer the last part of my question?" Steve moved to stand in front of Chester.

"I found my room off-putting. I didn't feel alone there, so I meandered about." Chester crossed his leg and set it in motion, like a cat releasing energy with his tail.

"I'm going to ignore your room accommodations not meeting expectations, but I'd appreciate knowing more specifics on your meandering." Steve typed a few notes before looking down at Chester. "Did you see anyone suspicious? Did you happen to meander to the gardens?"

Page knew Steve's interest was piqued. She wondered if he would bring up Chester's two threats in front of the others.

"I might have. I can't recall. I don't like your tone or implications, Detective." Chester looked away.

Steve ignored the barb. "You know, Mr. Tickle, you're a most interesting man. After this interview, I'd like to continue this conversation with you alone."

"I have no wish to speak with you further, Detective, whatever your name is." Chester twisted to face the window. The sound of material tearing caused him to look down at his trousers. A splintered piece of wood from the chair had delivered instant karma. A gaping flap of purple, plaid boxers exposed a near-hairless, white thigh. Chester released a loud groan, ignoring the chuckles and mumblings. His hand closed the flap and glared at Steve. "We're done. I'm returning to my room with whoever unseen is occupying it with me." Chester rose and attempted to walk bent over, holding the fabric.

A smirking Koch approached the man. "Hey, Tickle, you mustn't hurt Detective Tanner's feelings by declining his invite." Koch lifted Chester under the arm to encourage him to stand straight. "Come on with me. Don't worry about showing off those gams of yours. I think the ladies can resist."

Chester's anger simmered in the look he gave Koch. "Your attempt at humor is wasted on me. You forget words are my business, and yours are quite unimaginative. Get your hand off me."

Koch gave a gentle shove toward the door. "Right now, I'm imagining a lovely room in my jail for you if you don't act cooperatively. Some say I have a knack for matching roommates. You might get on with Hefty. We picked him up last night for brawling at our local pub, as you Brits call them."

Chester's eyes widened. "I've no desire to meet anyone named Hefty. He's not of my station."

Koch snorted. "Then why don't we put the kettle on and see if a cuppa will sweeten your disposition?"

Page watched as Koch escorted a flustered Chester Tickle from the library.

Steve rubbed his hands together. "Okay, folks, you've witnessed how a lack of cooperation gets handled. He sat in Chester's empty chair and faced his last suspect. "You know what to do. Let's hear your account?"

"My name is Ruby Reed. I'm an author and long-time friend of Evelyn's. I will cooperate fully because I want to know what happened to Eve. Like the others present, I spent the afternoon in my room, except for a brief trip to the kitchen. I fancied a cup of Rosey and one of your mangos. Sugar cravings, don't you know?"

"I gather Rosey is a drink of some kind?" asked Steve.

"Tea." Ruby leaned toward Steve. "You see, I hadn't much faith that the attempt at an English tea party would be palatable. Making a proper pot of tea takes skill. I wanted to have my afternoon tea the way I like it. Proper." Ruby leaned back in her chair, wearing a smug expression.

Steve's fingers typed at an impressive speed. "Tell me, when you and Rosey were keeping company, did you observe anything unusual?"

Ruby bobbed her head. "Perhaps I did, Detective, but I'd rather discuss it alone. Why don't we have a cozy drink at that pub the other detective named?" Her fingers touched the metal clip holding her platinum hair off her neck. Her eyes batted a flirt toward Steve.

"We can certainly have a private chat, but it'll be on

the veranda." Steve rose and stood in front of the group. "One final question for now. I want to know who had reason to harm Evelyn Potts?"

Fiona lifted her hand, signaling she wished to reply. "I think I can speak for everyone that Evelyn was difficult to like. I rather think she didn't want us to like her. But does that mean one of us wanted her gone forever? Of course not. We each found ways to adapt to her shortcomings."

The group mumbled in agreement.

"All right then. Contact me should anything come to mind that might shed light on this case. I believe someone pushed the statue on Evelyn either by some unfortunate mishap or deliberately. Should we raise fingerprints off the statue, we'll want to take yours. If you're innocent of any wrongdoing, you'll want to cooperate. You are free to leave."

Page watched as the group filed out of the library.

"Did you get a read on any of them?" Steve rubbed his forehead.

"These interviews drain you." Page stood and kissed his cheek. "Nope. They're guarded and untrusting of the police. After all, this isn't their country."

"True enough." Steve leaned against the door frame.

Page's mouth thinned as she pondered what more to say. "Fiona spoke truthfully about how they felt about Evelyn. That makes me think something the author did or said triggered her death. It wasn't premeditated. Do you agree?"

Steve laced his arm around Page's waist. "Perhaps. Have I told you lately how much I appreciate you?"

"No, but you can tell me over dinner. Remember? You're buying, and I'm starving."

"Let's go finish up with the three employees. Then, I want to hear what Ruby alluded to knowing. We'll save colorful Chester for last. Let him stew while waiting. Maybe I can tickle something out of him." Steve's lips twitched.

"Yeah, you try and tickle his fancy. Come on." Page squeezed Steve's hand as they entered the hallway. Another inkling came, telling her the day wasn't done with her.

CHAPTER 11

Alice met Steve and Page in the entrance hall. "The three staff are waiting in my office. I hope that's an acceptable place. It's the door directly behind the check-in desk."

"It's perfect. Thanks, Alice. We'll go there now." Steve motioned for Page to continue ahead.

"What's my role here? Truthfully, I don't see a need for me to attend." Page saw Ruby making a beeline for Steve. "Ruby alert on your starboard."

"Detective, how about we get cozy on the veranda now?" Ruby moved within a foot of Steve. Her cloying perfume caused him to cough.

"Ms. Reed, I'll join you there after speaking to the inn's employees." Steve kept walking and waved the air.

"I'll be waiting!" hollered Ruby.

Page poked Steve in the ribs. "Seems I have competition. Should I worry?"

"You definitely should worry because I have this thing for over-bleached hair that looks like a haystack piled on a maneater's head." Steve tweaked Page's nose. "To answer your question, do you need to attend this interview? Yes. Sometimes your inklings reward me with an insight."

"On behalf of my inkling gift, thank you." Page watched Steve open the office door. Meeting Mara and James held interest because of what she'd overheard them discussing on the beach. Maybe she'd get a sense of what they were up to, if anything.

Entering the room, Page settled for a ladder-back chair

waiting in a corner. The office was nondescript. An oak desk sat facing a window with two filing cabinets flanking it. A portrait of a couple dressed in attire from another era acted as the focal point on the wall behind two wood armchairs. The way the artist captured them, it was as if they were watching the room's activity. Their faces looked kind, although attractive wouldn't be a word Page would choose to describe their countenance. She assumed they were the original owners. Turning her attention to Steve, Page folded her hands in her lap and waited.

"Hello, everyone. This interview won't take long. I'm Detective Tanner." He glanced at his tablet before returning his focus to the three seated.

"Mara and James, I understand you are brother and sister." Steve faced them.

Both nodded but said nothing.

"And you're Ralph—"

"That's right, but folks call me Rake because I'm a gardener. So, Rake's fine." He nodded his head nervously. "Just Rake."

Steve cut amused eyes over to Page. "Rake it is." Grabbing his tablet, Steve typed.

Page studied the three. Mara was dressed in black slacks and a white button-down cotton shirt. James matched. Grass-stained overalls dressed the gardener, whom Page guessed was in his early fifties. His deep-blue eyes exuded a gentleness of spirit. Perhaps Alice had a keeper with Rake, but with the other two, she'd withhold judgment.

"I know you all have work to do, so I'll get right to it. Detective Koch told you that a death happened on the inn's property sometime between one and three this afternoon. I'd appreciate knowing if you saw anything unusual or anyone in the statue gardens around then. And I want to know your movements during that time. Mara?" Steve stepped closer and put his discerning gaze on the young woman.

"First, I'd like to say this is so horrible. Unfortunately, I saw nothing out of the ordinary to report. You see, James and I only began working here yesterday and haven't had a chance to explore the gardens. I was nowhere near the place," said Mara with a quiver in her voice.

Steve typed on his tablet. "Anything else, Mara?"

Mara looked at James. "Just that we like Shell Isle and need our jobs to stay at the beach. We'll do anything to help Alice keep the inn open."

"I feel the same. We want to assist." James checked his watch. "May I jump ahead of my sister and answer your questions? Alice has a food truck arriving any minute. She asked me to handle the delivery."

"Sure. Go ahead." Steve focused on James.

"I had front desk duty this afternoon because Alice needed to oversee teatime, or whatever it's called. The inn's rooms are fully occupied. None of the guests passed by my reception desk, so I had nothing to observe. Sorry."

Steve looked up. "No problem. And can you verify Alice was in her office?" He typed more on his pad.

"Yes, Alice only left the office once to go to the kitchen. I could see her enter and leave the room from the hallway. She spent the rest of the time in her office on the phone. I could hear her talking about needing an extension to make her mortgage payment. Mara and I sure hope Three Fables isn't in financial trouble. As my sister said, we like working here." James scooted forward in his chair, ready to rise.

Steve studied the young man for a moment. "If you have nothing further to add, you may see to the delivery. Thank you, James." Steve waited for the door to close before turning his attention to Mara. "Back to you. Please continue where you left off."

Mara shrugged her shoulders. "As I said, I've not visited the gardens, so I'm afraid I'm no help either. I was cleaning the first floor this afternoon. I'd finished tidying the upstairs earlier. It was challenging because most of the guests were in their rooms. I had to work around them. They're not the tidiest bunch."

Steve made immediate eye contact with Page. "That information could prove helpful. When were you tidying the upstairs?"

Mara looked up at the ceiling. "I finished a little after noon because James asked me to make sandwiches." Her lips moved in a momentary smile. "James still loves peanut butter and jelly. He's so basic."

"Let's focus on the point. I'd be interested to know if you observed any guests coming or going between one and three since you weren't stuck at reception like your brother." Steve returned to the oak desk and sat in Alice's swivel chair.

"Let me think a sec." Mara held up each finger. "Okay, I ran a tally of each guest. I only saw a lady guest who wasn't with the author group. I think her name is something like Chandelier. She acts very boujee."

"It's Chandelle," Steve corrected.

"Right. I heard Chandelle tell Alice she was going shopping. She's the only one I saw moving about. Is there anything else? I really should help James put away the food." Mara rose.

Steve cast his eyes toward Page.

She knew what the look meant. Page shook her head, signaling she'd picked up nothing from James and Mara that warranted more investigation. She admitted they seemed nice enough, but job desperation often bred bad decisions. Perhaps a chat with Alice about securing her cash wouldn't hurt. Page returned her attention to Steve's voice.

"You may go, Mara." Steve waited for the door to close. "Okay, Rake. What do you have for me? Since you spend your days outside tending the grounds, I hope something might have caught your attention. Also, I'd like to know why one statue base was cracked and the other appears in good shape." Steve sat in the now-empty chair to face Rake.

"I'm glad you didn't begin with me. I prefer to do my telling without others hearing." Rake pointed at Page. "Is she police?"

"Not exactly, but you can speak freely." Steve winked at Page.

Rake's thumb tugged on his overall strap. "Well, it's like this. I was laying cypress chips in the azalea beds around lunchtime when I heard two women talking from the gazebo out back. Their loudness alerted me that things weren't hunky dory between them. Naturally, I keep an eye on guests who don't behave nicely. Alice likes me to do that. I snuck closer to see." Rake craned his head to look at Page. "You a friend to Alice?"

"I'd like to think so." Page met his eyes, knowing he was sizing her up.

"Please continue, Rake. Could you hear their words and see them? Did you recognize the two women?" Steve typed more.

"I heard and saw them just fine. The one with the bunched-up, bleached hair told the other one she wasn't paying her another plug cent." Rake paused. "Plug cent are my words. She said another quid. She called the woman Evelyn."

"Duly noted," responded Steve. "The blonde's name is Ruby Reed. Continue."

"Right. Then the Ruby lady gets really mean and says

she has ways to shut someone up who talks too much. And this Evelyn had more to worry about than collecting hush money off others. Ruby said it was a big mistake threatening to tell Fiona about her DUI."

"To be clear, are you referring to Ruby, who has the DUI?" asked Steve.

"Yep, Ruby must have a problem with the sauce. Next, she declared she'd had enough of Evelyn's intimidation and blackmailing." Rake waited for Steve to quit typing. "You got all that? Should I continue?"

"Hang one a minute. Your information is already proving valuable." Steve rested the tablet on his thigh. "Go on."

"Anyway, this Evelyn gets all ruffled. She tells Ruby to pay, or else she'll ensure the publishing contract won't be renewed." Rake rubbed his chin. "What happened next surprised me. It's like what you see on television."

"I'm all ears." Steve leaned in.

"So, Ruby goes and smacks Evelyn in the kisser." Rake repeated the action on his face. "Pow. Like that. Next, Evelyn gets plenty riled and throws her glass of juice in Ruby's face."

"Then what happened?" asked Steve.

"Nothin'. The show ended. They stomped off in opposite directions. Ruby returned to the inn, and Evelyn walked toward the statue garden. I needed more bags of chips from the nursery, so I took off in my truck. When I got back, I heard the news."

Steve closed the tablet's cover. "I appreciate your coming forward. On a personal note, I like that you're looking after the premises because my aunt is a guest here."

"It must put a damper on her vacation to be staying at a place where someone got injured and died. I'll make sure to keep an eye on her."

"Thank you, Rake. Don't hesitate to contact me should you see or hear anything of concern." Steve stood and handed the gardener his card. "You're free to go."

Page gave Rake a friendly nod as he passed. She waited for the sound of the door closing before rising.

"We now have two suspects, Chester and Ruby, who threatened the deceased. And they're waiting for a chat. Shall we go ruffle more feathers?" Steve extended his hand toward Page.

"Sure. Let's go find your girlfriend." Page opened the office door and waved to Alice behind the desk.

Steve approached. "Alice, I've completed my interviews with the three employees. Once I speak with Ruby and Chester, I'm heading out, but you'll have an officer on the premises this evening."

"Thank you, Detective Tanner. I'll feel better with a policeman at the inn." Alice refilled the mint dish.

"Steve, I want to chat with Alice about something. I'll join you in a sec." Page watched him move toward the veranda.

Alice frowned. "Is everything okay?"

"As okay as it can be under the circumstances. Would you consider a suggestion?" Page leaned across the counter so her voice wouldn't carry.

"Of course. What is it?" Alice's frown lines turned into crevices.

"Because Mara and James are new hires, I assume you haven't had a chance to check references."

"No, I haven't, but I will tomorrow. Why the concern?"

"I believe they're lacking money and—" Page let her words sputter out. "Never mind, I'm overreacting."

Alice lifted her hand. "Say no more. James doesn't have access to the cash box." Alice patted the locked drawer.

"Don't worry. What else?"

"Nothing more for now." Page had a niggling ghost question. It could wait, but not for long.

CHAPTER 12

The afternoon sun had grown tired and dipped behind the stand of trees. Page tuned in to read the sky's colors. They seemed to portend what was brewing with the Potts case. She frowned, seeing the clouds hanging overhead tinged in indigo and grey. Absent were the rich apricot and rose shades that always reminded her of the inside of a conch shell. A sensation of heaviness descended upon her.

Page forced her attention from the sky and hurried to find Steve and Ruby on the veranda. She chose a rattan swivel chair with floral cushions off to the side and waved when Steve glanced her way.

Ruby continued prattling, unaware of Page's presence. "I'm enjoying your quaint little beach hideaway compared to our English fog's dreariness. However, I find the food here unappealing. No morning kippers or crumpets."

"Ms. Reed, I'm not here for your take on English weather or a disappointing breakfast. Please, have a seat." Steve's voice sounded exasperated. "Let's get to this. What do you have to tell me regarding this case?" He took the chair opposite Ruby.

Ruby's fingers stroked her décolleté, drawing attention to the low-cut, silk blouse. "You probably know I write bestselling mysteries. I'm well-versed in murder motives. Perhaps you'd like to know who amongst us fits the bill, so to speak." Ruby's hand moved to twist at her string of red beads.

Page bit her lip to avoid laughing at the ploy to entice

Steve's eyes to her endowed bosom. Ever the professional, he showed no interest in her feminine wiles.

"Ms. Reed, I'm eager to hear who you think might have been involved with Ms. Potts's demise." Steve grabbed his phone. "Would you mind if I record this information? I don't want to slow you down with my typing."

"Of course, anything to help you, Steve." Ruby's eyelashes went to work again.

"It's Detective Tanner." Steve placed the phone on a nearby glass table. He dictated who was present and the time. "Please begin."

Ruby crossed her leg and arranged her skirt to expose a knee. "With the juicy tidbits I'm going to share, I feel sure you'll want to take me for drinks afterward."

"Ms. Reed, this is strictly police business. You'd do well to remember that fact. Now, tell me what you have to say regarding the death of Ms. Potts." Steve sent an intimidating stare the author's way.

Ruby sat up straighter and tilted her double chin higher. "I must say I prefer our British coppers to you. They're friendlier."

"I'll make a note of that. Please, I find my patience evaporating." Steve glanced at Page.

Seeing Ruby now fiddling with her phone, Steve reacted. "Ms. Reed, perhaps you'd like Detective Koch to step in to do this interview." He moved to rise from the chair.

Ruby laid her phone in her lap. "No, no. Apologies. I had an important message to respond to. Very well, here's what I have for you. Evelyn always confided personal things to me. I know she and Leo had some trysts, shall we say. Evelyn ended things a few weeks ago. She told me that Leo took the news rather badly." Ruby studied her nails.

"Define badly." Steve leaned forward.

"Leo told her no woman broke up with him first. And things weren't over until he said they were. Evelyn told me he shoved her down on the bed — and had his way with her."

"I assume you mean against her will?" asked Steve.

"Well, of course, against her will. He left her rather in tatters. The next day, Evelyn said Leo showed up at her writing studio and threatened her well-being if she breathed a word about what had transpired." Ruby dabbed a non-existent tear.

Steve paused playing along with her performance. "Do you have more?"

Ruby nodded. "You didn't know Evelyn, but she'd never let any man dictate what she could do or say. They had a row. Evelyn told him she was considering filing a police report, telling all. Eve zinged him, saying she'd already contacted two friends who were gossip columnists. Hearing that, Leo stormed out of her studio, yelling that she'd be sorry. That's what she told me. I'd say he has a definite motive, and you'd best see to Leo straight away."

"Thank you for this information, Ms. Reed. I appreciate your coming forward." Steve checked the phone.

Ruby did a bit of preening. "I know a baddie when I see one. I write about them. Leo fits the mold."

Steve leaned back in his chair and studied Ruby. "You know who else has the motive to want Evelyn Potts gone?"

Page hid her amusement. He'd set the hook.

Ruby's eyebrows shot up. "Let me think for a moment."

"No need. You, Ms. Reed, strike me as someone who has secrets better left in the shadows, too. I've learned you and Evelyn had a heated exchange in the inn's garden earlier. I'm curious about that meeting. It smacks of motive to me." Steve's grey eyes locked on her.

Ruby made sputtering sounds until her words came.

"All right, yes. It wasn't anything of consequence. Friends sometimes have little spats."

Steve's fingers tapped the glass table. "Really? I'd categorize slapping and throwing a glass of juice in someone's face as more than a little spat. I'm tired, so here's how I view this. Evelyn had you paying for her silence about your DUI. If Fiona learned that you'd been charged and could be incarcerated, your contract with the publisher would end. An author's reputation is important."

Ruby's cheeks flushed in anger. "I seriously doubt that I'd have to serve time—"

Steve raised his hand. "Let me finish. Your livelihood was in jeopardy, too. Evelyn had the power to unravel your life. Now factor in that I know you exhibited physical aggressive behavior toward your friend. I think you were motivated to harm Ms. Potts."

Ruby huffed and cast her eyes toward Page. "I told you. It was a minor tiff. We always worked these things out. I resent your making more of this."

Page remained expressionless, letting Ruby know sympathy wouldn't be found with her.

Steve rapped his knuckles on the table. "Ms. Reed, here's my plan of action. I will determine whether you had the opportunity to solve your problem. Someone pushed that statue on your friend." Steve grew quiet, observing Ruby. "Unless you'd like to confess now, I'll soon have my answers."

Ruby rose. "I have nothing to confess, Detective. You'd do well to seek out others in our group, like Leo, for your confession. I've broken no law by slapping Evelyn or throwing her a tuppence to appease her mouthiness. You'll have no further cooperation from me. And all's the pity because I might have shared additional tidbits."

Page wondered if Steve would allow Ruby to leave. His methods were unpredictable but always spot on when dealing with suspects. Weariness claimed her as she watched. It had been a long afternoon. Witnessing interviews had drained her last energy reserve, and Chester still awaited his turn.

Steve clicked off the cell phone. "I tell you what, Ms. Reed. I will excuse you, but count on us chatting again soon. Whatever bee you still have in your bonnet, I'll discover one way or another."

"I didn't have anything to do with Evelyn's death. That's the only bee you need to hear buzzing. Now, I'm going to seek refreshment after this unpleasant ordeal." Ruby moved past Page but said nothing.

"Madam, you'd be well advised to keep your refreshment alcohol-free," Steve said somberly. He watched Ruby leave before joining Page.

"Wasn't that loads of fun? Last up is Chester. I'm past ready to be done with these chats. Too many folks are milling around wearing the suspect label." Page hung her handbag over her shoulder and sighed.

"Come on. I'll knock this one out fast, then we can look forward to the Crab Shak."

Another inkling came. "Something's up, Steve."

"An inkling?" He touched her shoulder as they moved toward Detective Koch.

"Yes." Page pointed toward Koch, motioning them from the door. "What's got him acting animated?"

"We're about to find out," said Steve. "What's happened, Detective Koch?"

"He gave me the blasted slip." Koch's arms waved like a bird, ready to take off.

"Who gave you the slip?" Steve's expression turned serious.

Page sensed the answer was tied to her inkling.

CHAPTER 13

"Chester Tickle took off. He asked for a beverage. I stepped out to the kitchen to snag one from Alice, and when I returned to the library, the rascal was gone." Koch activated his arms, flapping again. "Gone. No one pulls that stunt on me. Don't you worry. I'm going to find him."

"We'll help. Tickle's around here somewhere." Steve smirked.

"Normally, I'd take advantage of this situation and give you a sassy retort, Koch. But all I want to do is have Steve get this guy in the wringer and go home." Page released an exasperated sigh.

Koch left to hunt, wearing a mutinous expression.

"Let's divide and conquer," offered Page. "Koch headed toward the parlor. Why don't you take the outside, and I'll go upstairs?"

"Okay. We'll meet back in the library. If you score the runaway, ring my cell phone. I'll do the same. No doubt we'll hear Koch if he nabs him." With a chuckle, Steve jogged down the veranda's steps.

Page passed Alice on her way to the entry hall stairs. "I'm still here. I may need a room tonight if we don't finish these interviews soon."

Alice's smile peeped through. "I'm sorry today ended up being so horrible. It's all my fault. If I hadn't asked Betsy about catering, you'd have a typical day at Honey Bees surrounded by delectables."

Page hugged Alice. "I'm where I'm supposed to be.

Have you seen Chester Tickle?"

"I saw him heading upstairs muttering and swatting at the air." Alice looked bewildered. "What now?"

"Nothing at all. We need Chester here to finish the interviews. I'll say goodbye to you now. We'll chat tomorrow. Call Steve or me if you need anything. Promise?" Page voiced, climbing the stairs.

"I promise." Alice disappeared through the kitchen's double doors.

Page spent the next few minutes searching the second floor for Chester. Spying a narrow set of stairs at the end of a hall, she hesitated. Why would the man bother going to the third floor? She felt a gentle nudge on her back. "Fine. I'm going." Page crept up the stairs, trying to avoid creaking the treads.

The smell of old wood wafted toward her nose as she opened the door to a narrow hallway. The windows trailed down the outside wall and were draped with cobwebs. Four doors lined the opposite planked once-white walls. Page spied what looked like an expansive room at the end of the hall. She could see a high-arched window, capturing what sunlight was left in the day. Walking past the other open doors, Page glanced inside each. Two sparsely furnished bedrooms, with a single bed, chair, and dresser, appeared occupied. A bottle of perfume and a hairbrush rested on the dresser's top in one bedroom. In the next space, a laptop bag and a pair of men's sneakers sat beside the foot of a bed covered with a patchwork quilt. Page surmised the rooms belonged to Mara and James. The others were used as storage for pieces of furniture and whatnots.

Page paused in the doorway, taking in the sizable room with the arched window. What sounded like babbling came from behind two walnut clothes presses. Creeping closer, Page peered around the pieces of furniture at a figure hugging the wall.

"Tell them to leave me alone." Eyes full of fear stared at Page. Chester's toupee was askew on his head, and the signature bow tie faced north.

Page kept her distance and found her soothing voice. "Chester, calm down. There's no one here but you and me. Everything is okay." She could tell the author was experiencing some mental episode.

Chester focused on Page. "I'm not barmy. You can't see him, but he's in this room messing with me. The other one is with him." Chester tried to adjust his hairpiece.

"Who's messing with you?" The scene seemed laced with humor to an observer, but Page felt something else was afoot. "Chester, who's messing with you?"

"A ghost. A specter. An apparition. Call it whatever you like," said Chester. "This inn has them, and they've been stalking me since I checked in." His eyes darted to Page and back to the room.

"You're telling me a ghost has bothered you and chased you upstairs? And that's why you left the library?" Page struggled to take in Chester's words. She didn't discount the paranormal nor Alice's account of the inn's unseen guests. The author's emotional state appeared questionable and more likely the cause of his agitation.

"Yes, isn't English your native tongue? He keeps sending a rush of air to blow my toupee. Then my bow tie gets turned cockeyed." Chester's fingers straightened his tie. "I've had enough of this place and am booking the next flight home."

Page's expression showed amusement. "This ghost sounds harmless. Just a prankster type of—"

"I find your attitude offensive." Chester's tone shifted

to anger. "I'm well versed in our English ghosts, but yours —
I've had my fill." He moved toward the door.

"Hang on a sec. There's a police investigation
unfolding, and your cooperation is needed. Right now, two
detectives are looking for you." Page blocked the door. "Why
don't you and I mosey down to the library so you can put the
interview behind you?"

Chester ignored Page's words. "He's gone. There. Did
you feel the change in the air? It's warmer now."

"I did feel something." Page made a circle in the air
with her hand and sniffed. "And I just got a whiff of perfume
that smelled like lilacs." Was she joining Chester in his
alternate reality?

"See? That's the other one. She's still here. Now you
believe me. This inn will take you off your trolley if you stay
here." Chester pushed past.

Page dialed Steve's cell as she followed on Chester's
heels down the hall. "Mr. Tickle is heading downstairs," she
whispered and then hung up.

Koch met them on the second floor. "Hold up there,
Tickle. I don't like runners, so I'm here to personally escort
you to our little interview session. Your cooperation isn't
optional, so let's go."

"I refuse to enter that library again. If you want to talk,
it's going to be outdoors." Chester shook Koch's hand from
his shoulder and continued down the stairs to the main floor.

Page came alongside both men in the reception area. She
noticed James was busy putting together guest information
packets. He watched with interest their movement toward
the front porch.

Steve entered the room and quickly sized up the scene.
He said nothing but followed the procession out of the inn's
front entrance.

Page signaled Steve to relax. "Shall we all choose a chair? Mr. Tickle has experienced some rather unnerving encounters while being a guest at Three Fables. I'm sure, given a chance, he'll explain why he fled the library." Page gentled a smile on Chester. "How about this rocker?"

The author nodded and sat. Chester pulled a handkerchief from his pocket and wiped his forehead, but not the frown of worry away.

Koch took a stance on the porch steps, blocking any further attempts to escape.

"Alrighty, Mr. Tickle, let's get this interview done. My phone will record our conversation." Steve parked the device on the table. "Let's begin."

Page wondered if Chester would share his ghostly encounters or stick to answering the questions. What role was she willing to play in supporting his accounting? She'd soon have both answers. Glancing at her cell, Page read Betsy's text asking when she was coming home to sample her latest tea. Page replied and stowed her phone. It was Betsy's first day back at Hibiscus, and trouble was already brewing in Aunt Tilly's tea pitcher. She watched Steve open his tablet.

"Mr. Tickle, I'm giving you one last chance to expound on what you saw on your garden meander, as you referred to it. Before you respond, let me make something crystal clear. I expect you to be forthcoming with any information regarding Evelyn Potts's death. Failing to do so will earn you a visit to the station and a possible introduction to…who was it, Detective Koch?"

"Hefty." Koch cocked a sideways glower Chester's way. "I'd sing like a canary, Mr. Tickle, if I were you. I don't think Hefty cares for you bow-tie types."

Chester set his rocker at a faster pace. "You made your point, Detective. Now, I'm going to make mine. I'd prefer you to go first with whatever lingering questions you have for me. Then, depending on your attitude, I might feel inclined to tell you who I think took Evelyn's life." Chester cast his eyes at Page. "And I want her present."

Steve raised an eyebrow at Page. "I'll accommodate that request, Tickle. Here's what I know and why I've decided to put you at the top of my suspect list. Earlier today, a Three Fables guest overheard you arguing with Evelyn. I'm told you made some veiled threat to this guest afterward. So why don't you spin your version and convince me you weren't involved in Evelyn's death? Start by explaining why you wished one of her murder characters would come to life and take her out."

"Oh, that." Chester waved his hand dismissively. "You're making something out of nothing. Evelyn and I always tapped our characters in jest to make a point." Chester fiddled with his tie and looked uninterested.

"Okay, I'll put that to the side for the moment. Let's look at your motive for wanting Evelyn gone. She was blackmailing you. Why don't you tell me the reason?" Steve delivered one of his intimidating looks to Chester. "And before you try and paint it as nothing, hear this. I don't appreciate having my time wasted by uncooperative suspects. What did Ms. Potts have on you, Mr. Tickle?"

Page watched Chester's façade evaporate. She sensed the earlier experiences still had him emotionally rattled, and his pressure valve was ready to blow.

Chester picked up a cocktail napkin on the side table and wiped his face. "All right, but I need you to promise to keep this from Fiona. You could ruin my career and reputation."

"I can't promise you anything but a night in a cell if you don't cooperate. As I said, you're my number one suspect, and that's reason enough to book you on suspicion. My patience has expired, Tickle." Steve looked over at Koch. "Go ahead and take him."

Koch nodded and moved toward Chester. "Okay, princess."

Chester jumped up. "No. I'll tell you everything. You'll see you're barking up the wrong tree." Chester watched Koch return to the doorway. "Evelyn was blackmailing me, in a manner of speaking. The woman ran through money like a loser always betting on the wrong ponies. Evelyn craved fine things and did whatever it took to have them. That included finding any weakness or dirt on someone and using it to her advantage. So, yeah, she scored on me." Chester collapsed into the rocker.

"What did Evelyn have on you?" asked Steve.

Chester lowered his head and stared at the porch floor. "I had writer's block—a bad case of it. Fiona had been pushing me hard to deliver a manuscript or face a breach of contract. That meant I'd have to return the advance money for the book. Money which I had spent."

"That's a tough position." Steve made a note.

"Quite so. Desperate, I got my postgraduate school teaching assistant to finish the novel. She'd just written a paranormal story and asked for my help to get a query submitted to a publisher. I called the debt due and collected."

"Sounds like you and Evelyn share a playbook," said Steve.

Chester raised his hand in defense. "I know it was dishonest and unethical, but I was desperate. Somehow, Evelyn got wind of my actions. She threatened to tell Fiona unless I paid her." Chester released a sarcastic laugh. "Because I didn't have the lolly, she offered to put me on a monthly payment plan. Isn't that rich?"

Steve nodded. "Very magnanimous of Ms. Potts. So, you got tired of paying her, argued in the garden, and pushed the statue over on her. Problem solved."

Chester left the rocker. "What? No. I did not accidentally or on purpose kill Evelyn. I don't possess the nerves for such an act. I can write about it, but I can't do it. That's the truth." Chester's eyes darted from Steve to Koch. "Want me to tell you who killed Evelyn Potts? Do you?" Chester's voice rose enough octaves to sing soprano.

"I'd appreciate having you solve the case for me so I can enjoy my weekend. Please, Mr. Tickle, enlighten us." Steve pointed to the empty rocker. "Sit down."

Chester glanced back at Page. "A ghost here at the inn caused Evelyn's death."

Koch choked on his drink of soda. "Did you say a ghost?" He turned his attention to Steve. "I made a mistake thinking Mr. Tickle needed to bunk with Hefty. He needs a specially made jacket and a padded room at Happy Home."

Page felt the nudge to intrude. "Detectives, I think you should listen to Mr. Tickle."

Chester nodded his thanks. "May I explain?"

"By all means, continue this haunted tale," replied Steve.

Chester rolled his eyes skyward. "I'm an expert in the paranormal. I've written ten books in this genre, so when I say there's a ghost, there's a ghost. Evelyn came to me in quite the tizzy at first light. She'd experienced some disturbing things happening in her room."

"For example?" asked Steve.

"For example, a wind came from the open window and blew her manuscript pages into the rubbish bin. Then another instance, she reached for her box of sweets, but it moved away from her hand. She told me it was a female presence because the room smelled like a bouquet of fresh-cut lilacs."

"Fresh-cut lilacs? Isn't that lovely?" interjected Koch.

Chester delivered a sigh. "That's a similar response to what I gave Evelyn. But what gutted the woman was when she woke up to find the bed's quilt covering her entire body, like a shrouded corpse." Chester gave a shiver. "You see, the ghost was foreshadowing her death. And it happened. They don't want us here. And one of them did in the old dear. Worse, I fear another from our jolly group could be next... me."

"You're serious, Mr. Tickle? You expect us to believe tales about the inn being haunted and taking out unpleasant guests?" Steve laid his tablet aside.

"And toppled the statue over on Evelyn. Why yes, I do expect you to believe this. The apparition hasn't neglected me either, which I told Evelyn. I even warned that blabbing guest, Chatty, to tread carefully." Chester glanced at Page and pointed. "Ask her about the ghost."

Steve raised his hand in protest. "Hang on. I'm still processing this nonsense regarding Evelyn. Your blackmailer chose you to confide in? And you validated her fears because of your paranormal writings and experiences at the inn? I'm struggling with how you two were all friendly and consoling, only threatening each other a few hours later. Mister, your story is more twisted than a pretzel."

"Alas, it does sound a bit daft to my ears after telling it. Still, I'm convinced ghosts are also trying to run me off." Chester touched the top of his head. "No one would ever guess, but I wear a rug. And they keep blowing it askew and causing my bow tie to turn north." Chester twisted his tie to demonstrate. "Just so."

"Do tell?" Koch's smirk returned.

"As I'm endeavoring to do, sir. It's why I left the library. The phantom was tormenting my person. Will you tell him of my fright, madam?" Chester implored Page.

Three pairs of eyes turned to Page. "I found Mr. Tickle hiding behind two clothes presses in the attic room. He relayed that a ghost had been tormenting him. I can attest he appeared convinced and frightened." Page folded her hands, considering her words' impact on both detectives.

"Don't leave out that you felt the air change and smelled lilac perfume. That's proof a spirit is around," stated Chester, smacking his leg for effect.

"What a bunch of blarney. A ghost moving a toupee and blowing ill winds. Simply too much," declared Koch.

"I can't believe I'm going to ask this. Page, did you feel some strange air currents and smell something?" Steve walked to where Page sat.

"I did feel something out of the ordinary that I can't explain. And the scent of lilacs was quite strong. It's a matter I'd like to discuss with Alice privately."

Steve stared at Page in disbelief. "Fine. Talk about this haunted inn with Alice. I deal with facts. Mr. Tickle, do you have anything else to add to this lunacy?"

"I remain steadfast in my denial of involvement in Evelyn's death. I admit she was blackmailing me and that I made an idle threat, but I wasn't in the statue garden this afternoon. I detest heat and gnats. And you've no shortage of either in this beach dive."

Koch made a groaning sound and left the porch.

Steve motioned to Chester to rise. "Mr. Tickle, I will let you go about your evening with the ghosts. You remain a person of interest and are not to leave Shell Isle. Do you understand me?"

"Yes, but know that I possess the desire to return home post haste. And for that reason, may I suggest you expend your investigative energy elsewhere? Perhaps you'll find skeletons in other closets besides mine." Chester pivoted and left the porch.

Steve came to sit next to Page. "You know what?"

"What?" Page beamed a smile.

"They all did it. Every living and dead person here at this establishment did it." Steve hesitated. "Minus Alice and Aunt Chatty. And they've succeeded in making me doubt reality. Are we to believe ghosts have taken up residence in our quiet little beach town?"

Page burst out laughing. "Well, I'm considering buying a second suspect board for Betsy and me to include ghosts."

"Ah, the infamous Sherlocka board." Steve tweaked Page's nose. "I'm going to ask Koch to do the follow-up interviews with the lot of them. I'm ready to get out of here."

"Sounds like a solid plan. I'll swing by in the morning and talk further with Alice about her nonpaying guests. All right by you?" Page slung her tote over her shoulder and stood.

"Yes. The day I start interviewing ghosts is when you check me into Happy Home with Tickle." Steve pointed to the parking lot. "I'll walk over to Hibiscus later for the Crab Shak date. Page?"

"Hmm?" Page spun to face Steve. "Sorry. I was thinking about something else."

"Thanks for your presence this afternoon. You'll let me know if you glean any information or have more of those inklings. Right?"

Page smiled reassuringly at him. "Right. See you in a bit." Stepping toward her SUV, she noticed the officer on duty standing nearby. Having observed Chester and hearing his side, she no longer felt concerned for Chatty's safety. Whoever had a hand in Evelyn's death wouldn't want any attention directed their way. They had solved their problem, or had they?

CHAPTER 14

Page reflected on her life at Shell Isle as she drove home. Her relationship with Steve was in a good place. Even Betsy had found a healthy rhythm to life at the beach. Having the anchor of Honey Bees served them well. They'd meshed within the eclectic community and achieved acceptance and town support for their shop. Page felt she and Betsy were now officially Shellers. For the most part, lighthearted defined their days. Their routine only changed when inklings activated her sleuthing gifts and pulled them into solving a case.

At last, Betsy had found a fellow who understood her flamboyant personality. Andre and Betsy jelled as a couple and were enjoying no-strings time together. Hearing Betsy express loneliness living at her bungalow had taken Page by surprise. She made a mental note to ask her cousin to elaborate on that statement later.

Page pulled into the cottage's driveway and saw Barnacle running toward her. The spaniel excelled at finding escapes from Steve's fenced backyard. Exiting the vehicle, she bent down to pat the dog. "Gracious, your muzzle is covered in dirt, and so are your paws. Barn, you certainly put max effort into digging for your freedom this afternoon."

Barnacle stood on his hind legs, trying to kiss Page.

"No love or entry into Hibiscus until you're cleaned up." Page moved toward the hose.

Betsy opened the door. "It's about time you showed up. We've got an hour before we taste our Clam Po Boys."

"I know. The interviews took longer and were

exhausting. I'll catch you up while I change for dinner. First, Barn needs a tidy." Page turned on the hose.

Betsy came alongside. "Give me that. I'll clean up Houdini. No doubt he's come calling for a new rawhide stick. Go on inside."

"Thanks, Bets."

"Give a good sniff of what's baking in the oven. It's a new recipe. It's for us to enjoy later. The Crab Shak's Velma can keep her seven-layer fudge cake for the pool-playing bikers. I've got something healthier."

"I'll peek at your latest creation." Page released a sigh. Betsy hadn't wasted time settling back at Hibiscus and activating her culinary debacles. Hanging her tote bag on the foyer's wall hook, Page was greeted by a whiff of cinnamon and something unknown. One glance and sniff inside the oven sent her to the screen porch.

Inhaling the salt air, Page slowly released the stored stress. She watched the waves roll in, teasing abandoned sandcastles that would soon become a memory of the builder. The predictability of the tides brought a kind of comfort to each day. Page chose to draw on that occurrence to ground herself each morning. She glanced at her watch. There was enough time for a quick refresh before the evening ahead.

***

Page entered the kitchen, casually dressed in her white jeans and a polka-dot peach top. Her honey-blond hair was clipped away from her face, showcasing aqua eyes that matched the ocean's color. A dusting of freckles across her tanned cheeks created an image of someone who loved the outdoors. Gold hoop earrings and light makeup application completed the desired look of a woman possessing an innate style.

She found Betsy busy piling her baked delights onto a

floral ceramic plate.

"You look nice, Page. Here you go. Sample one of Bets Best Brownies." Betsy placed a bar on a napkin. "Guess the surprise in it."

Page's eyes looked suspiciously at the brownie, having smelled them cooking. "Maybe I should wait. I don't want to ruin my dinner."

"A tiny bar won't spoil anything. Taste it first, and then I'll share my secret ingredients." Betsy plopped one in her own mouth. Her wardrobe of colorful and roomy muumuus allowed for frequent sweet indulgences. "So good. I've outdone myself yet again."

"Yep, you excel at outdoing." Page broke off a morsel and put it in her mouth. With Betsy cooking at the cottage again, she'd need to check the supply of antacids.

"Well?" Betsy poured a small glass of purple tea for Page. "Here's your chaser."

"Well, the texture is a surprise." Page forced herself to swallow.

"That's the black beans." Betsy delivered a pleased expression.

"Black beans?"

"And carob instead of chocolate is another surprise," replied Betsy.

"For sure." Page chewed. "I taste cinnamon, and whoa!" The spice hit came next. Page grabbed the glass of tea and took a gulp. "What the heck caused the fire?"

"Cayenne, of course. It's to put the pep in your step." Betsy leaned over the kitchen island, whispering, "It's my ta-da secret. Cayenne burns off the calories so that you can eat more of them."

Page set the other half of the brownie on the counter. "I'd say it burns off more than calories. My esophagus may never recover. And what's made the tea purple?"

"Grapes give the tea pizzazz. You have the weakest constitution, Page Wright. I'm going to work on improving that whilst here."

"I've told you a gazillion times, leave my constitution alone, Betsy Ross." Page sipped from her glass of tea. The taste was tolerable. She'd ignore what it looked like. "Come to the porch so I can update you on our case before the guys arrive."

"Right behind you, but you gotta know I'm not a bit happy we're involved in another caper." Betsy settled into the hammock.

"That's the one fact I'm sure of right now." Page spent fifteen minutes sharing the afternoon's doings with her cousin. "So, there you have it. My colorful visit at Three Fables."

Betsy shook her head. "It's mindboggling how Evelyn managed to find dirt on her peers. The woman's death confounds me. Never mind the ghostly parts, I can't begin to process right now. I guess we'll drag out the suspect board tonight." Betsy made a face.

"Yes, the board will make its debut. We need it to get these suspects sorted around motive, means, and opportunity. Then maybe we can better noodle out things. With luck, the whodunit will be revealed in the next couple of days." Page went to the kitchen to wash her tea glass.

Betsy followed, after sending Barnacle home. "All I've got to say is may the inkling gods hear you."

***

Tucked into a booth at the Crab Shak, Page's eyes observed the Saturday night scene. The crunch of tossed nut shells on the pine floor provided the ambiance as patrons came and went. Planked walls held fishing nets strung with all manner of ocean treasures. But it was the pool room that delivered the local color. Page's mind flashed to memories of interacting with the bikers from their last case. A slight smile found her face as she spied a familiar face heading their way.

"Hiya, Peanut. I see you're still attached to that cop." Cueball nodded to Steve, seated next to Page. A red bandana hid his bald head.

"Yep, still attached. I see you're raking up the balls tonight," replied Page.

"Yeah, a new guy in town fancies himself a player. I'm about to prove him wrong. And, gal, you know I can."

Page bobbed her head. "That I do."

Cueball shuffled his feet. "I'd better get back. I wanted to say hi to you, Peanut. Holler if you need anything tonight. Me and the guys like to look out for you." He grinned at the other three, displaying his latest missing tooth.

"Will do, Cue. Good to see you." Page poked Steve to respond.

"Yeah, take it easy out there, Cueball." Steve nodded.

Betsy offered a wave. Andre followed suit.

"Peanut. I see I've still got competition. Shell Isle's resident bikers have taken a real shine to you. Clearly, your Cueball holds out hope of having you for his ol' Lady," teased Steve.

Page smacked his shoulder. "You leave my Cueball alone. He's my second-best snitch after Mickey."

The four enjoyed a laugh as they watched him clank his beer stein with his sidekicks.

Betsy recovered first. "Shh. Here comes the biker's babe, Velma, with her endowments front and center." Betsy's expression showed a flicker of irritation.

"Evening, everyone. Hey, handsome. Catch any bad guys today?" Velma's eyes locked on Steve's.

"As a matter of fact, I'm hosting another jail slumber

party tonight," bantered Steve.

"That's my tough guy. What are you having, honey pie? Say the word, and I could be your dinner special tonight." Velma puckered her painted scarlet-red lips. Her blouse's first two buttons, always left undone, presented an open invitation.

"We're all having the Shak's special Clam Po Boy basket." Ignoring Velma's typical teasing come-on, Steve glanced at the other three. "Right?"

Three yesses had Velma writing the ticket. She turned her attention to Betsy. "And for the big eater, I guess you want an extra order of fries and a full ketchup bottle. Same as always."

Betsy pulled a face. "Velma, one of these days, your overdone sense of humor—"

"Double that extra order, Velma. The lady and I like our fries crispy." Andre jumped in to answer before the rest of Betsy's sassy retort could escape.

Velma popped her gum and winked. "Can do, Detective. You can play second fiddle for Steve anytime with me. I dig your French-Canadian accent."

Betsy eyed Velma as she walked away. "If the Shak's food weren't such fried wonderfulness, I'd never set foot in here. That woman lives to aggravate me."

Page rallied for her cousin. "Ah, Bets, don't you know Velma sees you as tough competition? Doesn't she, honey pie?" Page teased a smirking Steve.

"Velma thinks I'm her competition?" Betsy reached for her hand fan. "In that case, I suppose I can ignore her barbs. She's suffering from envy. You'd think with all those enhancements to her person, Velma could find her own man."

Andre and Steve exchanged amused looks.

"Oh, please. Surely you can see what's been enhanced

on our server?" volleyed Betsy.

Wanting to shift attention, Page turned to Steve. "Did you happen to hear from Koch after he interviewed Leo? I've already enlightened Betsy on our afternoon."

Steve set his water glass down. "He called me. It seems Leo told a different version of the story."

Page's eyebrow lifted. "How so? This literary group knows how to spin more yarns than an Irish weaver of wool shawls."

"That reminds me." Betsy leaned forward. "I once dated this sheep farmer from Ireland. He had the blackest hair. I loved to run my fingers —"

"Not now, Betsy." Page waved her off. "Steve, what did Leo say?"

"I'm interested in hearing what Leo said because I've something to add to this conversation." Andre reached for Betsy's hand. "By the way, I'm glad you didn't stay in Ireland with the sheep."

"How sweet of you to say. There were too many rocks. I found myself eating pasture grass daily," replied Betsy.

Steve looked confused. "Okay, I'll join you two on this side trip for a minute. What in the heck do you mean by eating pasture grass, Betsy?"

"Betsy means she kept tripping on Ireland's topography of rocks and falling face down." Andre unfolded his napkin. "The green of those hills is like no other. It's such a beautiful country."

Page waved her hand in front of Steve's face. "Hello? Still waiting for the answer about Leo, if everyone is caught up on hearing Betsy's Irish blarney."

"To continue, Leo said he ended things with Evelyn when he found out she threatened to tell tales on her author friends if they didn't give her hush pounds." Steve paused. "I will quote him. 'Evelyn lived to tell porkies. No one paid her any attention. After a few tumbles, I lost interest in her and moved on.'"

"A few tumbles, geez. The Brits' language is so colorful. I fancy it over ours." Betsy tucked napkins under her chin, readying for her meal. "Who do you believe?" asked Betsy.

"I might be able to shed some light on that answer." Andre's eyes saw Velma coming their way with a tray. "Hang on. I see our baskets. We're sure getting fast service tonight."

Velma placed the orders before everyone and promised to return for drink refills. She swayed toward the bikers signaling her from the pool room.

Andre passed the bottle of ketchup to Betsy's outstretched hand. "Before we gathered the group in the library, I went to my vehicle to grab some evidence bags, should I happen upon something. I saw Leo and Fiona in a clinch."

"What kind of clinch?" mumbled Betsy with a mouth full of fries.

"A kissing clinch. I'd demonstrate, but your mouth is occupied." Andre patted Betsy's hand.

"It's quite all right. We get the picture." Page took a bite of her sandwich, considering Andre's words. "I guess my vote goes to Leo as the truthteller. Either Ruby lied to get attention off herself, or Evelyn lied to save her facelifted face."

A slight smile flickered on Andre's lips. "You women excel at noticing—"

"Fake women. Yes, thank you very much," supplied Betsy. "Natural women unite." Betsy raised her glass of punch to clank Page's glass of lemonade.

"Okay, so did Evelyn have any dirt on Leo or not? Did Koch confront him about forcing himself on Evelyn?" asked Page, taking another bite. Tartar sauce landed in her lap.

"Great. I would be wearing white jeans."

"Need some help with that?" Steve moved his napkin toward her thighs.

"Stop that." Page smacked his hand away. "I need help with answers." She grabbed a napkin and blotted her leg.

Steve chuckled and continued, "Koch said he had to wait for Leo to stop laughing over the question. He maintained that Evelyn or Ruby fabricated the ridiculous notion from one of their debauchery novels. Leo quickly informed Koch that women sought him out, and he had no need to force himself on anyone to get bedded. He suggested we confirm this with Fiona."

"Did Koch confirm it and prove Andre correct in what he saw?" asked Betsy, dragging another French fry through a pool of ketchup.

"Yep. Fiona admitted to having a thing with Leo. She told Koch that Evelyn wouldn't speak the truth even if hooked to a polygraph machine. It appears Leo is Fiona's author with the most potential to deliver continued bestsellers. They're using each other to achieve their goals."

"This feels like a dead end with Leo. Truthfully, I welcome having suspects who don't fit the template of wanting Evelyn gone. We can focus on Chester and Ruby." Page stole a fry from Steve's basket.

"I'm all for having fewer names on our suspect board for a change. Two's a good number." Betsy tucked another napkin under her chin, creating a bib.

Page shook her head. "No, we still must list them all. Them's the rules."

"To change the subject, I'm already thinking about a sweet," said Andre.

Velma appeared on cue, asking about dessert. Steve ordered a slice of key lime pie to take to Chatty.

"Shall we order something?" asked Andre.

Betsy leaned over and pecked Andre's cheek before giving the server the eye. "Velma, just bring our checks and the pie slice."

"Okay, toots." Velma moved on to the next table.

"I've got dessert waiting at Hibiscus. Don't I, Page?" prodded Betsy.

"That she does. Lucky me got a sample." Page waved goodbye to Cueball and his entourage as they headed for the exit. She hid her amusement at the worried expressions on Andre and Steve's faces. "It's a surprise kind of brownie."

Steve found his words first. "Betsy, that's nice of you, but I'm craving ice cream tonight. I thought after Page and I stop by to check on things at Three Fables, we'd grab a scoop from—"

Betsy waved her fan in Steve's direction. "No need. I'm serving ice cream with my brownies. Gotcha covered, Detective."

"Brownies sound safe—I mean good to me," said Andre.

"Page?" asked Steve, casting a skeptical glance her way.

"Would you all stop? My brownies are a feast for the taste buds. You'll see. Here comes Velma with our pie and bills."

"Alright, let's head out. Betsy, I'll drop you and Andre at the cottage. Page and I can enjoy that surprise dessert after checking on Chatty," said Steve.

"Okay, but you two make it a snappy stop. Page and I still have to work on our suspect board later." Betsy tucked her fan into the straw handbag.

"At least Honey Bees is closed tomorrow. We can sleep in." Page took the last sip of water. "Those clams were fantastic. I usually get oysters."

"And I like it when you get oysters. It makes you frisky," joked Steve.

"Don't you two start up the hanky-panky talk." Betsy stacked her empty basket on top of Andre's and cleaned up the table. She shrugged. "Just giving Velma a hand. Shall we go, chickadees?"

Steve tossed some bills on the table, and Andre added his.

"Wow, you guys are giving Velma a hefty tip. That'll buy more enhancements." Betsy looked at the money.

Andre chuckled. "So we are. She works hard waiting tables."

Scooting out of the booth, Page felt an inkling. "Why now?" she mumbled. Remembering she'd agreed to ride with Steve to the inn answered the question. The night wasn't done with the guests at Three Fables or her.

CHAPTER 15

Steve parked his black SUV in the Three Fables parking area. Holding the pie container, he turned to Page. "You've been quiet the whole ride here." He studied Page's face from the glow of the full moon. "Another one, huh? I'm on point. Let's see what your latest inkling has in store for us."

Page reached for the door handle. "You keep reading me. I'm not so sure I like it." She came alongside Steve as he waited in front of the vehicle. "And for the record, I was about to tell you."

"I'll take your word for — the inn's lights are out." Steve pointed at Three Fables draped in darkness. "Let's go."

"What in the world?" Page jogged next to Steve. "I see lights on at the manor house next door."

They reached the front porch steps and spied Leo and Fiona sitting on the porch swing. Their faces wore the same confused look as Page and Steve's.

"What's with the lights? We kept thinking they'd come back on," said Leo, pulling his arm away from Fiona's shoulder.

"We're about to find out. You two stay where you are." Steve motioned for the approaching duty officer. "Go around back."

"Yes, sir. I'd just completed my check of the grounds when I noticed the inn was dark." The young man took off running, unholstering his gun.

"Page, you stay on the porch. I'll come back once I know what's going on." He passed the pie to her.

"Forget it, mister. My inklings aren't meant for me to hang back. I'm going in with you, but I'll gladly carry Chatty's pie so you can act stealthy if needed."

"Okay, but no more talking." Steve opened the screen door with a slowness a tortoise couldn't match. He pulled a flashlight from his back pocket and pushed the button.

Page glanced back at Leo and Fiona, who hadn't budged. Satisfied they were staying put, she crept behind Steve. Her mind didn't waste time wondering what they'd find. Maybe a logical explanation awaited, and nothing of consequence had occurred. A woman's scream told her differently.

Steve broke his silence. "It's Detective Tanner. Where is everyone?" he called out.

"In the music room!" shouted a male voice that sounded like Chester.

As they moved down the hallway, Page caught sight of Alice and Chatty sitting at the kitchen table. A lit candle cast a warm glow on their frightened faces. Page left the pie container on the counter and gave a thumbs-up.

Steve motioned the two to remain there as he continued past them.

Page signaled him to make a right. The sound of muffled voices grew louder as they turned the corner. "In there." She cocked her head.

Steve's flashlight circled the music room, landing on three faces as he entered. "Is everyone all right? Who screamed?"

"It was Grace," replied Chester. "One of the ghosts sent a mouse scurrying over her feet."

Grace sat hugging herself at the piano while her feet dangled in the air. "I'm sorry for screaming. It was dark. I couldn't see what it was." Her meek voice trembled with fear.

"Other than a mouse, did anything else happen?" asked

Steve, impatience evident in his tone. He walked around the room.

Page remained at the door, taking in the scene. Her inkling didn't send her to this room. She was needed somewhere else. Hearing Ruby speak, Page turned her attention to the woman.

"Here's what happened, Detective Tanner." Ruby pursed her lips at Steve before continuing. "We were simply biding away another boring night in this dreadful place, listening to Grace play Bach, and then the lights went out. You showed up to save the night, only I don't see much that needs saving." Ruby found a pillar candle on a table and a box of matches next to it. She lit it and placed the candle on the piano top before returning to a gold brocade cushioned chair.

Chester fidgeted on the velvet settee. "Please, won't you get the lights switched on? I feel vulnerable sitting here, all ripe for the ghost plucking."

A surprised Page glimpsed Chester's toupee move a smidge sideways. She swallowed her words.

Chester's hand grabbed hold and repositioned the hairpiece. "Did anyone see that?" He jumped up and went to Steve on the opposite side of the room.

"See what? You're such a drama queen." Ruby took a sip of her sherry.

"My rug moved," exclaimed Chester.

"Maybe the mouse is under it? We all know you don't have a brain, so there's plenty of room for the rodent." Ruby set the glass on the antique filigree metal table. "Are you going to do something about the electricity, Detective? Where's that inefficient, Alice?"

"Ms. Reed, respectfully, I say be quiet. Everyone, stay here until I return." Steve scanned the room once more before leaving with Page by his side.

Out in the hall, Page whispered, "What next? Want me to get Alice and have her direct me to the breaker box?"

"I'll do that myself after seeing if the officer discovered anything. Go back to the kitchen and check on Alice and Aunt Chatty. Wait for me there."

"Sure, if that's what you want me to do." Page turned toward the kitchen.

Steve shone the flashlight down the hall. "Don't you dare do anything sleuthy."

Page kept walking and ignored his taunt. A strange sound came from the library's location. Page mouthed, "I'll be back," to Alice and Chatty as she passed the kitchen doorway. She remembered her key chain had a penlight hanging on it. Fishing it from her purse, she crept quieter than Grace's mouse toward the sound.

Page entered the library. Her eyes locked on a figure frantically examining books. Leo's flashlight, parked under his chin, provided light as he pulled three books from the shelves. The electricity came to life, illuminating the room. Page advanced and yanked a canvas bag from his arm. "What are you doing? You were told to stay put."

"Give me that. You'd do well to leave here and forget you saw me."

The menacing voice caused Page to step back. "I'm not leaving, and neither are you."

Steve appeared in the doorway. "Mr. Birdwhistle, what's going on? I distinctly told you to remain on the porch with Fiona. And yet, here you are." Steve came alongside Page.

"As usual, you're making a big deal out of nothing. I came here for a book to read. Simple." Leo tried to walk past.

"Not so fast." Page turned to Steve. "Mr. Birdwhistle

was in here pilfering books and threatening me, I might add. He's got three tucked in his little canvas bag." Page reached inside and pulled one out. "Let's see what makes this one special."

Steve looked over Page's shoulder as she thumbed to the page. "Ah, a first edition of a classic. It's in great condition. The leather isn't marred. Good choice, Birdwhistle."

"This is ridiculous. Of course, I'd choose a quality novel to read." Leo huffed.

Page ignored him. "Let's see about the others. We have two more rare first editions. I bet Alice doesn't even realize her library has such collectible treasures."

Steve's eyes fixed on Leo. "You're despicable to try to steal from your innkeeper, Mr. Birdwhistle. These actions carry a substantial penalty."

"Don't be absurd." Leo switched on his indignant look. "I wasn't stealing. I wanted the books for reading."

"I think not. You threatened me to keep quiet." Page pivoted toward Steve. "The man's plenty guilty." She pointed her finger at him. "Besides, if you wanted to simply read, you'd have chosen one book, not three. Hang on." Page squinted. "Steve, check his coat pocket."

"Hand it over, Birdwhistle." Steve's outstretched hand moved toward the man. "Now." The loudness of his voice brought Fiona to the room.

"Leo, what's going on? You said you needed the loo again." Fiona looked confused.

"Shut up, woman." Leo placed a small, leather-bound book of sonnets into Steve's hand. "Careful. It's an extremely rare, eighteenth-century edition and is fragile. It must be handled with the utmost care to protect its extreme value." Leo's expression turned dark as he realized what he'd said.

Steve passed the book to Page and grabbed hold of

Leo's jacket. "You needed the loo again? It's all becoming clear now. You shut off the breaker to keep everyone literally in the dark so you could sneak in and steal the books you'd already discovered."

"I won't stand for these accusations." Leo's cheeks flushed crimson. He tried to step back. "You've nothing to base this farcical accounting on."

"Mr. Birdwhistle, I'm being factual. Facts are my stock and trade just as words are yours. I noticed the breaker box on the wall inside the inn's front entrance. How convenient for you to flick the switch and set your plan in motion." Steve released Leo. "But I'll bet you weren't clever enough to wear gloves flipping that breaker."

Leo's expression changed to worry. Moisture beaded his forehead. His eyes darted toward the hall.

Steve continued, "I didn't think so. We'll lift those prints easily enough. Prosecuting you will be a snap, Birdwhistle."

"You're an idiot, Leo!" Fiona shouted.

Alice appeared. "Whatever is happening now?"

Chatty came from behind. "Steve? Why is this man wearing guilt all over his face?"

"We've discovered Mr. Birdwhistle possesses an impressive knowledge of valuable, first-edition books. And you, Alice, seem blessed with some of your own." Steve never took his eyes off Leo.

"My gracious. I had no idea these books were worth anything much. I bought the place from an estate 'as is'." Alice's hand found her locket and twisted it nervously. "This news is most advantageous. Why, thank you, Mr. Birdwhistle."

Leo muttered something unintelligible about lunacy and tried to move further away.

Chatty tapped Alice's shoulder. "Dear Alice, I fear thanking this man isn't appropriate."

Page joined the two women. "Alice, you certainly have some treasures at Three Fables. The two clothes presses upstairs are quite rare, too. I believe you have more assets than you realize." Page caught Steve's attention. "Maybe we should save this discussion for later."

Fiona spoke out, "Am I to understand Leo is being charged?"

"You grasp the situation perfectly." Steve turned to Fiona. "I'm going to read your author boyfriend his rights and arrest him. Leo has an outing to look forward to this night."

Fiona tried and failed to tug Leo from Steve's grasp. "Arrest him? You mustn't. His book is set for release next month. Between Evelyn's death and now this, my career as an editor will be in tatters."

"That's unfortunate. However, you might want to consider hiring an attorney for this guy," said Steve.

Fiona's hands cupped her face. "Please, can't we work something out? We're scheduled to fly out Tuesday night. Maybe you could forget it happened. You have the books," Fiona's tone turned pleading.

Steve remained silent.

"This retreat has been an utter disaster. Leo, you're a fool." Fiona's hand slapped the author's face before moving away.

"On that, we can agree. There's nothing I can do but uphold the laws of our land." Steve marched Leo past the four women. "Page, I'll return in a few minutes after I have the officer escort Mr. Birdwhistle to the station. I need to call our forensic guy here to lift prints from the breaker box." Steve scanned the room. "No one goes near that box, or you will suffer severe consequences."

Page gave a nod of understanding.

Steve shoved a nearby magazine at Leo. "There you

go. Take this for reading pleasure. It's no classic, but you'll learn about deep-sea fishing and meet your cellmate, Hefty. No doubt he's been lonely tonight."

Page felt satisfaction wash over her. The inkling had prevented a sizable loss to Alice and possibly offered relief from her financial problems. Leo had earned a higher rank on the suspect board. Perhaps what Evelyn told Ruby had been true. The author had proven two things that night. Leo Birdwhistle was a thief and a liar.

"I guess devouring my key lime pie comes next now that order is restored." Chatty turned back to Page and Alice. "How wrong for me to harbor concern that I'd spend days bored silly visiting my nephew."

"I know, Chatty. It's all too much. And because of these upsetting events, I'm making your stay at Three Fables gratis," said Alice.

"Absolutely no gratis," responded Chatty. "You should charge me double. I've never experienced anything so enthralling. The one exception being Ms. Potts's demise."

Page applauded Chatty's way of seeing her world. "Count on seeing Betsy and me in the morning. We'll bring our sleuthing questions and soon discover the guilty one. Fear not. Peace will return to Three Fables." Page followed both women to the reception area.

Alice turned her attention to Page. "I appreciate your help more than words can say. I'll have my answers ready. The hot coffee and freshly baked cinnamon rolls will greet you." The innkeeper acknowledged Grace and Ruby, heading upstairs.

Page slipped out the front door and waited for Steve. The night air had a chill wrapped in the ocean breeze. She shivered and rubbed her arms as the sound of nature's night shift drew her attention. The crickets' ratchety voices competed with the resident frog's ribbits coming from a small pond on the inn's property. Page wondered how much land belonged to Three Fables. With Shell Isle property being scarce, owning more than a small lot was unusual. Perhaps if Alice tapped into her entrepreneurial skills, she'd find unlimited potential to grow her enterprise. Page's eyes squinted to see the occupants of a car pulling into the parking area.

Mara and James exited a silver compact sedan and walked toward the front porch.

Hearing their laughter pleased Page for some reason. Despite feeling an undiscovered story followed them, her face presented a pleasant expression to greet James and Mara. "Hello, again. It sounds like you've had some fun this evening."

"Yes, Alice gave us a free evening," answered Mara.

"We visited the pier and watched people night fishing. It was cool seeing them fight the reel to bring in the catch. I may have found my next hobby." James paused on the porch steps while Mara continued inside.

"The pier is a happening place. Folks fish from sunrise until midnight there." Page kept her tone light.

James frowned. "Excuse me, but are you here to cater something again? It's kind of late."

Page shook her head. "No catering tonight. I'm sure Alice will fill you in on what transpired."

Without saying another word, James disappeared inside the inn.

"I don't know. Something still doesn't ring right with those two," Page muttered. She spotted Steve's silhouette coming her way.

The police car with a dour-faced Leo Birdwhistle in the backseat drove past Page. Someone from the group would need to post bail for the scoundrel. She wondered if Alice would allow him back to Three Fables for the remaining days. What a group of characters they'd proven themselves. Loyalty seemed in short supply, never mind the one who'd seen fit to cause Evelyn to leave her earthly home.

"Had enough action for the day?" Steve came alongside Page and kissed the top of her head.

"More than enough. Can we go?" Page laced her fingers through Steve's.

"Yeah, I'll drop you home before I go to the station. I need to file a report on Leo and see about his accommodation. Hop in."

Page closed the passenger door and took a cleansing breath. Restoring her balance needed to happen before explaining the recent events to her cousin.

"You've got Betsy's so-called brownies to look forward to. Thanks to Birdwhistle, I don't." Steve took one final glance around the area and started the engine.

"The culinary gods show me no sympathy when it comes to Betsy's food fiascos. And because of you, she's ensconced back at Hibiscus feeding me."

Steve maneuvered onto the main street. "Ah, come on. Betsy adds flavor to your life."

"Very funny." Page sent him a sideways look. "So, what's next with this case?"

Steve silenced his phone dinging. "I'll have the DNA results Monday or Tuesday on the button you found in Ms. Pott's hand, along with the fingerprints for the breaker switch, her phone, and the statue. I'm anxious to learn if Evelyn tried to call for help, though I doubt it."

"I agree. It's unlikely," added Page. "What else?"

"I'll run a check on Leo with Scotland Yard. They're top tier for outstanding police work. I've had the privilege of working with the Yard when I was with the FBI. I expect

Leo will be released after we process him and do a formal interview."

"Leo majorly botched his pilfering. The only thing he did right was killing the breaker to buy uninterrupted time in the library," said Page. "Tell me more."

"You're persistent in probing me for info, Sherlocka."

"I want to get the answers to what happened so my life returns to its sublimeness. Are you running background checks on the whole gang?"

"Absolutely. It just takes longer since it's international. We'll glean something from the reports soon enough." Steve reached for Page's hand and bestowed a light kiss. "I haven't told you tonight how nice you look in those white jeans, Peanut."

Page felt the ridiculous flutters activate. "Stop taunting me." Her voice sounded breathless. *Blast his keen observation skills.* He knew the effect he was having on her. She pulled her hand back to the sound of his laughter. "No time for hanky-panky. What else you got for me?"

"You sound like your cousin. While we wait for the reports, we need someone or something to surface and point us toward—"

"Whodunit," finished Page. Her cottage was a block away. "I'm seeing Alice and Chatty in the morning. And I plan to delve into the ghostly encounters. It's an area in which I have no experience but plenty of growing fascination, thanks to Chester. Maybe I'll turn up something."

"I'm ignoring the ghost talk. I have two things to say." Steve turned into the cottage's drive and cut the engine. He twisted to face Page. "First, tomorrow I'm taking Aunt Chatty out for brunch at Azalea and a visit to the Shell Point Lighthouse. Despite this case interfering with her visit, I want to enjoy her company."

"Of course, and you should. Your aunt is wonderful and so full of vigor for her age. It's nice that she and Alice have forged a bond." Page reached for her tote.

"Hang on. Second, I'm inviting you to sail on Carpe Diem tomorrow afternoon. Interested in escaping with me for a while?" Steve leaned across the console. His fingers stroked Page's cheek. "Don't think. Just say, 'Yes, Steve.'"

"Yes, Steve." Page gave an indulgent laugh and felt passion stir at the thought of them being alone. She climbed out before he could kiss her and activate things. The suspect board awaited her and Betsy's attention.

CHAPTER 16

Barnacle greeted Page as she entered the cottage. "Hey, Barn. Don't worry. Steve hasn't forsaken you." She paused to pat the spaniel's head before looking for Betsy.

"What did I miss now? You were gone an age. So far, this case has snubbed me every step of the way." Betsy inhaled. "Wait. I shouldn't complain. Snubbing is good."

Page pointed to the sofa. "Park your snubbed self while I grab a juice and the suspect board. I'm ready to update you."

"Not yet. You need a brownie to go with your juice." Betsy started to rise.

"Sit. I'll get my brownie." Page poured cranberry juice into a glass and reached for the smallest brownie on the serving platter. She tossed half into the trash and pretended to chew. "These have such an interesting flavor, Bets."

"That's what Andre said. Poor guy had a coughing spell and had to go home. I told him the oak pollen was terrible this spring."

Hearing Andre's reaction and recalling her earlier taste of a crumb, Page placed the brownie on a napkin and hoped it wouldn't catch fire. Pulling the suspect board and bag of markers from the hall closet, she returned to Betsy. "I'm sure he's fine by now. It's better if the guys aren't here tonight because we need to organize the board."

"Before you list everyone, tell me what happened tonight." Betsy leaned back against the sofa cushions only to sit up again. She shook three of them. "These pillows need to go. They've lost their fluff. I thought you'd planned to redecorate and get rid of Aunt Tilly's hodgepodge furnishings."

"It's on my list, but opening Honey Bees pushed decorating down in importance." Page noticed Barnacle climbing into Betsy's hammock. It was funny how she still thought of it as her cousin's. Page focused on detailing the events at Three Fables, including the interactions with Mara and James.

Betsy resurrected her neon-green fan lying on the coffee table. "Hearing all that produced a flash. I'm still hung up on the ghostly parts. People misbehaving, I get. People acting a touch strange, like James and Mara, I get. But spirits making mischief — that I don't get."

"That's why we're visiting Alice first thing in the morning. I want to hear what else paranormal she's observed since purchasing Three Fables. Let's focus on our suspects until we can garner more on the ghostly subject."

Betsy nodded. Okay, here's the black marker."

Page wrote headers across the top for means, motive, opportunity, and clues. "Done. Now the names. Hand me a colored pen."

"Here's red for Ruby. Put her first." Betsy tapped her chin with a marker. "Since I've missed so much fun, can I do this part?"

"Have a go." Page waited.

"First, put a check by motive. Ruby had reason to hate Evelyn. She was paying her to keep quiet about the DUI and who knows what else. As for means, we have the statue as the means that any of them could have used. That leaves the question of opportunity for Ruby."

"What do you think?" asked Page.

"Hmm." Betsy stared off.

"Let me ask you a question. Do you trust and believe any of the group's alibis? Most were weak."

Betsy went to get a brownie and brought Page her half. "That gets to the heart of this mystery solving. We can't trust them. We never trust our suspects. That's rule number one. Since their alibis are lousy, I suppose opportunity gets checked for them all. Right?"

"For now, yes. I'm going to list the rest of the bunch." Page wrote Chester, Leo, Fiona, and Grace's names. "Do you agree that we can eliminate James and Mara? They lack motive and were working."

"I do agree. Five suspects are my limit." Betsy bit into her brownie. "I'm addicted to these. Eat yours."

Page eyed it. "After we finish. It'll be my reward. To continue assessing, we agree that all had the means and opportunity. What about the motive for Leo, Grace, and Fiona? What do we know there?"

"Leo checks motive if Ruby's story about Evelyn breaking up with him is true. What says your intuition?" Betsy grabbed a throw pillow and hugged it.

"For the moment, I think Leo's an opportunist first and a guy looking for a tumble second. He proved that tonight, trying to steal the first-edition books. Who knows what he's capable of doing if super angry? I say Leo remains a suspect but lower on the list," replied Page.

"How about Fiona and Grace for motive? We don't know much about them regarding Evelyn."

Page uncapped the marker. "True. Fiona, being their editor, she carried some sway. Without her, the books wouldn't have been published. And without publication, no jingle flowed to anyone, including Fiona. So, while the editor might have disliked Evelyn, they needed each other—sort of a symbiotic relationship. I don't see a strong motive at this juncture. Agreed?"

"Yep." Betsy watched as Page wrote notes beside Fiona

and Leo's names. "And that mush mouth Grace depended on Evelyn for a job. What's the idiom? 'Don't bite the hand that feeds you?' Plus, didn't her alibi receive support from Leo?"

Page pursed her lips. "Leo did say he heard typing and Grace talking to herself while he tried to have a kip."

Betsy's head popped up. "What's a kip? Is it edible, and how have I missed tasting one?"

Page rolled her eyes over Betsy equating food to everything. "It's a slang word for a nap."

"Gotcha. I confused it with kippers. Those are edible, though not for me. Too fishy."

Page made a face and continued writing. "Moving along. We're together that motive is strongest for Chester and Ruby. I suppose we should award Leo third place."

"And it's a tie between Grace and Fiona for lacking a real motive. Next, we talk about who we think did the deed. It's the part where I show off my deducing talents." Betsy's hand moved the fan faster while she lifted the hair off her neck.

"Deduce away, and then we'll tuck the board away and call it a night." Page sat in the chair, awaiting Betsy's usual lengthy summation. Glancing at Aunt Tilly's cuckoo clock, she noted the hand nearing eleven. "Well? Who's earned the coveted honor?"

Betsy nodded her head vigorously. "Chester Tickle did it. Evelyn nailed him good on not writing his current bestselling book. It was a legal nightmare unfolding and big-time trouble for Mr. Bow Tie. Plus, his whereabouts this afternoon seemed suspicious as all get-out. He told Steve he was on a…what did he call it?" asked Betsy.

"A meander," answered Page.

"Here's what happened. On Chester's meander, he and Evelyn had another row." Betsy gave a confident nod.

"I'm learning the Brits' lingo. They were plenty steamed with each other. Evelyn pushed his buttons, and Chester Tickle returned the favor by pushing the statue on her. He had the strength to do it, though we now know the base was a teeter-totter."

"It could have happened as you stated." Page swiveled in the chair, taking in her cousin's words.

"Remember, Chester and Evelyn had a heated argument earlier, and he refused to pay her more money. And Chester pretty much threatened Chatty to keep quiet about what she overheard." Betsy bobbed her head. "Yes, he's my man. It tickles me to say Tickle checks all the boxes, and the clues lead us right to his ugly bow tie."

Page's eyes glinted in response. "You made some valid points. I assume you're dismissing Chester's claim that the ghost did it."

Betsy slid the uneaten brownie toward Page. "Until the ghost visits me with a confession, Tickle stays top of my list. Eat."

Nodding, Page took a tiny bite and went for her glass of juice. She saw Betsy's hurt expression. "I'm savoring."

"Fine, but I expect to see that square of perfection devoured. It's your turn to choose whodunit. Hang on. Barnacle wants out to do business."

Page watched as Betsy opened the screen door for the dog and hurried to slip the brownie into the kitchen's garbage can. The whodunit answer eluded her, and that was atypical.

"Who did it?" asked Betsy, settling back into the sofa cushions.

"I'm so cloudy on this, Betsy." Page lifted her arms in defeat. "You made a strong case for Chester. I know my inklings will lead us to the answer."

Betsy leaned over and patted Page's arm. "It's okay.

This is one of those instances where I'm on the fast track ahead of you. Follow my lead to solve this case, and we'll soon return to our beach and baking fun."

"Well, that's a huge relief," replied Page, swallowing the words that wanted to escape. A helpful Betsy chose to ignore the fact that the inklings were what guided them.

"Did you finish the brownie?"

"I finished it right off. It's right where it belongs," answered Page.

"Good girl." Betsy paused. "Wanna visit for a while longer before bedtime? I've missed evenings in the hammock with my historical romance novels." Betsy took their glasses to the kitchen.

"Sure, a few minutes to unwind sounds good. This day seemed never to want to end." Page tucked the suspect board in the closet, went to the porch door, and let Barnacle inside. "Are you coming, Bets?"

"As soon as I set out the breakfast items for tomorrow. I brought the fixings for my Slam Bam Ham Hash. I've never made this recipe for you."

Page gulped as panic set in. Betsy was notorious for her fire-starter breakfasts. "You don't need to trouble yourself. We can grab a bowl of cereal before going to Three Fables."

"Nonsense. You know I like to earn my keep." Betsy hung the dishtowel on the hook and joined Page. "You'll love the hash. It was a favorite of this guy I dated from Georgia."

A resigned Page sat in her favorite rattan glider as Bets continued yapping.

After shooing Barnacle, Betsy carefully positioned herself in the hammock, minimizing the swing. "Anyway, Arnie's company sold country hams. He kept me supplied for the two months we saw each other. I learned a lot about curing ham and bacon. He didn't use sodium nitrite as a preservative, which was a good thing. Nasty stuff, those nitrates. It's too bad I discovered his one character flaw. Otherwise, things might have progressed."

"Betsy? There's something I want to ask you." Page tried to shift the subject.

Raising her fan, Betsy continued, "Arnie loved to imitate a pig squealing whenever he got excited. And he got excited a lot." Betsy paused. "What were you saying?"

Page couldn't help but laugh, hearing another of Betsy's dating fails. "Is there any state you've missed having a beau?"

Betsy twisted her mouth. "Let me think. I haven't dated anyone from the Dakotas or Utah…or Alaska. Too cold for me to go up there and connect. I've missed Rhode Island. It's so small, the odds of meeting a guy from there are low."

"For now, you have Andre as a new guy in your life. You crossed the border to Quebec." Page offered a bemused expression. "Listen, you mentioned in passing that you felt lonely, Bets. It registered with me because I care about you."

"Yeah, I remember saying it and wishing I hadn't." Betsy tugged at her muumuu and encouraged the hammock's movement with her foot. "I love how my bungalow's renovation turned out. It's a sweet place to nest. But once the sun sets, I'm alone there. Honey Bees fills five days, but not the rest of my time." Betsy wiped a stray tear.

"I had no idea you were feeling lonely," replied Page, full of concern.

Betsy sniffed. "I know. Even cooking for myself isn't any fun. I don't have hobbies except bowling with the Mermaids. And Andre and I aren't serious or anything. It's fine because I like the way you and Dreamboat have things working. I'm following a similar pattern with Andre." Betsy grew quiet.

Page's thoughts rushed in. Betsy played a significant role in her everyday life. They'd been close since birth and shared so much over the years. If she were honest, a part of her felt a degree of loneliness, too. Maybe soon, a solution would present itself. For the moment, she could offer Betsy understanding.

"What are you thinking about? Don't you dare feel sorry for me." Betsy closed her fan and laid it on her lap.

"I don't feel sorry for you except for the flashes. I'm glad they've stayed away from me." Page's eyes danced in merriment. "You've got me thinking about things…things I'd ignored. What if we talk about our living arrangements when we aren't tired? We can let it percolate and see if an answer comes."

"Percolate? I forgot to bring my organic coffee beans to grind in the morning. I need them for—"

Page rose and inhaled deeply. "Betsy, my favorite cousin, stop all the fretting."

"I'm your only cousin, and I'm good at fretting. Please give me a hand. I can't get out of this Venus-flytrap hammock."

Pulling both of Betsy's hands, Page succeeded in freeing her. "As I was saying, we don't need a special coffee. Let's keep the morning simple. We've got an important visit at Three Fables."

"Okay on the coffee, but I'm getting up early to make my Slam Bam recipe." Betsy headed for her old bedroom as the cuckoo clock sounded. "I hate that bird. Him, I don't miss."

"You certainly did your best to shut him up, but Aunt Tilly prevailed from heaven. He lives to cuckoo another day." Page hesitated at her bedroom door. "Night, Bets. Let's find out what happened to Evelyn, and then we'll focus on ourselves. Deal?" Page extended her hand.

"Deal." Betsy shook.

"Ruff." Barnacle waited at the front door.

"My gosh, we forgot about Barnacle. I'll walk him to Steve's backyard now. He should return home soon from the station," said Page.

"No hanky-panky if Detective Dreamboat shows up," teased Betsy and disappeared into her room.

Opening the front door to a mist of rain, Page grabbed her umbrella. "Alright, Barnacle, your doghouse awaits." Page glanced up at the sky. The fast-moving clouds hid the stars as she crossed the yard, blanketing her in inky darkness.

Thunder clapped, causing Barnacle to whimper.

Page unlatched the gate and led the spaniel to his doghouse that matched the color of Steve's bungalow. "It's okay, buddy. The thunder won't get you in there."

Barnacle stepped halfway inside only to turn and bolt toward his latest escape hole dug under the fence.

Steve's black SUV pulled into the driveway. He exited to the happy barks of his dog. "Hey there, Barn. Why are you out?" Steve glanced up to see Page approaching.

"Barnacle spent the evening with us, and I was trying to entice him into his house when he heard you." Page felt the first serious raindrops hit her open umbrella. "It's about to bucket out here."

"Yeah, you'd better get home. The weather should clear by the morning. We're still on for a sail?" Steve pointed his dog toward the porch.

"You know it, captain." Page walked halfway across the lawn and stopped. "Hey, what's the latest on Leo?"

"Out on bail and back at Three Fables, thanks to Fiona ponying up the dough and Alice agreeing to his return with a few conditions."

"Like, banned from certain rooms," replied Page.

"Something like that."

Lightning cracked. The zigzag pattern illuminated the sky.

"That's my sign to adios. Night, Steve." Page waved and made it to her door as the deluge arrived.

Turning out the lights, she padded down the hall, hearing the snores from Betsy's room. "I swear. You could sleep through a hurricane raging outside." Page closed her bedroom door on a day that brought more inklings and the call to serve. She knew more would soon be asked.

CHAPTER 17

The aroma wafting into Page's bedroom clued her that the Slam Bam Ham Hash had become a reality. Judging by the past, her breakfast plate would soon hold an overly generous serving. The sun streaming in her window promised an ideal spring day. Page pulled a pair of cream, linen slacks and an aqua blouse from her closet to match the ocean's hues. Adding a floral-print, silk scarf lifted her spirits. The happy feeling lasted only seconds before an inkling hit. She sat on the edge of the bed and waited until the sensation passed.

A light tap on Page's door brought her cousin's cheerful face into the morning. "Good. You're awake and dressed. Breakfast is served, and you'll take to this recipe—what's that puss face?"

"Puss face? What in the world is a—"

Betsy pointed at Page. "It's the 'I had an inkling' face. I know it. And I'm seeing it. Please tell me we've got time to eat the delicious hash I've labored over this past hour."

Page moved toward Betsy. "You and Steve are getting too perceptive with reading my expressions. Of course, we can indulge in the Bam Ham. Lead the way." Page relaxed her face to cancel the frown lines.

"It's Slam Bam Ham Hash. You know I specialize in clever recipe names," replied Betsy over her shoulder as she walked toward her self-declared domain.

"Yes, special names are you and so much more," Page muttered under her breath, tucking two antacids in her mouth and following Betsy to breakfast doom.

***

Page parked her vintage British SUV at Three Fables. Another inkling had visited her while driving to the inn. She'd soon learn their reason. "Ready to talk ghosts?"

"You betcha." Betsy bobbed her head, showing enthusiasm. "I'm determined to embrace our ghostly talk and keep an open mind. Don't look at me that way."

Page's eyebrow stayed lifted.

"Humph, you'll see. My mind is one hundred percent open to paranormal doings." Betsy clutched her straw bag to her chest and stared out the windshield.

"I'm pleased to hear this. I was waiting to hear you dated a guy who did ghost tours," teased Page.

"No, but this guy Freddie gave Tarot readings. I ended things when his cards predicted I'd develop a stomach ulcer from my diet."

Page's laugh returned. "Betsy, you won't do."

"What? I'm not dating any man who tries to mess with my love of spice—enough said. Listen, before we go in, let's make a plan for later. I know you and Detective Dreamboat are sailing this afternoon, but how about we drag our lounge chairs from the storage chest and enjoy the beach before you go?"

"That's a delightful idea. I've got deli turkey for sandwiches and a new bag of blue corn chips. We can have lunch with the seagulls. Let's go, cuz." Page released the door quickly before Betsy could alter the lunch menu.

James greeted both women as they entered the inn. "Good morning. Alice told me to tell you she's on the veranda."

"Thanks. You're leaving?" asked Page, noticing James putting up the "Ring Bell" sign.

"Mara and I have the day off. We're going sightseeing

at a lighthouse. See you." James rushed down the porch steps toward Mara.

"Lighthouses seem a popular destination today," said Betsy. "Aren't Steve and Chatty visiting Shell Point?"

"Yes, and he's taking her for brunch at The Azalea." Page straightened a stack of Three Fable brochures on the reception desk. "Steve's doing his best to adjust his schedule to show Chatty some fun. Having a new case makes it difficult."

"Chatty seems to love being at Three Fables with Alice."

"Did I hear my name?" Alice popped around the corner. "Hi, ladies. I have a basket of cinnamon rolls and steaming coffee waiting on the veranda. Shall we go out?"

"By all means. I'm sure Page will devour three. She only had the smallest serving of my Slam Bam Ham Hash." Betsy made a pout.

Page jumped in to answer. "I told you I needed to save room for Alice's rolls." With its heavy dousing of red pepper flakes, one bite of the casserole had her crunching ice cubes like a high-powered blender.

Leading the two women outside, Alice wisely steered the conversation to the perennials that Rake was busy planting. "The kind man wouldn't hear of me paying for the flowers. He insisted living and working at Three Fables has restored his soul."

"What a nice thing for you to hear in lieu of what's been going on," said Page, choosing the wrought-iron chair facing the statue garden's direction. "Your table setting has such old-world charm, Alice."

"I'll say." Betsy adjusted the seat cushion and sat. "The coffee service matches the dessert plate and cups." Betsy's mouth dropped as she turned over the cup. "Alice, these are priceless and rare."

"They are? I didn't know. It seems I've acquired an inn with all manner of treasures, not to mention the maintenance issues which keep surfacing." Alice sighed and poured the coffee.

Betsy put her hand over the delicate porcelain cup. "We really shouldn't use these."

"Don't be silly. The delicate rose design cheers me. Now, how about a roll?" Alice passed the basket lined with an ivory linen napkin to Page. "Please have two."

"Thank you. Do I smell hazelnut in the icing?" Page took a bite.

"You do. Your nose is astute to pick up on that." Alice waited for Betsy to take a roll.

"Page's taste buds have awakened since I began cooking many of our meals. My culinary creations have opened new vistas for her. Isn't that so?" Betsy sipped, looking over her cup at Page.

"So many spicy vistas are opening almost daily." Page winked at Alice. "Would you mind if I get right into the discovery questions? We're committed to finding out what happened so you can focus on the inn."

"Please ask whatever you'd like." Alice dabbed her mouth with the napkin.

Page smiled, appreciating Alice's willingness. "First, I'd like to discuss Three Fables' growing list of maintenance issues. Things may not be as dire as you imagine." Page paused. "As a matter of fact, I think the solution is right under our noses, literally." Her hand pointed to the coffee pot and dishes.

A confused expression passed over Alice's face. "I'm afraid I don't—"

"Page is asking you to consider selling or auctioning some of your treasures. Doing so will give you cash to make repairs and updates." Betsy licked her fingers and snuck a third cinnamon roll to her plate.

"Offering some of your collectibles to a reputable auction house is what I was about to suggest. The clothes presses, the first-edition books, and now these dishes hold significant value. I don't know your cost estimate for the work needed, but selling several pieces could free up some money. What do you think?"

Color returned to Alice's cheeks. "What a wonderful idea. I'd have funds available to begin some minor restorations."

"That's right," said Betsy, her voice enthusiastic.

Alice looked at the cousins. "I'm blessed to have you as friends and your wise counsel. Could you help me find an antique dealer as soon as this horrible tragedy is resolved?"

"We'd be happy to," replied Betsy.

Page turned to the sound of voices. "Where's that bunch traipsing off to?"

"An arranged sightseeing excursion of lighthouses. Everyone is going, save Leo. He's been shunned and for a good reason. Despicable man trying to thieve my books." Alice tilted her chin, watching the door close. "Where were we?"

"Generating money, and now on to the next thing Page wants to discuss," answered Betsy.

Page shifted the subject to the statue's cracked base. "Alice, we know the statue of the woman—"

"Her name is Althea. She and her husband, Julian, are the original owners of Three Fables. The bronze figures are of them." Alice paused. "As for the statue that fell, Rake had provided me a growing repair list, and Althea was on it. I didn't prioritize her because truthfully, I placed more importance on leaking pipes and frayed wiring." Tears pooled in Alice's eyes. "I never dreamed...."

Betsy patted the innkeeper's hand. "You couldn't know someone would push Althea off her base."

Alice placed her cup back in the saucer. "Last winter, I came here looking for my next adventure. I fell in love with Three Fables and felt an immediate connection. And despite the home inspection report illuminating problems, I believed destiny tapped me to become the next innkeeper. To put it bluntly, I financially overextended myself to have it."

"You followed your heart. And Page has taught me that's always the right path." Betsy took a sip of her coffee. "Right, Page?"

"Yes, it's been my experience. Don't try to second-guess your decision, Alice. Rather, move forward in the present moment with us," suggested Page.

"Well, right now, I fear my bookings will suffer because of the poor woman's death happening here. It's all overwhelming." Alice wrung her hands.

Betsy poured Alice more coffee. "Now, now. I'm sure everything will work out splendidly for you. You're much too wonderful for it to go any other way, and you belong at Three Fables."

Alice leaned back in her chair, releasing a pent-up sigh.

Betsy eyed Page. "What else do you want to chat about? Something more pleasant."

"I wouldn't exactly call this subject pleasant, more like necessary. What I'm about to ask sounds out there, even to me." Page forced a smile. "Alice, it's about the ghosts Chester and Ruby believe are haunting them. Do you have something more to tell us regarding this subject?"

"Well, I've been fretting about how to broach certain odd occurrences with Detectives Tanner and Koch. I can tell those men will react as skeptics." Alice rose, walked to the veranda's low wall, and gazed at the gardens. "Come with me. I have something to show you that might illuminate this controversial subject." Alice proceeded down the stone steps.

Betsy's eyes shifted nervously. "You go first. You're the brave cousin." Her hand nudged Page.

"No, ma'am. You declared yourself the lead on this case," whispered Page.

"I spoke too hastily. You're always the one who solves the mysteries. I know my place. It's behind you and acting in support. Go on. Alice is waiting." Betsy dropped her sunglasses down over her eyes.

"If only I'd recorded those words to playback later. All right, let's go." Page almost missed the subtle flushing sensation to her body as she stepped into the sunshine. "Bets. We need to pay attention to our surroundings."

Betsy scurried to Page's side. "Did you get an inkling? Say no. I beg you."

"Shh." Page glanced around before taking a step.

"Ladies? Is everything okay?" Alice stood still, waiting.

"Peachy keen!" hollered Betsy. "We had to get our sunglasses positioned. The sun is certainly bright today, but beautiful."

"We're ready, willing, and able." Page motioned skittish Betsy toward a waiting Alice.

The innkeeper waved to Rake, pushing the wheelbarrow toward the plant shed. "I'm taking you to the statue garden. The police removed the yellow tape this morning so we can enter again."

"That's a good sign." Betsy's voice quivered.

"I'll say. The officer was kind enough to help Rake set Althea back in place before he left. I put up a 'Do Not Touch' sign until she is secured." Alice held the gate for Page and Betsy to enter.

"I must say things look shipshape." Betsy approached the bronze statue.

"Thanks to Rake. He worked hours this morning to restore and renew the space."

Page turned in a circle, taking in the garden. "Remarkable. It's like nothing happened. It feels tranquil and inviting as it should."

"You must tell him that before you leave." Alice's fingers touched the statue's base. "You asked me about the Three Fables ghosts."

Page and Betsy nodded.

"I'm ready to tell you what I know and beg your indulgence on an off-putting topic."

"Of course, Alice, we're keeping open minds," replied Page.

"Yes, open minds," Betsy parroted and looked uneasy.

Alice turned and looked directly at the cousins. "When I first heard from the locals about the occurrences, I laughed them off. You see, I'm a realist. If I can't see it, I doubt it." A hint of a smile appeared on her face.

"Me too. I'm one of those." Betsy activated her hand fan and stepped into a shady spot.

"Please continue, Alice." Page's gaze turned to admire the ironwork on a nearby bench.

Alice leaned down and sniffed a yellow rose. "Since moving in, I told you some odd, almost comical things keep happening."

"You did share that with us, although you didn't elaborate," said Page.

"I'm ready to give you examples." Alice inhaled. "I forgot to turn the burner off under the teakettle the other day. When I went back to the kitchen, I found the kettle safely slid to the side." Alice gave an impish smile.

"Whoa. That's a bit much," voiced Betsy.

"I know. What captured my attention most was the odd guest who would complain nonstop. They were handled most peculiarly, and not by me."

Betsy chuckled. "We get those aggravating customers sometimes at Honey Bees. 'My cookie is crumbly. There isn't enough buttercream on this cupcake.' Poor Daisy had this la-di-da woman the other day who insisted—"

"Betsy, let's let Alice tell her story," interjected Page.

"It's true, Betsy. People can be quite demanding. In my case, these ornery ones have been dealt with in unusual ways." Alice's eyes sparkled. "I'm sure Chester told you about his toupee being tousled on more than one occasion."

Page and Betsy laughed and nodded.

"So, I ask you both a question. Who do you think did that? Chester swears no one was nearby." Alice's expression grew serious.

Betsy offered a shrug.

"After wrestling with my logical mind, I tend to believe Chester's ghostly answer to your question." Page grew thoughtful. "Is there some sort of pattern to these occurrences?"

"Most definitely. Each instance something happens, it's to a guest who isn't polite. Alice's fingers touched her mouth as a grin appeared. "And the actions perpetrated are pranky and most entertaining. Nothing harmful or mean-spirited. Pardon the pun."

Page and Betsy looked at each other.

Alice continued. "I can't say one hundred percent a spirit is doing these things, but I haven't found another explanation."

A look of understanding flickered across Page's face. "I'm certainly not discounting that there's an energy here.

Remember, I'm the one who gets inklings and nudges that call my tune."

"I'd hoped you might understand if I told you." Alice glanced at Betsy. "Because of this, I want to show you what Rake discovered this morning. He was putting the statue back to rights on its inferior base." Alice moved closer to the statue and motioned for Page and Betsy to draw near.

"Consider this your introduction to Althea and her husband, Julian, who resides at the other end." Alice pointed to the statue of a man.

"Althea was a plain woman," said Betsy, staring at her face. "But she had a nice figure. Lucky gal."

Alice's mouth moved to a smile. "Yes, she and Julian made a fine couple. I discovered a journal giving accounts of the property's history. Every owner has added to it."

"How amazing to have a recorded chronicle of Three Fables," replied Page.

"It's been beneficial to me in so many ways." Alice brushed a fallen leaf off Althea's arm. "I read that Julian and Althea had the statues commissioned when they were in their forties. They designed the inn's grounds, and each subsequent owner has honored their vision. This resplendent, gated statue garden has always been their home in more ways than one."

"You just lost me." Betsy lifted her sunglasses to glance around the area.

"I'm about to lose you even more." Alice moved closer to the front of the statue. "Today, we discovered something extraordinary thanks to Rake's spiffing Althea. Are you ready?"

Betsy stepped back, wearing apprehension on her face. "I think so."

"We're ready." Page stayed put, expecting the

unexpected.

Alice's hand pushed on Althea's shoe, and a metal door opened.

CHAPTER 18

"Wait until you see what's inside." Alice pulled a box from the opening.

"Holy cow and calf. Is that chest real gold with precious gems?" Betsy bent down. "Looks like rubies, sapphires, and emeralds. Page, are you seeing this?"

"I'd like to, but your head is in the way. Let me have a squint." Page studied the box in Alice's outstretched hands. "It looks precious in value. There's a latch. Have you opened it?"

"I have. Let's sit on the garden benches and I'll show you."

Once Page and Betsy had settled, Alice lifted the box's latch. Her fingers pulled out an aged envelope and held it up. "Whatever they used to coat this paper has protected it for a couple of hundred years. Touch it."

"It's a kind of wax," said Page, running her hand gingerly along the front.

Betsy took her turn. "Everything seems well preserved. Are those Althea's initials embossed on the stationery?" She passed the envelope to Alice.

"Most definitely." Alice carefully unfolded the lilac-colored paper. Shall I read to you what Althea left behind? I think you'll find her words fascinating."

"Read. Even my hot flash is waiting," answered Betsy.

Page sensed her traditional beliefs were about to be challenged. "Please introduce us to Althea."

Alice closed her eyes for an instant, inhaled, and began

reading.

Dearest trusted caretakers of Three Fables,

I bid you greetings on this fateful day. You have discovered this missive penned in my time in hopes of meeting you in your time.

I'm called Althea, and the statue you undoubtedly reside near is of me. The other your eyes see is dearest Julian. You know not of my Julian and me, but we are the ones who dreamed and thusly created Three Fables that you now call home.

We charge you to be good property stewards in all ways, honoring our vision of the gardens now embracing you.

Our attachment to Three Fables is timeless and boundless, and that truth tasks me to prepare you for our involvement. We endeavor to remain here in our fashion, to oversee our home and who cares for it. Kindly embrace us as we shall you.

Faithfully yours,
Althea and Julian Marchant

Alice folded the paper carefully, tucked it in the matching envelope, and returned it to the box. "Excuse me for a moment while I return this to its home."

Betsy and Page nodded.

Alice settled on the bench once more and continued. "Finding this letter changed everything for me. I must consider the likelihood that Althea and Julian have managed to move around in time. I don't pretend to grasp the universe's workings. Still, I can grasp the meaning of Althea's letter and the happenings I'm witnessing. And in doing so, I've found a strange kind of peace."

Page frowned, attempting to process her own

acceptance of the curious encounters. She'd experienced firsthand Chester's attic episode. The smell of lilacs and the air change in the room were real. His active toupee left her befuddled and amused. If not for her inkling and nudging gift, Page's logical mind would call it strange and move on. Instead, she allowed the otherworldly explanation to play in her head. Like Alice, the thought left her believing that Althea and Julian's presence was real. Betsy's voice interrupted Page's musing.

"I think we need a new noun besides ghosts for Althea and Julian's presence at Three Fables. And I'm inclined to name them something they'd approve of. No need to get them riled. I'm going to ponder what we should call them." Betsy turned to face Alice, adjusting her hat to block the sun. "Can we agree that ghosts aren't befitting? Page? Alice? Anyone who's living?"

"Sure. I agree." Page nodded but kept her frown in place.

"I second it," said Alice.

Page leaned forward. "Here's where my thoughts have landed me. Somehow, Althea and Julian seem capable of transcending time to oversee Three Fables, proving their attachment to the property can't be denied. And while we're unable to know how any of this happens, acceptance is required if we want to move on. And we want to move on."

"I must move on, Page," responded Alice.

Betsy nodded. "I'm trying to catch up here."

Page peeked at the statue. "So, let's continue traveling down this unknown road. Alice, I'd say Althea has undoubtedly enlightened you to their expectations of you acting as the current caretaker of Three Fables."

"My traditional role as innkeeper has been upended." Alice clasped and unclasped her hands. "It's so much to take in. Really, it is. It's best if I don't ponder any of this too deeply. Rather, I'm choosing to see Julian and Althea as permanent unseen residents and keep it to myself as much as possible."

"That's the spirit." Betsy's eyes widened, realizing what she'd said.

Page looked askance at her cousin.

"Sorry. I needed a dose of humor." Betsy looked sheepish.

"I will accept their ways and go along." Alice lifted her shoulders in resignation.

Betsy gave a quick glance around and lowered her voice. "Speaking of their ways, how about the way they treat guests who don't pass muster?"

Alice's smile peeked through. "Thank you, Betsy, for interjecting another dose of levity. I neglected to share that Chester's toupee has gone missing. Sitting at breakfast with his shiny, bald head exposed, he was quite distraught. Do we think my unseen guardians of the inn had a hand in this?"

"No doubt from my perspective," Page said, chuckling. "I definitely want to stay on the good side of Althea and Julian."

Betsy rose with an air of excitement, amplifying her always flushed face. "I've got their names. They're going to love it, too. Let's call them Influencers." Betsy scanned the garden. "How about it, Althea? Julian?"

A breeze of intention blew a red rose at Betsy's sandaled feet. Her hand trembled and pointed down. "Did I just get an answer from…from them?" she stammered.

"I can't believe I'm saying this, but I think they approve of the name," replied Alice.

A recovered Betsy picked up the rose and slipped it through her bonnet's ribbon. "Althea and Julian like me, and I like them back."

As Page tried to absorb what had happened, she managed to string some words together. "So, we're thinking a *spirited* breeze brought Betsy a rose as a positive answer." Page stared at the flower tucked in Betsy's straw hat while her mind struggled to process this latest incident.

"Seems so." Alice's voice was laden with emotion.

Glancing at her watch, Page stood. "We've taken you away from the inn too long. Thank you for trusting Betsy and me with the discovery and for being so open about your unseen residents."

"Influencers," corrected Betsy.

"I'm grateful you didn't suggest a psychiatric workup," said Alice.

Page chuckled. "No way. That would mean we'd each need counseling. And Betsy and I made plans to lounge on the beach. No time to get shrunk by a shrink."

Betsy chuckled. Her eyes caught Page's signal, and she reached for her handbag. "Yes, it's our day off, and we plan to enjoy a few hours of sunning. It's our happy place."

"Of course, you deserve a beach today." Alice grew thoughtful for a moment. "There's one more fret I'd like your opinion on while we stroll back."

"I'm always a good choice for seeking opinions," replied Betsy.

Page half listened, recalling the earlier inkling. Something needed to happen before they left. She felt an immediate tug toward Rake. He'd reappeared with potted flowers to plant in the edible garden. The nudge came in support of the inkling. She'd wait for the right moment to excuse herself. Page shifted focus to Alice as they walked. "How else may we help?"

"It's this. Since we believe Althea and Julian are pranking unlikable guests, how will I attract people to Three

Fables once word gets out? Never mind, the tragic news of Evelyn's death that is already becoming town gossip." Alice hugged her arms. "To use a nautical term, I can't seem to escape the headwinds."

"Not to worry, Alice. You're looking at an expert in marketing." Betsy's chin lifted an inch. "I once dated this marketing guy from San Fran who was a whiz at writing jingles. The words were catchy as all get out. They'd stick in your mind forever."

"But his problem was?" Page decided to fast-track Betsy's tale.

Alice chuckled. "I need your banter. It's good for my soul. Continue, Betsy."

"Anyway, his problem was that he liked to sing his latest jingles to me repeatedly, employing different tones. I'd be in the shower, and the door would fly open and —"

"Skip that part. How does this make you a marketing expert? Pray tell, cousin." Page watched Rake dig his first hole. Counting only four plants, Betsy would need to share her wisdom pearls quickly. She couldn't miss acting on the nudge.

"For starters, he taught me how to turn a negative into a positive. In your case, Alice, don't hide your non-paying residents. Crow about them. I predict most guests won't fear encountering Althea and Julian mulling about the inn."

"They won't?" Alice's expression turned bewildered.

"Nope. You'll keep the promotion lighthearted while you plant some curiosity seeds in the crowing. People's interests will get piqued. They'll clamor to stay here so they can tell their friends. Your bookings will soar." Betsy set her fan in motion.

Page stopped. "Betsy Ross, I've never heard such impressive business pearls from those lips. I expect more of it directed toward our Honey Bees."

"Yeah? I'll put my thinking bee cap on first thing Monday."

Alice squeezed Betsy's hand. "I'm quite smitten with your concept. Once the police have put things right, would you stop by to give me more crowing lessons? I can't pay you right now because you know my funds are kaput, but I can feed you."

Betsy preened. "Why, Alice, I'd love to teach you Bets Crowing 101. I don't want any compensation. You know, I have an idea you can put to use immediately. It involves contacting past guests to write a blurb for Three Fables website. For example—"

"Ladies, please excuse me. I need to ask Rake something that's come to mind. By all means, continue with your discussion." Page took several steps and turned. "Betsy, I'll meet you at the SUV in about five minutes."

"Okay," Betsy answered absently. "Come on, Alice, let's pull up your website on the office computer."

Page shifted her attention in the opposite direction. She took a cleansing breath and strolled closer to the man creating beauty. "Good morning, Rake. Remember me? I'm Page Wright, a police consultant for Evelyn Potts's death."

"Of course. Hello, again." Rake stood and dusted the soil from his hands. He reached to shake Page's hand, only to withdraw his. "Sorry. My shaker is dirty."

"It's fine." Page glanced at the flowers. "What deep shades of hibiscus. I only recently learned they're edible." She'd ease him into trusting her. Rake had something meant for her, and she needed to hear it.

The gardener cast his eyes around the property. "I agree with you about the color of the flowers. I like to create interest in Three Fables' landscaping. Guests seem to enjoy seeing the uncommon plantings and my designs. The flowers depend on my care, and I honor our commitment to each other."

"What an interesting connection you share with nature. Have you always felt this way?" Page bent down and touched a flower. His energy matched the Three Fables' vibe. She smiled, wondering if Althea and Julian approved of Rake.

"Yes, ma'am. I got the love of flowers from my grandma. I replaced her, and eventually my father, as Three Fables' principal gardener." Rake picked up the shovel and scooped dirt out for the next bush.

"Gracious, but your family certainly has an impressive lineage here." The knowledge brought Page more questions. Denying her mind the chance to explore if the original owners had a hand in who cared for the property, she asked a different question. "I'm wondering. Do you have something to tell me?"

Rake planted the shovel in the ground. His blue eyes studied Page. "Did you come to me because you somehow knew I had a morsel or two?"

Page nodded. "Just as you have an unusual connection with the flora to help them thrive, I experience inklings when I'm needed to help others. Like Alice."

"I knew I liked you." Rake's brows pulled together. "I don't know if what I overheard a while ago is meant for you or one of those detectives." He reached for the shovel and made the hole larger.

"Why don't you tell me, and I'll pass it along to Detective Tanner. I'm seeing him today. Would that work?" Page handed him one of the potted, yellow hibiscuses.

Rake released the plant from the container and placed it in the hole. "I suppose because you're helping the police and Alice." He tucked the bush's roots with rich potting soil before standing. "Follow me."

"Okay." Page walked with Rake to a side garden where a six-foot hedge bordered a gravel drive leading to a small cottage on the property. It looked vacant and represented another place needing maintenance.

Rake halted. "I was standing right here a couple of hours ago assessing whether these uninvited dandelions would claim my Sunday afternoon. On the other side of the hedge, I heard a woman talking on her cell phone. She had the speaker on, so I heard both sides."

"Do you know who she was?" asked Page.

"I do. She's the one who bosses the authors. She's tall and brunette and keeps her nose in the air most times I've seen her."

"Fiona. Go on." Page sensed Rake had scored important clues by being at the right place and time.

"So, this Fiona's chatting with, I assumed, her boss. She's plenty worked up about things." Rake pulled a bandana from his pocket and wiped his forehead. "I'll tell you what she said, and you do with it what you will."

"Great, go ahead," Page said in a deliberate voice.

"Fiona said the problem of Evelyn leaving them for another publisher had been permanently solved. She told this fellow that her group of authors' shenanigans had crossed every line. Fiona went on a rant complaining that out of the hundred outstanding British authors they represented, she was dished out the tossers to manage. That's when she began ticking off her group's unsavory ways. They're quite a bunch—one with a DUI, one thieving, and another who has a DA writing books for him. No, wait. TA is what Fiona said."

Page nodded. "TA, teaching assistant. I heard something about that."

"I guess her boss had heard enough. He went on some

kind of tirade, calling Fiona inept and threatening to fire her. She kept interrupting him to say her job meant everything, and she'd do whatever it took to keep her editor position with the publishing house. The last thing I heard Fiona say was she'd handle the authors' misdeeds that had come to light in her way. And she'd return to work on Wednesday with all problems remedied." Rake rubbed his chin. "Maybe the detectives should investigate her or at least have another talk."

"You're absolutely right." Page considered her next words. "Tell me something. You're in tune with things going on around here. Do you get the impression that Fiona's capable of harming another?"

Rake stepped over to a dandelion and plucked the weed. "I take it at face value when someone says they'll do whatever it takes to keep a job. I don't know what role she played in Ms. Potts's death, but Fiona has big problems with her authors' misbehaving. She's caught in the middle and being squeezed by her boss to weed her garden, so to speak. I'd say it's survival of the fittest now. You know what I mean, Page?"

"I certainly do. And I appreciate your wise assessment. What you overheard will prove of great value to Detective Tanner. Is there anything else?" Page adjusted her tote higher on her shoulder.

"Two more things. I saw the woman who assisted Evelyn, crying in the gazebo." Rake pointed to the structure. "Guess the loss of her boss overtook her, but I didn't feel it appropriate to intrude."

"I understand. Sometimes it's best to let a person process their grieving privately." Page touched Rake's arm. "What's the second thing?"

"Just be careful. This group knows you're working

alongside the police, and you were the one who found Ms. Potts. One of them did wrong, and they might do it again, given a reason." Rake glanced toward the inn.

"I'll take care. You're a good guy, Rake. And there aren't many of you out there." Page extended her hand. "Give a shake. I don't care if it's a garden-loving hand."

Rake did another swipe down his overalls before shaking. "One more thing. Don't trouble yourself over Alice's safety. I'll see to her."

Page detected a note of more than fondness. "Alice is indeed fortunate to have you here and caring for things. Please contact Detective Tanner if you observe anything else concerning. I'll see you later."

"Under happier circumstances, I hope." Rake returned to his plants.

Page hurried to her SUV and a likely simmering Betsy. Thanks to the nudge, she'd scored more nuggets for their suspect board and info to share with Steve. Fiona had the scoop on her author's problems. Page bet they'd squealed on each other to the editor.

For now, she and Betsy had earned a break to decompress on the beach. The authors were occupied with sightseeing, and Leo wouldn't risk misbehaving. Page released a sigh and saw Betsy fanning herself by the vehicle, probably plotting their spiced-up lunch menu. *Time to embrace my karmic fate.*

CHAPTER 19

"I'm so hot right now. You could cook lunch on me. What took so long?" Betsy climbed into the passenger side of the vehicle.

Page laughed and started the engine. "It is a mite warm for spring. Sorry to make you wait, but it was worth it. Rake had tidbits for us."

"Fill me in on the drive back to Hibiscus because I'm declaring our beach time free of whodunit chatter once we arrive. I plan to read my new historical romance, learn about this dowager's escapades, and eat unlimited blue corn chips with a yummy dip I'm serving us."

Page swallowed. "About lunch. I thought we could keep it simple and get to the beach sooner. How about peanut butter and jelly sandwiches or the turkey I suggested earlier?"

"I used all the peanut butter last night. I'm ahead of you." Betsy tossed her straw hat in the backseat. "I did lunch prep while you and Dreamboat were at the inn. It's in the fridge for my final touches. Wait until you taste my dip." Betsy brought her fingers to her lips and made a smacking sound.

"You're too kind feeding me such culinary masterpieces." Page hoped the giant bottle of antacids had been delivered to her door. Every dip created by Betsy packed a wallop.

"Watch that big pothole." Betsy pointed out the windshield.

Page steered quickly around it. "I wish they'd fix the

Oyster pothole. It's going to ruin someone's tire. The roads in this country are a disgrace."

"You're so right. It's funny how Shell Isle's potholes get named. That speaks volumes about streets needing major attention." Betsy waved a dismissive hand. "Forget all of that. Are you going to update me on your chat with Rake or not? Talk fast. I want to get this over and think about lunch and the Dowager Eleanor entertaining the Ton."

"You and those uppity historical romances. Moving on." Page spent the next few minutes sharing Grace's emotional state and Fiona's phone conversation. "To sum it up, we've discovered a motive for the editor. She was losing Evelyn as a client, and her publisher was none too happy. Now, Fiona's faced with her authors having personal and legal problems jeopardizing their contracts. More revenue loss will cost her job."

Betsy gave a shake of her head. "Fiona sure drew the short straw in getting assigned this bunch. British authors are known for their manners and respectable standing amongst their peers. The ones who write my favorite books all hail from across the pond." Betsy grew quiet. "And you're right—Fiona's in a desperate place. And, as we always say, desperation breeds desperate actions. As for Grace and the crying, she's unexpectedly lost her job. I'd cry, too."

"Still, I sense there's more to Grace and Evelyn's relationship. Steve's doing background checks on everyone. That always illuminates something." Page popped a peppermint in her mouth, anticipating the dip.

"True." Betsy fiddled nervously with her beads. "I still don't like knowing someone bad is staying at Three Fables."

Page adjusted her sun visor and did a sideways glance at her cousin. "Maybe the two unseen residents will look after Alice and Chatty. If we're to believe they exist on some level, then—"

"Then Alice and Chatty aren't vulnerable." Betsy smoothed her muumuu's hem. "I like the two gals so much. Don't you? Chatty fits in so well to Shell's casual atmosphere."

"I agree." Page signaled a mom with a stroller to cross the street before she turned. "Hopefully, the next inkling will lead us to the truth of what happened to Evelyn. My intuition says we're close to a wrap. Having the contenders in one place helps." Page parked her vehicle. "We're home."

"Okay, no more case talk. I may not drink hot tea ever again after this caper. If I hadn't booked us to cater the tea party, we wouldn't be involved, and life at Shell Isle would have stayed sublime." Betsy hopped out of the SUV.

"You did nothing wrong. We're doing what we're supposed to do. Help when tapped." Page followed Betsy up the cottage's steps. "How about I update the suspect board while you make lunch?"

"Good idea. Let's change into our beach attire first. I brought my new cover-up to show off. It's a print with purple seahorses. And my flip-flops are the same shade of purple." Betsy placed her handbag and hat on the hooks.

Page shook her head and moved toward the bedroom. "Sounds like the perfect Betsy Ross beach ensemble." Closing her door, she inhaled the solitude.

Betsy hollered, "I'll pack the cooler with our lunch and drinks so we can soak up every minute by the ocean."

Page decided against wearing a bathing suit and changed into a pale-blue tee and a white skort. She'd sneak an apple and crackers in her beach bag for a backup lunch. The suspect board only asked for a brief update. She found Betsy swinging in the hammock and noticed the cooler's worrisome contents waiting at the screen door.

"All set?" asked Betsy.

"I just need to grab our two chairs." Page lifted the storage box's lid and hoisted out their loungers. "Lead on."

***

The early afternoon sun painted the sand a dazzling white. Surfers in wetsuits bobbed on the ocean swells, having patience for the perfect wave. Distracted parents with cell phones glanced up frequently to ensure their kids behaved. And a competitive group playing volleyball clapped and whooped at each score. Page waved to a toddler carrying a handful of shells toward her family.

"Here's good," declared Betsy, unfolding her chair. "The tide's going out, so we won't need to move."

"Nice choice to keep us away from the volleyball game." Page spread a navy striped towel in her chair and fished in the beach tote for sunscreen. Eyeing Betsy as she removed the lids from three containers, Page swallowed in preparation for the zing awaiting her. She grabbed the bag of tortilla chips and sprinkled them liberally on one of the empty plates. Learning to cover her plate with something tame meant less room for generous Betsy to heap mounds of the unknown on her plate. "What do we have here?" asked Page as she peered at the substance resembling dip.

"Let me tour you." Betsy pointed. "Here we have my Dippity Dagger recipe. I dried the Dagger peppers myself." Betsy scooped dip onto a chip and passed it to Page. "Try."

Page stared at the diced unknowns of red, orange, and purple. She smelled cumin. "How hot is this Dagger—"

"Take a bite and stop dissecting my creation." Betsy ate a chip. "Perfecto."

Not seeing a helpful seagull to feed it to, Page bit into the chip and waited. Nothing fire-like happened. The pepper's heat was palatable. "Why, Betsy, the dip tastes yummy. Tell me what's in your recipe."

"See? Another gold-star creation by me." Betsy spooned the dip next to Page's chips. "There's sour cream, Dagger flakes, roasted eggplant, yellow peppers, fresh chives, cumin, Worcestershire, which I'm super attached to lately." Betsy reached for the second container. "That's the basic recipe. Usually, I would add red pepper flakes, but I left them out for you."

"I appreciate the thought. What's that smell?" Page pulled back.

"Limberger pimento cheese." Betsy produced four slices of raisin bread. "We're going for sweet and savory tastes here."

Page felt her stomach turn over. "Ya know, I'm not feeling the sweet and savory today. That's your sandwich. I'm going to make a meal out of this dip starting now." Sparing Betsy any hurt, Page ate a chip. "So good, Bets."

"Okay, no sandwich for you. How about some Pumped Pineapple?"

Page nodded and held out her plate. "Just two or three chunks. What makes it pumped?"

"Hey, here comes Chatty and Dreamboat." Betsy stood and gave a big wave.

Taking the opportunity, Page buried her pumped chunks in the sand and twisted to see the duo heading their way. She laughed, seeing Steve acting as a pack mule. He wore his stealthy wetsuit, but the surfboard wasn't part of the tote.

"Hello, snoops." Steve opened one of the chairs for his aunt.

"How many times must I say, cut the snoops, or I'll tag you with Dreamboat at the station," threatened Betsy.

"Ditto that from me." Page smiled, rising to help Chatty get situated.

Steve handed his aunt sparkling water from a tote. "Yeah, yeah, copy that on the Dreamboat threat. Anyway, Chatty and I returned from the lighthouse earlier than planned."

"And I asked if we could enjoy a bit of the afternoon sun on the beach. Having you two to visit with while my nephew surfs is the cherry on top of my day." Chatty settled into her chair and took a sip from the bottle.

Steve surveyed the setup. "If you're situated, I'll grab my board and hit the waves." Steve lifted his eyebrows, seeing Page's plate. "Wanna walk me back to the bungalow? We can discuss what food to bring on our sailing."

"Sure." Page turned to Betsy. "I'll be back in a jiffy."

"Fine, but no hanky-panky. I'm timing you. You've got fifteen minutes starting now." Betsy winked at Chatty. "I must give them strict rules of engagement. They run hot, those two."

"I can see that." Chatty's eyes danced in merriment.

"I've heard enough of my cousin's malarkey. Come on, Steve." Page accepted his hand. "Talk food to me, handsome."

Out of earshot, Steve said, "That lunch looked and smelled worrisome. I figured I could offer you a cheese sandwich or something on the sly."

"Nah, don't worry about me. It's Chatty who's vulnerable," teased Page.

"We'll make haste. How did your visit to Three Fables go? And I suppose we might as well decide what to bring sailing." Steve lifted the gate's latch.

Barnacle came bounding toward Page, bringing a fresh bone that he had dug up.

"Hey, Barn." Page accepted the offering with two fingers and tossed it into the yard for him to chase. "Let's do food talk first."

Steve perched on his picnic table and pulled Page close. His lips brushed against her warm cheek. "Sure, we can talk food, but first some hanky. You smell like jasmine."

"I know." Page released a sigh and let the flutters come.

Steve's mouth found hers, and both became lost in the moment and feeling. He pulled away, releasing Page. "How many minutes do we have left on Betsy's timer?"

"Not enough. Better talk food."

"I hate your duenna." Steve tugged on Page's ballcap.

"Blame yourself. You decreed Betsy must stay at my cottage until this case is solved. Focus. Food. Give me choices," said Page.

"Okay. How about something light like sushi? I can order takeout from Wasabi."

"Sounds great. Order me whatever you're having."

"Done. Now about the inn visit?" Steve tried to pull Page closer.

"Behave. I can share what I gleaned in five minutes. First, I want to hear what you learned from bringing in thieving Leo."

"Nothing more, other than he finally admitted to trying to 'nick' — as he calls it — a few books. Monday, I should have a report on any priors for this clown." Steve shrugged. "Your turn."

"Listen and grow wiser, Detective." Page chose to omit the discovery of Althea's letter.

Steve kept quiet until Page finished detailing the visit. "Basically, we're assuming it's up to the phone or button's report to narrow our field of suspects. And if I allow this group to fly the coop on Tuesday without charging one of them, it complicates things. Without something that links one to Evelyn at the time of her death, the DA won't charge." Steve pushed his hand through his coal-black hair.

"That means I need another inkling or nudge, and fast. Let's hope I get one soon." Page grabbed Steve's hand and tugged playfully. "Time to go. Get your board."

"At your command, madam." Retrieving the surfboard from his patio, Steve joined Page on the walkway.

"Did you and Chatty have a fun outing?" Page changed sides as they walked to avoid the surfboard's movements.

"We did. My aunt's energetic and in amazing physical shape. I watched her climb the stairs to the top of the lighthouse like a thirty-year-old." Spontaneous laughter escaped Steve. "Get a load of this one. Aunt Chatty informed me she booked a three-hour cruise tonight. The theme is stargazing or something. She lives to chase fun."

Page added her laugh. "Chatty's a force. I aspire to pattern after her at that age."

"Don't we all? I adore the woman and miss having her in my life," said Steve.

Page tilted her head sideways, pondering Steve's words. "Well, you never know how things might change."

"Hey, what was on your lunch plate hasn't changed. It's waiting for you." Steve pointed ahead.

"And not a seagull to save me anywhere around. Go surfing and leave me to my destiny."

"A destiny I won't share. See ya later." Steve tweaked Page's nose.

While Betsy and Chatty discussed their favorite romance authors, Page munched a chip and watched Steve paddle past the wave break line. How she wished the summer would hurry. Just thinking about sitting on the board, snuggled against his tanned, muscular chest, amped her pulse. "Enough of these thoughts. You're tormenting yourself." She glanced to her right, ensuring Betsy and Chatty didn't hear her words.

Page took a read on the sky. Groups of passing white fluffy cumulus clouds gave no sign of an impending storm, but she knew how quickly their white could change to dark, foreboding grey. Being sensitive, Page knew time was choking the person who'd harmed Evelyn. Worry was probably their constant companion now. All she could do was wait for the next inkling or nudge's direction.

CHAPTER 20

Dressed for sailing in her denim jeans and sailboat-printed shirt, Page spritzed a citrusy scent on her wrists. Applying a mauve shade of lip gloss, she studied her image in the mirror. "I need mascara and my gold button earrings." She added both before slipping her feet into navy sneakers, draping a wide scarf around her neck, and giving the mirror one last smile. "Now, I'm ready."

"Let me see." Betsy appeared in the doorway. "Yep, you're good." She sniffed. "Hmm, fragrance means smoochin' with Dreamboat."

"Only if I'm lucky," teased Page.

"You're always lucky. It's me that has to date every… oh, never mind all of that."

Page scooted past Betsy, heading for the kitchen. "Need I remind you that you're on Andre's arm now? He's a super guy."

Betsy followed. "I like him. The Mermaids bowl tonight, and he's coming by to drive me. Andre insists on staying to cheer me on to bowl strikes." Betsy handed Page her baseball cap and canvas bag.

"Are you getting serious with him, Bets?" Page adjusted the cap and draped the bag's strap over her shoulder.

"I could, but I won't. Nothing's changed from when you asked me that last. I told you I'm following in your footsteps and keeping things light. It's better for me at this point in life to enjoy Andre's company and avoid vows of any kind. I've said them too many times. No more." Betsy walked to the glass door and gazed at the beach. "I just need to figure out the loneliness part, and I will. It's the nights, you know. The bungalow gets all quiet. I don't like quiet." Betsy turned toward Page, lifted her chin, and blinked away tears.

Page came to her cousin's side and bestowed a hug. "Betsy Ross, I hereby declare we'll find the answer to our evening loneliness."

"Our? Did you say our loneliness?" Betsy's expression changed to surprise.

The cuckoo came out of his house, reminding Page to leave. "I gotta dash. Steve's probably outside waiting. We'll chat more on this subject later."

"Sure. Go and have fun. You'll probably beat me home tonight." Betsy opened the front door. "I've got an opportunity to try and kill that cuckoo again."

Betsy calling Hibiscus home again wasn't lost on Page. She could understand why Betsy felt that way. They'd spent their summers at the cottage with Aunt Tilly since they were five. Page glanced back at a determined Betsy going for the step stool. "Leave Aunt Tilly's clock alone. That bird has bested you more than once." Chuckling, she hurried down the steps. Her date leaned against his vehicle, looking too manly and sea captain-like. Steve Tanner didn't play fair with her hormones.

"All set for some choppy water?" Steve opened the passenger door.

"How choppy? Do you want to reschedule?" Page tossed her things in the backseat. "We could go play miniature golf. I like winning."

"I let you win." Steve's dimples winked at Page.

Page tossed her hair back. "I win because I'm a confident woman, and your ego needs a smackdown."

Steve buckled his seatbelt. "So, this is how our

evening—hang on, course correction." He leaned over the console and kissed Page, engaging her senses. "That's also called a reset, Sherlocka."

Breathless and enjoying the reset, Page managed to get out four words. "What about that chop?"

Steve put his black SUV in reverse. "Carpe lives for a chop. We'll stay around Shell Bay. I promise you a fun sail and fresh sushi waiting in the ice chest. Are you my first mate?"

"Aye, aye, my captain." Page settled into the seat, anticipating a beautiful sunset with a man who knew how to deliver flutters.

The chime of Steve's cell phone interrupted their carefree mood, and a male voice boomed on the SUV's speaker. "What's up, Detective Koch?"

"Alice called me about two of her guests getting into some big blow. Are you ready for this one?" Koch paused.

"Lay it on me, but don't you dare ask me to cancel my sail." Steve reached for Page's hand.

"Our Chester Tickle accused Ruby Reed of taking his toupee, and she accused him of taking her wig. Alice said they started slapping the air at each other."

Steve sent Page an exasperated look. "Are you kidding me? You're calling me about a hairpiece brawl?"

"Hang on. It gets better. They return to their rooms after creating a stir amongst the others, only to find Chester's rug on Ruby's shower head and her wig draped over his bedpost." Laughter rang out from the other officers in the background. Koch joined in.

"And?" prodded Steve.

"And Chester and Ruby are convinced it's ghosts that are messing with them. They're all hyped up, demanding Alice have us guard their rooms while they sleep. Have you ever heard of such nonsense? Ghosts. Steve? You there?"

asked Koch, still snickering.

"I'm here." Steve winked at Page. "Listen, why don't you offer Chester and Ruby an empty cell and breakfast, compliments of Shell Isle's taxpayers? That should shut down any more demands on Alice."

Koch laughed again. "I told the guys here you'd come up with something. Ghosts. If there are ghosts at Three Fables, I hope they deliver to us the culprit who tipped the statue on Ms. Potts. Someone must explain to me one day why anyone wants to run an inn and put up with guests losing touch with reality. See you tomorrow."

Steve hung up. "It seems — what are their names? You told me earlier."

"Althea and Julian," replied Page, amused over the exchange. She reminded herself she'd held back sharing information about Althea's letter. It had nothing to do with the case and was Alice's story to tell.

"Right, Althea and Julian. Assuming we buy into this paranormal thing, it seems they're causing quite a stir. Why do you think? What should we do? This ghost business is hard for me to wrap my head around. I'd welcome some guidance from someone who has experience with woo-woo." Steve turned into the marina's lot and parked. He twisted in the seat to face Page.

"My woo-woo is quite different from spirits, or as Betsy's named them — influencers — hanging around Alice's inn." Page raised her hand. "Okay, I get your point. Give me a chance to ponder my answer. Let's go sailing into the sunset and eat sushi."

"I'm a patient man. I'll wait for your insights."

Page lifted an eyebrow.

"All right, I can behave like a patient man...sometimes." Steve tipped Page's chin. "I'm ready to claim our evening alone."

The two hurried down a walkway toward the boat.

Page felt happiness claim her as she boarded the thirty-foot Carpe Diem moored at the dock. They stowed their things before Steve made use of the sloop's engine to maneuver them out of the marina. Once on the open water, Page watched the transformation. Steve became one with the boat when he unfurled the sails, letting the wind grab them. The Bermuda-rigged main and headsail were perfect for sailing into the wind.

Page tucked her hair under the cap and assumed first-mate tasks.

"Come take the wheel so I can tighten the loose rigging."

"Got it." Page used her thigh to help maintain control of the wheel.

Within moments, Steve stood next to Page as the sloop skimmed across the white caps like a sea nymph. Their free-spirited delight built as the boat gathered speed. Feet firmly planted, they held on to Carpe Diem's lines while the wind directed them toward Shell Bay.

Page licked the salt spray from her lips. "There's no feeling like this, captain."

"Or this." Steve pulled Page into him and kissed her to prove his point.

"No argument from me after that kiss." Page repositioned her cap and sighed. "I adore how each sailing is unique. It's the intoxication from the sea's ever-changing moods. Know what I mean, captain?"

Steve wiped the droplets from his face. "I call it the sea's allure factor. Something you're most in tune with, and I enjoy watching."

"Do tell. Alluring, hmm." Page gave a sideways,

flirtatious glance.

"That look undoes me every time. Steady on, mate, or there will be consequences." His grey eyes roamed over her face and hair.

"Consequences, you say. Would I like them?" Page knew she'd sealed her fate.

"You need to find out, now." Steve's strong arms wrapped around Page. "You're my Calypso and need more kissing. Consequences are coming." For the next moments, he made good on the declaration.

Finally pulling away, Page gave in to the myriad of feelings Steve awakened. Her head lifted and met his gaze. "You don't play fair. You break our hanky-panky rules."

"Maybe they need breaking." Steve pressed his warm lips to her forehead.

"Tanner, the only thing we need to break is into the cooler and eat sushi. Park this sloop, will you?" Page needed to cool things down pronto. Escalating things to a more intimate level scared her. She wanted to keep their relationship light and fun with a bit of enjoyable kissing and cuddling.

"At your command." Steve's eyes locked on Page. "Your teasing wiles —"

"Forget my wiles. I'm starving. How about we anchor by the small island? The seagulls like it." Page pointed.

"Way to spot, mate." Steve made the adjustments. "Duck. We're coming about."

Page noticed the sun was saying its final goodbye to the day. The show craved an artist's brush. Its beauty unfolding distracted her from crewing until Steve's voice brought her back.

"Make ready to trim the sails."

"Aye, I'm dropping the jib first. Signal me when to lower the main." Page moved toward the bow.

Carpe Diem's anchor splashed within minutes, and Steve secured the sailboat. "We're all set. I'll go below and grab our dinner. Would you choose a place for us to eat?"

"Can do." Page arranged two cushions to face each other and spread a small, blue tarp as a makeshift tablecloth. She sat cross-legged, admiring that Steve had the agility to keep his balance while bringing their meal. Navy Seals excelled at prowess, and Page knew firsthand that Steve Tanner had an oversupply of it.

He plopped down on his cushion and began unpacking the containers. "I kept it easy and didn't order soup. But I took liberties with something else." His dimple flashed at Page.

"What kind of liberties?" Page leaned closer to peer at the round containers.

Steve lifted the lids. "Seaweed salad and calamari liberties. They don't spill on a choppy sea. You like?"

Page's expression changed to delight. "I like." Her fingers stole a bite of the calamari. "My kind of liberties. Have one." She placed a piece in his mouth. Her fingers touched his lips as their eyes met.

"I'd better feed myself." A grin edged Steve's mouth.

"Good idea." Page tried to ignore her rapid pulse rate. Her hormones seemed to pump like she was sixteen again. She focused on sprinkling soy sauce on the sushi. "Lately, I discovered that I love spicy crab rolls, and you chose six of those for me. Thank you."

Steve opened the paper holding his chopsticks. "You're welcome. I fear that's Betsy's influence. Next, you'll tell me you're eating hot tamales from Juan's food truck."

"Food truck? Where has this Juan and his tamales been hiding?" Page's voice had a haughty lilt.

"Juan's hiding in plain sight about twenty yards from the police station. There's an empty parking lot adjoining our building. He smartly requested a permit to be close enough to chum us for lunch. The guy makes a mean burrito." Steve released a slight laugh.

"Wait until I tell Bets. Maybe there's something tame on the menu for me? A taco or something."

"The tacos are amazing. Give Juan a go."

Carpe Diem bobbed enthusiastically with the waves, forcing them to keep the caps on their drinks. While they shared a meal, Steve detailed the next maintenance project planned for the sloop.

Page listened while he explained the steps to overhaul the auxiliary engine and the drudgery of removing barnacles from the hull. "You should give Barnacle the hull job," teased Page.

"Yeah, I should. That crazy mutt eats anything." Steve shook his head. "Anyway, both jobs require a lot from my day. But the good news is I've taken three weeks of vacation in June to tackle it. I need to wait until the water warms."

Surprise colored Page's face. "You're doing the work yourself?"

"I am." Steve's hand patted the railing. "She's my girl, and I know how to care for her."

"I'm impressed. I suppose I won't see much of you in June." Page felt sadness as she said the words. Was she already a goner for this guy? No. She refused to allow such thoughts to take root.

"What? Of course, you'll see me. I live next door. Besides, I hope you'll bring lunch on your days off and keep Carpe and me company." Steve tweaked her nose.

"Depends, Tanner."

Steve's eyes narrowed. "Depends on what, Sherlocka?"

"On if you're suckering me to swab a deck or something," retorted Page. "I don't do swabbing."

"Duly noted. How about waxing and polishing teak?" Steve ate his last sushi and tossed the empty containers in the trash bag. He held it open for Page.

"We might barter something around that job. Let me think about it." Page repositioned the cushion so she could lean back against a storage chest.

Steve's expression grew thoughtful and married to his silence.

Page could tell his mind held him captive. She listened to the colorful telltales flapping in the breeze, showing the direction of the wind. Their sound was hypnotic, as the water's negative ions bathed her in relaxation. The past twenty-four hours had exacted a toll, and Page knew she would keep paying the price until she discovered who had harmed Evelyn. Sailing with Steve served to fill her energy reserves.

Steve's voice interrupted her musing. "The sun's left us. Are you good with staying anchored a while longer? I want to delve into the subject we didn't finish discussing."

Page reached for her scarf and wrapped it around her shoulders. "I'm good right here. Betsy's bowling and won't be home until later. What's pressing on your mind?"

"Ghosts. Specifically, Three Fables' supposed ghosts. I need your insights to move forward with this twisty case." Steve inhaled deeply. "Are you a believer in them?"

Page studied his face and waited for the answer to come.

CHAPTER 21

"Am I a believer in ghosts sounds like a simple question, but it's far from it. I will endeavor to answer you. Be warned. My beliefs have changed in the last twenty-four hours. And I'm adding the caveat that my thoughts continue to evolve after being at Three Fables." Page took a moment to center herself and gain the clarity needed. "Okay?"

Steve gave a quick nod. "Okay, you're driving this ghost-busting vehicle. I'm a passenger going for the ride." Steve scooted his cushion closer to Page and draped his parka around her shoulders. "It's getting chilly. Your scarf isn't doing the job."

Page snuggled into the jacket's warmth and inhaled the masculine scent of its owner. It was time to lift the lid on Pandora's paranormal box. "First, I don't refer to those appearing at Three Fables as ghosts. I believe they're spirits. Just as we are, only ours live inside our bodies. We have shape. Those who crossed over have a kind of nebulous form. A subtle body, so to speak. Are you with me?" Page glanced at Steve's face. "You asked for this."

Steve rubbed his chin, looking perplexed. "I asked if you believed ghosts were real and causing mischief at Three Fables."

"Ah, you want a simple yes or no answer to those complex questions." Page gazed at a motorboat speeding past. She understood. This ex-Seal was wired for logic and provable facts. Neither could she provide. "Well?"

"I suppose. If that's possible." Steve's hand lifted.

"Page, I've got to be honest here. I don't get this whole higher-self thing. I don't get your inklings and nudges, but I believe it when you tell me you've experienced something that's guiding you. You've proven yourself over and over." Steve hesitated.

"Thank you for saying that." Page knew he was processing his thoughts and letting them trump his feelings.

"Here it is neat. When I ask myself, what's the source for your insights? I'm immediately lost. I'm partial to my explainable world. Truthfully, it's a place I prefer to reside." The corners of Steve's eyes crinkled.

Page reached for his hand. "I understand. Your thoughts are normal, though I can tell you feelings provide greater insights on this topic. Pay attention to them instead of your mind's chatter."

Steve opened his mouth to speak.

Page placed two fingers against his warm lips. "Hang on. Let me have the wheel. I've dealt with others' reactions to my gift for so long. You shall have the simple answers to your questions. Yes, I believe in spirits. And yes, I believe two reside at Three Fables. You got two yeses. Now what?" Page hadn't closed Pandora's paranormal box yet. She watched as the detective went to busy himself with tasks while he allowed his mind to torment him. She knew he wasn't satisfied with her two yeses and was about to realize it.

Steve checked the nearby riggings. He re-tied a nautical knot and coiled the rope before returning to Page. "Answer me this one. Do you think Chester's correct that the two ghosts, or spirits as you prefer, killed Evelyn Potts?"

"No." Page waited.

"That's it. Just 'no'?" Steve's expression turned puzzled.

"You want single-word answers. You got another one." Page removed the ball cap and fluffed her hair before securing it again with the rubber band. Feeling hot, she jettisoned the parka and wondered if she'd experienced one of Betsy's hot flashes.

Steve bent down and lifted Page's chin to meet his eyes. "How do you know these spirits or ghosts didn't harm Evelyn?"

"Because."

Steve threw up both arms. "Okay, you win...again. Answer me the way you want. I'll muddle through and extract what I need."

"Because they're not evil. Alice told Bets and me that Althea and Julian prank the guests who aren't nice. They don't want them in their home or bothering Alice. So, I've devoted the afternoon to pondering this subject and finding my truth."

"That I can believe. But how and why are these two spirits able to hang out—"

Page raised her hand. "For some reason that I can't explain, Althea and Julian's connection to Three Fables wasn't severed when they left their bodies. They maintain an ongoing relationship and love for the place."

Steve shook his head. "Of course they do. Here's an idea. Maybe we could invite Julian and Althea for dinner and ask Betsy to make one of her fire-breathing entrees. That might bring them back to life."

Page went along with his nonsense. "What a marvelous idea. Look, Steve, I know this is all far out. If you can try accepting what I say and move on, you'll have the answers you need. It's the method I had to employ to feel anchored. Pardon the sailing comparison."

"Fine. I'll play. I accept our imaginary new friends didn't have a hand in Evelyn's death, and they mess with the guests they don't like. Great. However, their messing is clouding my investigation and causing these suspects to behave strangely." Steve quit talking. His eyes widened with an aha-type look.

"What?" asked Page.

"Do you think Althea and Julian witnessed what happened to Evelyn Potts?"

"Gosh! That's an insightful question. We need to discover the answer." Page leaned over and kissed his cheek. "And this from a guy who doesn't believe what he can't see. You're making progress," chided Page.

"Very funny. So? How do we get Ally and Jules to point us in the right direction?" Steve pulled out his cell phone and answered a text.

Page grinned at the nicknames he'd bestowed on the spirit couple. While he fiddled with his phone, she took the opportunity to noodle his question around in her mind. Was it possible to communicate with Althea and Julian? She recalled the rose dropping on Betsy's feet. Were they around to see what happened? Her next step revealed itself in an instant.

"Well?" asked Steve, tucking his phone away.

Page slipped the parka back on. Now she felt chilled. That was a hot flash, she told herself. "I'm clear on my next move. I'll pay another visit to Three Fables tomorrow and knock on that door. I'll see if our new unseen friends are hanging around and maybe I'll ask if they know whodunit." Page gave a solemn nod. "That's my plan."

"I'm on board with your plan. Pardon the sailing jargon. I'll even meet you there. Julian might prefer to talk to a guy." Steve showed his perfect white teeth.

Page smacked his shoulder. "Now you want to buddy up with Julian? Sure, you do, Mr. Skeptic. Thanks all the same. I've got this outing covered."

"But it's my brilliant question that opened—"

"Pandora's paranormal box?" finished Page.

"Now, what are you talking about?" Steve rose. "Don't answer even with one word. Keep your box and hocus pocus talk. I'm pulling up the anchor. This outing has turned my rational inner world inside out." Steve extended his hand to Page. "Come on, first mate. Make ready to cast off."

Page accepted Steve's hand. Flexing her stiff muscles, she replied, "Aye, captain; I'm on the sails."

As they tacked Carpe Diem toward the marina, Page let her mind run free with the sloop. She had a myriad of questions. Assuming Althea and Julian maintained a connection to their beloved Three Fables, was it possible to elicit their help in solving the case, or was that another Pandora's box better left alone? Steve's question intrigued her.

Another niggling thought continued to play in her head. Page felt Mara and James were holding something back from Alice. They seemed friendly enough, but the conversation she'd overheard on the beach kept replaying. She'd snoop more on the brother and sister on her next visit.

There was one fact that Page couldn't ignore. Time was pressing to find the answers to what happened to Evelyn. With the author's group scheduled to fly out Tuesday, the window to discover who tipped the statue would vamoose. Was she willing to ask and accept guidance from unseen residents of Three Fables? The answer waited for tomorrow.

CHAPTER 22

Page bid Steve goodnight from his driveway. Even though the sail had been pure joy, their conversation left them adrift, floating in the unknown abyss of the unexplained. Coming from different viewpoints and beliefs, they needed to process the paranormal aspect of the case individually.

Hurrying up the cottage's steps, Page deposited her things on the bench. She flicked on the lights and grabbed a bottle of tea. The place felt empty, almost sad. Taken aback by the feeling, the idea of a walk along the beach came calling. She jotted a note to Betsy and left it on the kitchen island. She grabbed her windbreaker, cash, and a flashlight, and tucked her cell phone in her back pocket.

Slipping out the screen door, she inhaled the salt air, noting the full moon lit the beach in a silvery light. White caps on the ocean glistened from the orb's glow. In the distance, Page could see a shrimp boat's lights readying for a long night's work.

The inkling hit as she stepped onto the sand. Her mind struggled to grasp why she'd get one at this hour. "So much for a relaxed walk," Page mumbled to herself. Feeling the breeze shift direction, she zipped her jacket, wondering what the evening still held for her.

An unusual number of people strolled the beach. Their flashlights shone on tidal pools of small fish. The pier's lights twinkled, nudging Page to visit her favorite gelato shop and the night fishers. The inkling and nudge spurred her curiosity to walk faster. She wished her sleuthing buddy was by her side.

Page's cell rang. "Hey, Bets. I was thinking about you."

"I'm home from bowling a lousy game. I read your note. Where are you?"

"Starting a walk toward the pier." Page waved to a little girl swinging her shell bucket and flashlight.

"Wait for me. I'm heading your way," answered a winded Betsy.

"I'll do better than wait. I will turn back and meet you." Page caught sight of her cousin stepping lively on the beach. "I see you."

Betsy waved. "There you are. Ouch. I stepped on a shell. Hang on. I'm putting on my flip-flops."

Page reached Betsy. "All set?"

"Yes. What was I about to miss?" Betsy followed Page down to the firmer sand to walk. "Because if you're heading for the pier at night, it means you had an inkling or something. That also means I have a role to play."

A smile tugged at Page's mouth. "You're right. See? Everything aligned for us."

"So, we're going to the pier where we have an illustrious history of finding trouble." Betsy took a deep breath and jumped over a tidal pool.

"The pier is a magnet for mayhem, but maybe tonight we'll only need to do a bit of snooping. By the way, gelatos are my treat." Page tugged Betsy's arm to miss a jellyfish washed ashore.

"Gelato is my weakness. I think I'm feeling it for pistachio. This inkling had better not keep me from a confection." Betsy's flip-flops made a squishing sound.

Page glanced down. "Don't tell me you managed to get another pair of shoes wet."

"Forget them. They'll dry out." Betsy paused. "I've

changed my mind. I'm ordering banana gelato after we deal with this inkling."

"And a nudge," said Page.

"A nudge, too? That means we'd better walk faster, and you're treating me to a double gelato. It's good I didn't invite Andre inside for a root beer float as planned. Maybe I'm developing some Betsy-style inklings."

"Could be. You've been blooming with talents since we moved to Shell Isle," Page teased.

"Are you joshing me?" voiced a doubting Betsy.

Page aimed her flashlight at a sandcastle the tide hadn't yet claimed. "Nope. I'll even give you examples."

"I like how this sounds, although I'm wondering what I'm being buttered up for."

Page tapped Betsy's arm. "Stop and listen. You and Ina make a great baking team. You inspire her to take your recipe ideas, using our special jars of honey, and create delectables for Honey Bees. You oversaw the renovation of your bungalow, and look how charming it turned out."

"I agree. It's a darling place. Everyone who sees it says so. My neighbor is quite smitten with it. What other talents do I have? Don't stop." Betsy clipped her frizzing hair into a topknot. "Blasted humidity. Continue."

"You can grow anything, thus your blooming talents. We're almost there. I need—"

"I know. You need silence to receive direction. I'm hushing, but please let's not find a dead body this outing."

"We won't. The inkling came softly, as did the nudge to head to the pier. You'll have the gelato before Gumdrop's closes. Shh." Page cleared her thoughts as they approached the stairs to the pier. Entry was free on Sunday nights, encouraging the fishing folk's appearance.

Betsy opened the hinged gate for Page to proceed, but

said nothing.

Page read her cousin's anxious expression. "We're fine. Relax." The nudge came to walk to the end of the pier. "Come on. We're one step closer to solving this case and being beach and baking gals again."

"I hope you're right." Betsy's flip-flops answered as they walked. "Don't say I'm not stealthy. Next time we're out to reconnoiter, I'll consider going barefoot."

Page turned a bemused face toward her cousin. "Pay attention. Observe." As soon as the words slipped out of Page's mouth, she saw them. Her hand pulled Betsy over to the railing.

"What did I miss now? I always miss seeing what we're supposed to see. It's so annoying."

"Shh; look to your left and twenty yards." Page motioned with her head. "Do you see them? He's fishing and she's fiddling with her phone."

"Is that James and Mara from Three Fables?" Betsy's eyes squinted. "It *is* them. Are they who we're here to snoop?"

"Seems so. Let's try to get closer." Page led them to stand between a light pole and a fish-cleaning sink.

Betsy leaned in and whispered, "You chose the stinky sink station for us to slink beside? Next time, I'm picking our eavesdropping place." Betsy's hand covered her nose. "Phew. You're buying me a triple gelato."

Page bit her tongue to keep from laughing. "Listen. They're talking."

"Would you reel in the line? You're such a dud, James. The only thing you've caught tonight was someone else's line." Mara peered over the side. The floodlights showed several large fish swimming close to the surface.

Betsy chuckled. "Sorry," she mouthed to Page.

"Cut me some slack. I'm learning how to cast." James

tugged on his line. "I think something's nibbling."

"Has it slipped your fish brain that Grandfather expects our final report in an hour?" Mara's tone sounded anxious.

"Chill. There's no rush. Stand back. I'm going to cast this one way out." James released the line.

Mara laughed. "You're such a bozo. You hooked your jeans. Give me that rod. I'll do it for you."

"Fine. Let's see what you've got." James crossed his arms and stepped back.

Betsy leaned close to Page's ear. "Let's hear it for the women. Mara sent that shrimp flying out in the water."

Amusement glinted in Page's eyes. "Quiet. We have to listen."

"Okay, now you'll catch something. And then we can leave." Mara handed him the rod.

James placed it in one of the pier's mounted holders. "Why don't you figure out a way to get Alice's accounting book? And figure out how we can take some photos of the pages? I guarantee they'll show how bad things are at the inn. It'll drive our point."

"Did you discover where she keeps it? That was your job," replied Mara.

"I think she stashes it in the back of the office's metal filing cabinet." James turned his reel handle a few clicks. "At least she's old school and doesn't keep it on her computer."

"We need to try for tonight after she goes to her bedroom," suggested Mara.

"She locks the office when she's done for the day, usually by ten at night. Unless you've learned to pick locks, we have to do it before then."

"Thanks for telling me this when we're down to the wire in time." Mara's tone carried anger.

James cranked his rod and held up his baitless hook.

"Lost the shrimp. Alright, let's do this. Maybe the office is open."

"You'd better hope so. Grandfather's wrath has a long reach," said Mara.

Page and Betsy twisted to face the ocean as Mara and James passed, not wanting to risk being recognized.

"Who *are* these two? Why so much interest and snooping into poor Alice's financial woes? Something smells fishy." Betsy waved her arm in their direction.

"You're standing next to a fish cleaning sink." Page teased and motioned for Betsy to walk.

"Allow me a clever moment. Still, why the interest in Alice's debt load?" asked Betsy.

"Moreover, who is the grandfather? I'd like to know."

Betsy's face lit up. "Hey. Maybe the grandfather wants to buy Three Fables and has his grandkids as plants to assess the situation."

"That's a plausible explanation." Page frowned, considering the idea. "We'd better hurry to Gumdrop's if you want a triple-banana gelato. The open sign is still lit, but not for much longer."

"I'm on the move. Stand back. Fish out your money," said Betsy over her shoulder.

"Still working with the fish word, huh?" Page laughed and followed her cousin.

The sleuths sat on a nearby bench and spooned their confections into their mouths. Betsy spoke first. "So, are you going to call Alice and alert her about Mara and James being up to something?"

Page gazed at the moon hanging over the ocean. "I've been considering it and don't think I will. Alice isn't in danger from James and Mara, just her financial doings. Tomorrow morning, we're visiting Three Fables. The inklings will guide us and not our thinking on this one. Agreed?"

"Agreed." Betsy took another bite. "What are we doing with Althea and Julian? I'm hesitant about introducing myself to them despite bestowing them the terrific name of Influencers. I like my hairstyle, and they've got a thing for moving hair around." Betsy ran her fingers through her damp mop before clipping it back.

Page's laughter drew the attention of passersby. "I don't think they'll mess with your mop."

"Probably not." Betsy grew thoughtful. "Seriously, do you have any plans for them?"

"I'm working on that one." Page tossed her empty gelato cup. "In the meantime, let's head back to Hibiscus. I feel like we're working on two cases with way too many unanswered questions." Her intuition conduit needed a fast refresh. Page hoped some quiet reflection before bed would do the trick.

CHAPTER 23

"It's late. I wonder where Steve has gone?" Page pointed to the dark bungalow as she and Betsy walked Hibiscus's ramp over the sea oats. The stroll back had been uneventful.

Betsy shrugged. "Probably got a call from the station. Maybe Althea and Julian rattled chains or something that spooked the authors." Betsy held the porch screen door for Page to pass.

"You're developing quite an attachment to the couple." Page headed toward the kitchen.

"It's not every day I hear about ghosts hanging out at an inn nearby." Betsy glanced outside the window. "Speaking of Detective Dreamboat, I see his vehicle pulling in. Yep, that's him dressed in his stealthy black duds. Where are you going?"

Page opened the front door. "I'll be right back."

"Sure, you will," replied Betsy. "No, hanky."

"Hey, Detective. Hold up!" Page hurried to Steve's side.

"Hey, yourself, Sherlocka. What brings you my way this late?" Steve released the gate and whistled Barnacle out of his doghouse.

"Bets and I just got back from having gelato at the pier. Did you go off and score some info for me?" Page bent down to rub Barnacle's ears before he took off toward the front door.

Steve's eyes studied Page briefly before his dimples gave her a wink. "Depends. Care to barter?"

"Sure. I'm up for a barter. To show you my amenable

side, I'll even go first."

"Now, I'm worried you're setting me up." Steve motioned for them to move to the porch chairs. He opened the door for Barnacle. "Go in, buddy. Your chow bowl is full."

Page watched the spaniel give a thank-you lick to Steve's hand before bounding inside. "Maybe I need a dog for company. I've been considering getting one for ages."

"Dogs are the best. Barn would feel jealous if you gave his place at your porch dining table to another canine. He's already claimed your cottage as his other home," reminded Steve. "Page, I'm wiped and want to find my bed. What's your half of the barter?"

"Yeah, okay. I got an inkling to head to the pier."

"The place where you attract trouble." Steve rolled his eyes heavenward. "Go on."

"We saw James and Mara. He was attempting to master fishing. There's something fishy going on with them. Those are Betsy's clever words that I'm borrowing."

"Are they connected to Evelyn's death?" Steve leaned forward.

"No, nothing like that," replied Page.

"Then why should I care about—"

"Because we care about Alice, and they want to get into her office and take photos of her accounting ledger. And here's the real puzzling piece: these two are taking direction from their grandfather. What's up with that?" Page rubbed her arms together, feeling the evening chill.

"Hang on." Steve stepped inside and returned with a throw from his sofa. "Wrap up."

"Thanks." Page sniffed. "Barnacle has claimed this."

"Yeah, I thought I detected the scent of a rawhide chew. Sorry." Steve's teeth glinted in a brief smile. "Let's get back to James and Mara. What do you think needs to happen next? Have me question them if they do something wrong?"

Page deliberated on how best to handle the situation. Her intuition brought the answer. "This time, I'd like your blessing. Let me delve into why they're compelled to work at Three Fables."

"You are asking a detective to bless your snooping? You're off your rocker, Sherlocka. Go home."

Page tilted her head and met his eyes. "I simply wanted to make you aware of this situation. Keep your blessing. Your turn. What do you have for me?"

"Because I'm too tired to spar, I'll take my turn." Steve lifted his chin. "The detective inspector from London called me. Some background checks came in, and he wanted to pass the info to me."

"Super. We need something to shine the light on who took Evelyn's life. Your expression tells me you've scored something juicy." Page sat up straighter, anticipating getting closer to discovering the truth.

"First, I agreed to send Leo back to their chief. They've been tracking this guy and an auction house involved in black market dealings. Leo's passion for nicking first editions has filled his coffers with a few quid. The chief inspector is ready to charge him." Steve glanced at his watch. "Andre is escorting Leo to the airport as we speak. They'll have one of their detectives waiting at the airport with his party invitation."

"Wow! Leo's getting arrested a second time. That's some news." Page wrinkled her nose and laid the blanket aside. "Hold on here. What if Leo did the deed to Evelyn?"

"I don't think he did. But if it turns out to be so, we'll bring him back and let the FBI deal with the legal aspect."

Page rubbed her hands together to get warm. "I understand. What else do you have for me?"

"How about this? I confirmed Ruby has two DUIs

and is facing thirty days in the slammer and a stint in rehab. Fiona's arrest record is clean except for a bundle of unpaid parking tickets. The police in London continue to earn my respect."

Page stared off. "I can tell you hold them in high regard. Here's what we know. Evelyn had the goods on Ruby and was threatening to tell. I still think our Ruby was tapped out of money and options and needed to solve her Evelyn problem pronto. I bet Ruby's publishing contract would get canceled if she gets sentenced to time. And finding another publisher to take her as a client is unlikely with that dark cloud following her. She'd have to find a job, and Ruby doesn't strike me as the type to work for anyone. Remember, Fiona just learned of one DUI. Anyway, that was a powerful motive to do away with her Evelyn problem."

Steve checked his cell phone and laid it on the nearby metal table. "Correct."

Page tapped her chin, pondering Fiona. "And the leader of the pack, Fiona, had disloyal Evelyn jumping ship to sign with a different publisher. Her job was kaput if she couldn't corral Evelyn back and keep the others in line. We can't forget that desperation often results in bad decisions and actions. In this case, potentially deadly ones." Page nodded once. "Fiona remains on my suspect board despite her background check."

"They all remain on my list until we figure out who interacted with Evelyn last. She certainly racked up enough haters. Heck, even I don't like her based on how she portrayed herself to others." Steve's face showed fatigue. "In my line of business, there are days when people's baser behaviors make me want to—"

"Escape to your deserted island and live like a beach bum?" finished Page, adding a hand squeeze for sympathy.

"Live like a beach surfer, actually." Steve scooted to

the edge of his seat.

Page lifted her hand. "Wait. What about Chester and Grace?"

"No police record for either, but the full background check hasn't returned yet. Three of the five isn't bad for a late Sunday update, Sherlocka." Steve rose. The lines around his eyes showed he was spent. "Let's get to our respective beds unless you'd like to—"

Page hopped up. "Nope. My bed suits me fine, but I have a goodnight peck for you." Page moved closer. Looping her arms around his neck, she stood on tiptoe.

"I see your monkey business!" Betsy hollered from Hibiscus's front door. "I figured as much. I declare you two are worse than teenagers."

"Betsy, your timing is consistently lousy," answered Steve.

Page pulled back and sighed. "Goodnight, Detective."

CHAPTER 24

Shell Isle delivered another glorious sunny day. The cloudless sky showed off a shade of blue that tried to match the ocean. Joggers and walkers claimed the beach and were first to see what treasures the low tide had left for discovery. Page found fascination in what people chose to take from the beach. A pelican feather, a shark's tooth, and a piece of elusive sea glass made their shopping list. What intrigued her most was the shell selection process and the time invested in sifting through the many strewn along the shoreline. What made one acceptable and another rejected? For each person, the quest was different, much like one's life path.

Page abandoned her bedroom window's view. Her nose informed her that Betsy had breakfast waiting. She went to the kitchen, intending to find something positive to say about her cousin's effort.

"Here you are, just in time for my Sassy Sausage Surprise. Betsy set two plates next to juice glasses containing a worrisome dark liquid.

Grabbing spare napkins, Page sat on the island's stool and gazed at her plate. "What makes this sassy?"

"Ah, the sassy comes from another secret dried pepper I discovered when I dated, very briefly, this chef from Baja. He taught me how to make homemade breakfast sausage, which you'll enjoy atop yellow grits and grilled fresh pineapple. Of course, I added chopped jalapeños for the green color. It's what I call a fiesta—"

"For the taste buds." Page finished the sentence,

ignoring the reference to dating a Baja chef. She sent her fork toward the grits and away from the jalapeño garnish. She took a bite and glanced at Betsy, who waited for her compliments. "Um, the grits are sweet. Very nice, Bets."

"Taste the sassy already." Betsy came around to sit on the empty stool. She used a soup spoon to scoop a generous amount into her mouth. She chewed and watched Page take a bite. "Well? Enough sass? If not, I can get my bottle of pepper flakes."

Page gulped her glass of water, trying to find her voice. "Nope," she answered hoarsely. "I'm plenty sassed."

"Good. Eat up. I want to stop by The Perk and grab a frozen Irish coffee. It's this week's special, and according to Mickey, tastes amazing. Before you ask, he told me last night at the bowling lanes."

"Gotcha." Taking advantage of Betsy's wish to leave soon, Page pretended to take bites as she hurried to the sink and the blessed disposer. "Just finishing up here, and we can go." Page put her plate on the dish rack. She'd sipped the dark liquid that made her think of octopus ink flavored with something syrupy sweet. Page couldn't find a single compliment to offer Betsy for the vile-tasting drink. She apologized to her sink drain and washed the glass.

Betsy gobbled her remaining bites before meeting Page at the front door. "Did I tell you The Perk's Irish coffee is topped with green whipped cream and minty drizzle? I'm ordering the grandest size."

"You did not. I might want to try this Irish coffee," replied Page.

***

Entering The Perk, Page inhaled the enticing aroma of coffee filling the air. She followed a fast-stepping Betsy to the order counter.

"What size Irish do you want?" asked Betsy, pulling out her coffee stamp card. "It's my treat today. I get a free one."

"A small is fine." Page waved to Mickey delivering an order to four women playing cards. "I'll go claim us seats." A gentle sensation touched her solar plexus — a new inkling.

Betsy nodded and turned to the barista.

Two men wearing suits vacated her and Betsy's favorite club chairs. Page offered a nod as they passed. She reflected on how the coffee house had played an essential role in their past three cases. Whether it was Mickey bringing gossip to their table or someone who happened to be sitting close by, Page's inklings had a history of visiting her at The Perk.

Betsy came over and settled in the empty chair. "Hopefully, our order won't take long." She glanced at her phone. "We've got twenty minutes before we need to unlock Honey Bees. Ina and I have a new recipe for popovers we're trying this morning. I can't arrive tardy."

"We'll make it. I see Mickey bringing our drinks now." Page smiled at his approach.

"Here you go, ladies. Betsy, you took my advice and ordered the Irish cream this morning. It's a winner." Mickey handed off two straws.

"Of course I took your recommendation. You never lead us wrong in coffee or selling us enchanting honey. Speaking of honey, anything special from the bees?" asked Betsy.

"As a matter of fact, yes. I'll stop by with samples in a couple of days."

"Sounds good." Page reached for napkins. "I don't know how you find these uncommon honey varieties, but I'm grateful you share with Honey Bees."

"Let's say I'm tapped for the service. It's my honor."

Mickey turned to Betsy. "What do you think?"

Betsy took her first sip. "This is yummy. If you'd put an apron on, I'd marry you."

Mickey chuckled. "Bets, I'll give that offer some thought, but I don't think Andre would appreciate me making a move on you." He took a step to deliver his next order and halted. "Sit tight. I'm coming back with some gossip about two of those author types. I know you're involved in solving the tragedy at Three Fables."

Betsy nodded. "I like that guy. He's a true friend to us and our shop. And when we have a case, our Mickey is a reliable source about Shell Isle doings." Betsy moved her straw around her cup.

Page's expression grew thoughtful.

"You're thinking about Mickey's chin wag, and you got another inkling. Didn't you?" Betsy smacked the table. "I knew it. Coming here when we've landed a case never works out for me to enjoy a stress-free coffee."

"I'm sorry, Bets. I can't control when I get intuits."

"I know, but this coffee tasted scrumptious, and now not so much." Betsy lifted a gob of whipped cream toward her mouth and failed to connect. Her fingers tried to scoop up the green cream from her pale-yellow muumuu. "See this?"

An amused Page passed a napkin. "Here, you're making it worse."

"I would wear a solid color today. The front of my pretty muumuu looks like a green Rorschach inkblot test. Forget whatever Mickey wants to crow about. Let's go. Maybe the smear will come out if I can get to Honey Bees before it sets."

Page handed her cousin a second napkin. "Doubtful, Bets. You're dealing with green food color. Besides, we can't leave until we hear what Mickey has for us."

"Where's my Irish luck when I need it?" Betsy sighed.

"I'm back." Mickey grabbed a folding chair from a nearby card table and straddled it. He glanced at Betsy's ministrations to her dress and shook his head. "Listen up. Last evening, I was busy cleaning the tables and chairs before closing. I overheard two of those author people staying at Three Fables chatting. I recognized them because they've been coming here for pots of tea."

"Talk faster, Mickey. We have to get to Honey Bees." Betsy motioned with her hands for him to speed up.

"I'm hurrying. Anyway, the gist of their conversation was that I think the one called Chester was hitting up Faith to borrow money."

"Hold on. Who's Faith?" asked Betsy.

Page smiled a little. "I think he means Grace."

"Right, Grace." Mickey nodded. "So, Grace tells him she lives paycheck to paycheck, and she's out of paychecks now that her author employer is gone. She finishes by saying all she has is five hundred pounds put away to carry her until she finds another job."

"Poor woman," said Betsy.

"Yes." Mickey waved to a customer leaving. "This Chester tells Grace he'll hire her as a teaching assistant if she does an online transfer of that five hundred to his account pronto. He tells her he's typing a text to the human resource department and adding Grace to his staff. And the job is hers if she moves the money."

"Did she go for it?" asked Page.

"It sounded like it. Chester agreed to pay her back in three months with interest. You wouldn't catch me giving my last nickel to some guy wearing an orange, polka-dot bow tie." A glimmer of laughter came into Mickey's eyes.

Betsy tapped his arm. "Do you know why Chester

needed the money so badly?"

Mickey bonked his forehead. "Almost forgot that part. He'd overspent bigly on some crazy-named collectibles. It sounded like Netzers. Who knows."

"Ah, I bet he's collecting Netsuke." Page took a sip of her coffee.

"Artists sure love to collect. What in the world is a Netsuke?" asked Betsy.

Page pulled up a picture of them with her phone and held it up. "These are Japanese miniature sculptures dating back to the seventeenth century. As I recall, they were first used as some kind of button fasteners."

"Wow, they look tiny. Is there anything you don't know?" responded Betsy.

"Yeah, who killed Evelyn Potts." Page tucked her phone away and turned to Mickey. "Anything else?"

Mickey stood and returned the chair to a nearby table. "Only that Chester said he has two mean blokes chasing him for the money he owes. Grace seemed sympathetic enough and kept asking him about the job's details. He dismissed her, saying he'd tell her more once they returned to England. I hope that helps."

Page reached out a hand. "It does, Mickey. Thanks a bunch. Stop by Honey Bees after your shift, and we'll send you home with a dozen of your favorite toffee cookies." Page gathered her handbag and placed her empty cup on Mickey's tray.

Betsy followed suit. "And I'm making—"

"The cookies will do me just fine. Don't need another thing," answered a wizened Mickey, who'd sampled Betsy's wares more than once. He winked at Page and headed back to the kitchen area.

"We got a bonus of info and a free coffee which I

managed to tattoo on my dress." Betsy stared at the front of her muumuu. "What a way to start Monday. I'm unsightly." She headed for the door holding her straw bag in front of her chest.

Page followed her cousin, trying not to laugh. "Yes, we did get rewarded. And before this author bunch flies out, we must crack this case." Page acknowledged that the inkling had highlighted two more people's desperation for money. The whole bunch lacked jingle.

CHAPTER 25

Standing on the sidewalk, Page glanced at her watch. "We've got three minutes to get to the shop."

"And I'm going to look like a slob all day." Betsy made another swipe at the front of her shift.

Page took in her cousin's pouting face. "Hey, I've got your solution. Wear your flowered apron. It covers the front of you nicely."

"My apron. That could work." Betsy paused, considering. "It'll make the hot flashes worse, but that's the price I must pay." She nodded to the mayor and his wife as they strolled past.

Page opened the car door. "I almost forgot. You're going with me to Three Fables once you and Ina get the popovers and muffins baked."

"I can't wear my apron there," Betsy groaned and buckled her seatbelt. "Oh my gosh. I'm flashing, and it's a doozy. Turn all the AC vents on me."

Page cranked up the fan speed and adjusted the vents. "I'm giving you the max."

"This max is pathetic. I could blow more air out my mouth." Betsy plastered her flushed face in front of the vent. "I hate Mondays, and they hate me back." She gazed at the muumuu's stain, now the size of a lemon. "This thing has spread. Hurry and get me to the shop."

***

Betsy came from the kitchen carrying two boxes of popovers for Alice and her guests. "I'm ready. These finicky pops are sure to impress those authors. Ina declared the new recipe a dandy."

Page passed a waiting customer the sack of doughnuts and turned to Betsy. "Hey, where is your green tattoo?"

"Ina rescued me with a mix of club soda and something else. I'm telling you, that woman is a Honey Bees treasure."

"I heard that. I want a raise for going beyond the call of baking." Ina arranged a plate of honey oatmeal cookies and covered them with a glass dome.

"You got a raise last week, Ina Funk," answered Betsy good-naturedly.

"I need one every week. I've been on a losing streak at Mahjong." Ina gave a quick mock downtrodden look. "Before you skedaddle, Page, taste this cookie. I used Mickey's Buckwheat honey."

Page broke off a piece and chewed. "Gracious, but this cookie tastes amazing. Earthy but in a good way. I'm taking a half dozen home." Page took another bite. "Here, Bets. Try."

Betsy shook her head. "I already ate four. Ina smacked my hand, so I can't indulge on more."

"That's right, Ms. Ross. You'll end up looking like a *knadle* moving around in a muumuu if you don't watch out." Ina hugged Betsy. "You know I love you, Mermaid sister."

"Yeah, and I love you back, but whatever that Yiddish word means, I don't love. And don't think I won't look it up." Betsy waved her finger at Ina.

"You both won't do." Page finished her cookie.

"Is that the oven buzzer?" asked Betsy.

Ina shuffled toward the kitchen. "I'm on it. You two take off. Daisy finished frosting the blond brownies. I'll send her out to take care of the customers. Having her working with us is a blessing."

"I agree. Thanks. We won't be gone long." Page tugged on Betsy's sleeve. "Let's go attempt to meet two ghosts." Page waved at a confused Ina.

"Oy vey, what sane person chooses to meet ghosts?" Ina mumbled, continuing to the kitchen.

***

Page drove for a couple of minutes before broaching a subject they needed to discuss. "Bets? Are you up for this unknown we may experience?"

"Hmm?" Betsy answered absently, fiddling with her phone.

Page tried again. "Listen to me a sec. We've never been around anything paranormal before. These are uncharted waters for us." Page turned into the Three Fables lot and parked.

Betsy tapped Page's shoulder. "I looked up the history of ghosts. Listen to this. Did you know ancient Egyptians believed in ghosts, and they're referenced in the Bible?"

"The Bible talks about ghosts? No. Show me where you read that."

Betsy handed Page the phone and pointed. "Right there. It says ghosts are referenced in Deuteronomy and Samuel."

"I see it." Page felt her body react with a strange tingling. It didn't feel like an inkling but more like an external energy. She glanced around but saw nothing out of the ordinary. Rake was pulling weeds in the front planter. Everything appeared normal.

Betsy frowned. "Why are you acting all quiet and watchful? Don't tell me—"

"No inklings or nudges. Just taking in our surroundings before we get out."

"Does everything look okay? You aren't seeing apparitions or anything coming for us." Betsy's voice held a quiver.

"Stop being silly. No one is coming for you except maybe an ex-boyfriend. Hop out. Those popovers need to get to Alice before they collapse." Page tucked her cell and keys in her handbag.

Betsy came alongside Page. "Hold up. Suddenly, I feel strange. Kind of electrified. Do you?"

Page gulped. "I did a sec ago. It's probably nothing."

"Except this nothing happened to both of us." Betsy's hand swatted the air.

"What are you doing? Trying to catch a butterfly?" Page grabbed the other box of popovers before Betsy could send them skyward.

"I'm clearing my energy field." Betsy leaned over and repeated the same exercise around Page's head.

"Would you stop it?" Page pushed Betsy's hand away. "Pay attention to me. We need to keep open minds when we go inside. Our goal is to see if Althea and Julian want to help us. I don't pretend to understand any of the spirit world's doings, but I'm game to knock on their door since I'm flirting with believing."

Betsy's fingers touched her throat. "You're ahead of me on this whole spiritual business. I can grasp that Alice wants her inn to get past this unfortunate event. But chatting with Althea and Julian, I've changed my mind about talking to them." Betsy halted. "I'll wait in the SUV. I don't want to meet new people today."

Page laughed and reached back and grabbed Betsy's arm. "You thrive on meeting people. You're highly social. You even talked to a caterpillar yesterday."

"Because I could see him." Betsy stepped backward.

"Expand your horizons." Page looped her arm through Betsy's and pulled her along. "Let's go see if we can make new unseen friends?"

Alice greeted both women. "I hoped you'd arrive before my guests appeared for breakfast."

"We brought fresh popovers." Betsy passed the boxes to Alice.

"Delightful." Alice peeked inside the lid. "Come to the kitchen."

"I didn't see James at the reception desk." Page wondered if the brother and sister had succeeded in snooping into Alice's ledger the night before.

"Unfortunately, James and Mara are upstairs. Both are sick from eating bad oysters. They came in the door last night and rushed to their rooms. I've been supplying them with ginger ale and crackers." Alice shook her head in sympathy. "I expect they'll feel able to work by the afternoon. At least, I hope so." Alice reached for a basket and carefully placed the popovers on the green-checked cloth napkin lining it.

"So, it's been you alone handling things?" asked Page.

"That's what she just said." Betsy rolled her eyes. "I hear voices. Here, Alice, let me help with the tea."

"That must be the group waiting for breakfast on the veranda. I told everyone last night to expect something like baked goods due to Mara and James being ill." Alice placed the butter crock and different jams on the serving tray next to a bowl of fresh fruit.

"Shall I carry the teapot?" offered Betsy.

"Please. And Page, would you mind arranging the slices of cranberry bread on the milk glass serving dish and bringing it?"

"Certainly." Page washed her hands and began the task after she treated herself to a tiny slice. "Yum. I need this recipe from Alice."

"I can write it down for you if you like?" said a voice from behind.

Page jumped and turned to see Mara standing in the doorway. "Hello, Mara. Alice told us that you and James weren't feeling well."

"I think I can speak for both of us. Raw oysters will never touch our mouths again. I felt well enough to slip downstairs to get more soda. James said his stomach feels like a bull keeps charging him." Mara's face looked pale.

"It sounds like you're faring better than James."

"That's because he ate more oysters." Mara filled the glasses with ice and poured the soda. She moved toward the doorway and pivoted. "Tell Alice I hope to be well enough to clean the rooms in a few hours."

Page placed the last slice on the platter. "I'll let her know. Feel better." Page rinsed the loaf pan. "At least I know they haven't been snooping yet," she whispered to herself.

Taking the platter to the group, Page expected to see Alice and Betsy hovering around, serving the guests. They were curiously absent. Putting on her friendly smile, Page offered the group a serving of banana bread. She eavesdropped on their chatter, noting it seemed pleasant enough. "Excuse me. I'm going to leave the platter on this side table. Everyone, please enjoy." Page didn't expect an answer from them, nor did she get one.

Holding her hand against her forehead to shade her eyes, Page gazed toward the gardens. She saw no sign of the wayward Betsy or Alice.

Rake appeared, pushing his wheelbarrow full of weeds. "Top of the morning, Page. If you're looking for Alice and your friend, they're in the statue garden."

"Thanks, Rake." Page strolled toward the gate, admiring a new bed of pansies already showing their love by blooming. The marble fountain's trickling sound was inviting, but something else had trumped the fountain—a nudge.

CHAPTER 26

"Hallooo. We're over here." Betsy turned into a windmill, waving her arms.

Page waved back and moved in their direction. She felt a gentle push to veer to the right toward the tall hedge which wrapped the statue garden in privacy.

"Where are you going?" shouted Betsy.

"I'll come there in a sec." Page strolled the outside perimeter. *Why am I here? I don't see anything or anyone. Just grass and this hedge.* She stopped and stroked the shrubbery leaves, waiting for a sign. Nothing came. "Okay, I'm done." As Page circled back, a gust of wind blew a square of material from the hedge onto her foot. Stooping down, she saw the blood stains on a handkerchief.

Page's mind scrambled to her next logical move. Hoping Betsy and Alice were engrossed in chatting, she trotted toward the inn's kitchen. Within a minute, she found a plastic bag and rushed back to secure the evidence that chose today to reveal itself—the how and why of it she'd ponder later.

Using a stick, Page lifted the ivory-colored handkerchief to examine it. The initials, monogrammed by a delicate hand, identified its owner. She zipped the bag closed. Calling Steve could wait until she returned to Honey Bees. As for telling Alice about the discovery, Page decided to keep silent. The poor woman had enough to deal with at the inn.

"Page? Are you out there?" hollered Betsy. "We need you to join us inside the gate."

Tucking the bag into her tote, Page entered the garden. "Sorry. I had to run back to the kitchen." She held up her cell phone. "You have so many beautiful flowers blooming. I wanted some pictures." Page snapped photos of two roses and hoped perceptive Betsy didn't question her excuse for the delay.

"Yes, the flowers are putting on quite a show. Rake deserves all the credit." Alice lifted one of the yellow roses and sniffed.

"Enough posey talk. Ask us what you missed?" Betsy pointed to the statue of Althea.

"Okay, what did I miss?" Page moved closer to the figure accompanied by the two women.

Betsy pointed at the base. "What do you see that's different?"

Page bent down. Her lips formed an oval surprise. "The crack in Althea's foundation base is gone. Where's the crack?" Her fingers stroked the base, which now matched Julian's. "Alice?"

The innkeeper shrugged. "I've no idea. It's all too much for me to process. I thought I'd move here, buy this quaint historic inn, and live happily ever after. Instead, I'm living in this curious place and sharing it with who I now believe are Althea and Julian."

"Who, I might add, help you run Three Fables and look after you," volunteered Betsy. "I'm kind of digging them and their ways again now that I see this fix. And I think Althea and Julian like you. You're golden. If they didn't, they'd employ things like the wind to make a point."

Page paused and considered the wind connection to the ivory handkerchief's appearance. Did the unseen residents of Three Fables deliver the evidence for her to find? She hadn't yet asked for their help. "Betsy, do you believe Althea and

Julian fixed the statue and are responsible for blowing things around?"

"Yes, that's what I'm saying. Plus, how else can you explain Ruby's wig and Chester's toupee movement?" posed Betsy. "I'm embracing this explanation."

Alice released a loud sigh and touched her throat to self-soothe. "I'd rather think one of the guests was doing a bit of tomfoolery, though I can't explain how. I vacillate and can't keep straight what current belief I'm clasping in desperation."

Page motioned Alice to the bench. "Treat yourself to a few cleansing breaths before I ask the next question."

Alice sat down. "I'm feeling more myself now. Please ask."

Betsy joined Alice and gave her hand a squeeze of assurance.

"Detective Tanner wants me to ask you something that will sound farfetched. Can Julian and Althea help us discover what happened to Evelyn?" Page watched the changing expressions play across Evelyn's face as the woman processed a question that belonged at a séance.

"You mean we ask them to show us something clue-like?" Alice's voice quivered.

Betsy nodded. "Yes, we simply say, 'Althea and Julian, if you're really and truly moving about here, we'd appreciate it if you could help us solve this case.'" Betsy looked upward. "Yeah, that sounded good to me. What do you think, Page?"

Page kept her voice steady. "That was straightforward. Alice, tell me something. Have you experienced anything since living at Three Fables that would make you think your unseen residents respond to you?"

"I keep trying to ignore these things or dismiss them quickly to my guests. I don't wish to talk to spirits, even the kindly ones who likely live with me here. No. I don't have proof they respond to me." Alice rose.

"That's okay. Please don't give my questions another thought." Page knew Alice was emotionally spent, but one more matter needed airing. She felt obligated to warn Alice about Mara and James' snooping desires. She wondered how best to broach the subject.

Betsy stood and hugged Alice. "This nasty business will work itself out soon. You'll see."

"I do hope you're right, Betsy. At least I have Chatty around. She has such a calming influence on me."

Page nodded in agreement. "Chatty's personality fits at Three Fables."

"I hope to look as good as Chatty when I get her age," added Betsy.

Alice touched a white rose. "Such delicate beauty. If you'll excuse me, I need to check on the guests. They're due to leave on a last sightseeing excursion."

"Good. The group will be out of your hair for a while," said Betsy.

"We'll walk back to the inn with you and be on our way." Page waited until they reached the now-empty veranda before speaking. "Alice, I must share one more thing with you."

Alice halted. "Dear, oh dear, what is it now?"

"It concerns your two new employees. I overheard Mara and James at the pier last evening saying they wanted to look at your accounting book. I have no idea why, but I felt you needed to know." Page stood, waiting for Alice to respond.

"Gracious, why would they have any interest in my financial affairs? I can't imagine they wish to cause any harm. They're a nice addition to the inn, and both are willing to do extra whenever I ask."

"That's good to hear," responded Betsy. "Isn't it, Page?"

Page turned back to Alice. "I'm relieved to know they've been kind and helpful."

"And I do like them so much." Alice grew quiet. "Nothing makes sense anymore. My mind is a jumble. What do you both suggest I do?" Her eyes darted from Page to Betsy.

Page jumped in to reply before Betsy offered some Betsyism. "I suggest two simple things. First, put all of your financial papers and accounting ledgers in a secure place. And second, stay aware of Mara and James's activities at the inn."

"She means to keep an eye on them. Nothing more. I'm sure there's a logical explanation for their interest. Alice doesn't need to fret. Right, Page?" Betsy's tone turned to cajole.

"Right. No fretting over any of these matters we discussed." Page motioned to Betsy for them to go. "Wait. It slipped my mind. Mara said to tell you she hopes to clean the rooms in a few hours."

Alice paused with tears in her eyes. "Please figure out who did this horrible act to Ms. Potts. In the meantime, I take solace in the group's plan to leave tomorrow." The innkeeper hurried inside.

Betsy pulled the purple-floral fan from her straw handbag and put it to work. "At least the flash waited until we finished here. For pity's sake, don't ask Althea and Julian for help now. Tanner's the detective. He can have a visit with them."

A laugh escaped Page. "I may suggest that very thing to him."

"Good. Can we please, and thank you, go back to Honey Bees so I can pretend things are hunky dory in my small world?" Betsy headed in the direction of the parking lot.

"We can and will, Bets." Page thought about the blood-stained handkerchief and its telling initials as she followed Betsy. Whether the breeze that delivered the evidence came from Althea and Julian's assistance or nature's breath didn't matter. What mattered was the answer to who took Evelyn's life could be tucked inside her handbag.

CHAPTER 27

Page and Betsy met an enthusiastic greeting from Daisy as they entered Honey Bees.

"I'm so glad to see your faces. I've been a busy bee buzzing around, selling potions and scones like there's no tomorrow. Ina's in the kitchen whipping up another batch of honey-date ones." Daisy hesitated. "What's with all the scone love today?"

Betsy passed the young woman heading for the kitchen. "Me thinks it's the new honey we purchased from Mickey." Betsy pointed to a jar of honey behind the counter. "That's the one. We may have another enchanted honey here."

"Well, whatever it is, Mrs. Droodle made three return trips for more scones. Her husband told me this was her last visit for the week." Daisy's lips turned into a smile. "I think we'll see her tomorrow for more scones, but without him."

Page chuckled. "Sounds like we've got a winning recipe. Listen, Daisy. I need to make a quick call. I'll come back and take over so you can have a break."

"Thanks, Page. It's such fun working at Honey Bees. I've got an idea for our summer season inventory. I want to share it later." Daisy picked up the tongs and arranged the remaining cookies on a tray.

"Excellent. I look forward to chatting as soon as things calm down." Page moved toward the storage room for privacy with her cell phone in hand. She liked Detective Koch's daughter and valued her devotion to Honey Bees. As Page walked past the kitchen, she motioned for Betsy to follow her.

"What now?" Betsy came into the hall. "We've only been here five minutes tops. I've got an idle mixer waiting on a recipe I created for honey cornbread."

Page whispered, "I've got something to show you before I call Steve. Come back here with me." Opening the storage room door, Page waited for Betsy to enter. She pulled the plastic bag from her tote and waved it. "I got a nudge in the garden. And take a look at what blew out of the thick hedge."

"Did this come from the statue garden's location?" asked Betsy eyeing the bag's contents.

"Yes, a strong breeze appeared, and viola, it landed by my feet."

"That's weird. Is that blood?" Betsy stepped back.

"It's not beet juice." Page glanced at the bag and wrinkled her face. "I was meant to find this handkerchief. I never got a chance to ask for Julian and Althea's help earlier, but I suspect they're behind this."

"Yeah, okay." Betsy's eyes remained fixed on the handkerchief.

"And don't forget we know of Althea and Julian's affection for making things blow around. I believe that's what happened. The cloth was probably hidden in the hedge by its owner. The same person who harmed Evelyn."

Betsy nodded. "I understand where your head is now." Betsy took a gulp of air. "Althea and Julian are assisting us. We needed this evidence since we've heard zippo on Evelyn's cell phone and the button DNA."

"Exactly. We're seriously leaping into the unknown dimensions here, but it seems we're being assisted." Page laid the bag on top of a cardboard box.

"I'd say so, although I don't plan to go blabbing that we're working with ghosts. I mean Influencers." Betsy looked up. "Sorry."

Page appreciated the timing of Betsy's humor.

"Hey, I wonder who owns this hanky? It would get Detective Dreamboat's goat if we knew that."

"We know," answered Page.

"We do? How—"

Page flipped the bag over and pointed to the handkerchief. "Give a squint at those two initials."

"You're kidding me. Someone's goose is cooked and about to be served with a nice Yorkshire pudding. Call Dreamboat. We're celebrating. I'm making extra cornbread to take home for our dinner tonight. I've got a Mex Monday menu planned to go with it. Let's invite Dreamboat and Andre to our fiesta since we're so close to solving this one."

Page dialed Steve and ignored the dinner talk—one fire to put out at a time.

"Detective Tanner," he answered.

"I've got some evidence I discovered at Three Fables this morning. It's here at the shop waiting for you." Page returned the plastic bag to her handbag for safekeeping.

"What kind of evidence? I'm busy now."

"The kind of evidence that will have one of your suspects sitting in the interrogation room post haste. See you soon." A smile flickered across Page's face as she disconnected.

Betsy reappeared. "I called to check on Alice. I wanted to make sure she'd calmed after we swooped in."

"And how is she?" asked Page. "I hated to upset her, but the questions were timely."

"Alice said the group had left. Chatty was keeping her entertained with past travel adventures, so that's good news. I think we can breathe easier until those teatime troublemakers return."

"Chatty's presence is a breath of fresh air for all of us.

Steve is fortunate to have her in his life."

"Still, I feel sorry for Alice. She's alone, trying to create a life here at Shell and run a profitable inn. And what happens? Althea and Julian are making unexplained mischief, while two new hires want to snoop in her finances. It's all too much." Betsy flapped her arms again.

"Relax. We're about to discover what happened to Evelyn, and the guests will soon take their problems back home, except for one." Page moved past Betsy. "Go tend your mixing bowls while I tend our customers. I expect Detective Tanner to barrel through our door any minute."

"It won't be a pretty sight. Dreamboat will be chapped when he sees what evidence his guys missed. I'm staying in the kitchen."

"That's probably wise." Page gave a throaty laugh.

Page had dusted two display tables of honey bath potions when the bell announced Detective Steve Tanner, badge clipped on his belt and his pistol parked on his hip. The black polo shirt and jeans gave an informal vibe to complement Shell Isle's lifestyle. Still, his no-nonsense expression was directed right toward Page. She pulled her shoulders back and prepared for the onslaught. "You got here fast. Did you speed?"

Steve came alongside her and took the feather duster from her hands. "Don't start with the jokes, Sherlocka. Show me this evidence. I'm in the middle of dealing with some thugs who thought Shell Isle made a good target for breaking into vacant beach homes."

"Geez, we don't need them here." Page frowned. "Did you arrest them?"

"No, I thought I'd invite them for tea. Care to bring your trouble-making tea trolley to the station?" Sarcasm deepened Steve's voice. "Of course, we arrested them."

Page jerked the duster back from his hand and waved it like a wand in front of his chest, followed by a quick swoosh over his face. "Shazam. You're pleasant-natured again. Let's test it."

"What the h—?" Steve sneezed. "Give me that thing." He tried to grab it from Page's hand, but she slipped behind the counter.

"Stop right there, Detective. No one is allowed here except employees." Seeing Steve undeterred, she hurried out the other side heading toward the hallway with him on her tail.

Betsy and Ina poked their heads out of the kitchen as the two ran past.

"It's just Page and Steve gearing up for more hanky-panky and behaving like teenagers again. Let's get back to frosting the cupcakes."

Page entered the storage room. "Behave, Detective, or I won't hand over the goods."

Steve pulled her close. "This is me behaving the way I like." He kissed Page's forehead before moving down to her lips.

Her eyes closed as she gave in to the feelings and flutters only Steve Tanner could incite. Page returned his kiss before backing away. "Remind me to take that red feather duster home with me," she said breathlessly.

"I'll do better than that." Steve's grey eyes settled on Page's aqua ones. "I'm stopping at the home store and buying every duster in stock. All colors, and we'll leave a trail of them at Hibiscus, my bungalow, Carpe Diem, maybe even the Crab Shak." Steve delivered another kiss to Page's cheek.

"I'm a fan of your idea, but my duenna, Betsy, will have plenty to say." Page went to her purse and pulled out the plastic bag. "Okay, let's do police business. Here you go.

A nudge sent me to discover it. The handkerchief was stashed in the hedge bordering the statue garden. You might say a ghostly wind blew it at my feet."

Steve examined the bag. "You didn't touch it, right?"

"Come on. I know the rules. Turn it over, and you'll see its owner." Page pointed.

"How about that?" Steve looked up at Page. "Your tinklings and—"

Page's eyebrow shot up.

"Correction. Inklings. Your inklings and nudges keep amazing me. Great work, Sherlocka." Steve took several shots of the handkerchief with his phone. "I gotta dash to deliver someone a special invite to the station."

"Hang on. The invitation must wait until the group returns later from their afternoon sightseeing. And one more thing you might want to know. Althea's foundation is miraculously fixed." Page heard the shop's bell. "I need to go take care of the customers."

"Go." Steve walked behind Page. "I'll swing by the inn around three or four this afternoon. I will look at the statue and check on Chatty."

"That should work. And I expect my reward for this great find to be an invite to observe the interrogation." Page approached a young boy staring at the tray of cookies.

"Okay, but do you have to bring Betsy?" asked Steve, opening the door.

"We're a team." Page turned to the boy. "What's your favorite cookie?"

"Fine. I'll text you when. Thanks, Sherlocka." Steve and his dimples disappeared out the door.

After sending her young customer on his way, holding two free cookies and money still jingling in his pocket, Page leaned against the counter, contemplating the next move.

They had a suspect who could no longer deny involvement.
She'd wait for the interrogation to chart the course.

CHAPTER 28

Page and Daisy were discussing what inventory to order for the upcoming busy summer season when Page's cell phone dinged. Steve's message gave her a measly fifteen minutes to hustle to the station for the interrogation. "Daisy, I need to dash, but I like your ideas for the table display and new product line. Go ahead and order everything."

"Cool. Thanks, Page. I have my list, so I'll take care of this now. I can do it and mind the shop." Daisy gathered drawings and stuck them in her file.

Page twirled her hair into a topknot and clipped it. "Excuse me while I go speak to Betsy." Hurrying to the kitchen, Page found Betsy's face and hair wearing green batter. "What happened to you?"

"Her mixer's beaters weren't inserted properly," answered Ina, trying to wipe the sticky mess from Betsy's red hair.

"And I thought this day couldn't get worse after the green whipped cream on my favorite muumuu. I'm a complete mess." Betsy's fingers touched her hair. "The batter is making me frizz."

"Aw, Bets, I'm so sorry. Is there anything I can do? I came back to tell you we need to leave for the interrogation." Page handed Ina another damp paper towel to clean the mess on the counter.

"There's no way in Hades I'm going to that station and have Andre see me looking like—what do I look like, Ina?"

Ina rubbed her chin. Her dark curls framed a round

face. "A Martian? No. More like a witch who had a cauldron misfire."

"A witch?" Betsy's voice rose three octaves.

"A very nice witch," amended Ina and turned back to her tarts.

Page's hand covered her grin. "Okay, I get the picture. I'll go alone and meet you at Hibiscus. You close up the shop."

"That's a better plan. I can shower and then prepare our Monday Mex Fiesta." Betsy wiped another glob from her neck. "You did remember to invite Dreamboat?"

"Oops. I'll ask him." Page pointed to another splash of batter on her cousin's upper arm.

With an exasperated sigh, Betsy grabbed the roll of paper towels from Page and wiped more splatters. "Good luck. I don't envy you stuck in that room smelling of stale coffee, not to mention the creepy observation mirror."

"It's worth it to see Steve interrogate our prime suspect. Our detective puts on quite a show himself. See you soon." Page waved to Ina.

**

Page stood before the desk sergeant and waited for him to wand her.

Andre came around the corner. "Hi, Page. I see you've passed muster. Steve told me to escort you to the observation room. Where's Betsy?" Andre led the way down the hall.

Two officers recognized Page and nodded.

"Betsy needed to stay and close Honey Bees. She's going home to prepare dinner. Be warned. It's Tex-Mex Monday. She's on a Mexican cooking theme."

"That tells me she's going to be liberal with spice." Andre patted his stomach. "I'll down a glass of milk before coming to your place."

"You're a brave man, Andre, to keep showing up for

Betsy's meals," said Page.

The detective's eyes changed to amusement. "A brave one or a masochist. Isn't Steve dining with us?" Andre opened the observation room's door.

"I forgot to invite him. Don't you dare warn Steve. It'll give him time to make up an excuse."

"Warn me about what?" Steve appeared in the doorway. "What trouble are you brewing for me now?"

"Tex-Mex Monday." Andre smacked Steve on the back. "See you in the next room. I'll bring the suspect."

"What's Tex—no way. It sounds like a Betsy dinner invite. Not happening." Steve backed away from an approaching Page.

"Now, Detective, be a sport." Page made a pout.

"I've been a sport too often. You're on your own, and don't you dare feed Barnacle any of that Mex under the table. Besides, I'm going to visit Aunt Chatty." Steve looked through the glass and saw the suspect taking a seat at the table.

Page's thoughts raced to gain control of the situation. "Tell you what. If you come to dinner, we can cuddle at your bungalow afterward."

Steve's eyes gazed at Page's lips. "What time?"

"Come after you visit Chatty. Now that we've got things settled, dazzle me with your interrogating skills." Page took her seat and texted Betsy that she'd have four at her Tex-Mex table. She watched through the two-way mirror as Andre and Steve assumed their typical stances.

"Detective Lyon, did you Mirandize our guest?" Steve stood at the head of the table. His laptop lay open, and a file sat next to it.

"Yes, and I'm promised full cooperation," answered Andre.

"That's an excellent beginning. Let's hope it continues.

Please start recording. "Present this day at four o'clock p.m. are Detective Lyon, Detective Tanner, and Mr. Chester Tickle." Steve's eyes narrowed. "We've brought you in for questioning regarding the death of Evelyn Potts."

"And I've already told you that I know nothing about the woman's death. Forcing me here smacks of harassment. I have a reputation to uphold. Parading me out of the inn in front of others is unacceptable. When I return home, my solicitor will hear of this." Chester clenched his hands.

"Have you wound down? Because I'd like to proceed. As for your solicitor, I have little doubt you'll need his services." Steve picked up the file and flipped through it.

Page's eyes stared at Chester's purple bow tie with fuchsia polka dots. His canary-yellow suspenders and plaid trousers competed for attention. The whole ensemble looked like a magic mushroom trip.

"Let's go back to the afternoon Evelyn died. I have in my notes that you were meandering—and that's your word—around the inn's property at that time. And that stroll provided you with no alibi." Steve put a stare on Chester.

"So? I meandered. There's no crime there. I didn't harm Evelyn, although most of us wanted her out of our lives. She loved to stir trouble. What's your point, Detective?"

"My point is establishing that you had the opportunity to murder Ms. Potts. The statue gave you the means, which leads me to motive." Steve walked around the table.

Page had neglected to tell Steve about Chester having asked Grace for money. She rushed to the door and signaled an officer in the hall. "Please ask Detective Tanner to step in here. I must speak with him right away."

"I understand, ma'am, but please remain in the observing room with the door closed. It's for your protection."

"Sorry." Page closed the door and waited.

Steve stuck his head in. "What's so important that you pulled me from the questioning?"

Page came closer to where Steve stood. "When you said motive, I remembered it slipped my mind to tell you something Mickey said this morning."

"What did the town gossip have to say that's related to this case?" Steve entered and shut the door.

"He overheard Chester asking Grace to loan him five hundred pounds, which is all her savings. In return, he promised her a job at the college as his teaching assistant." Page grabbed a breath. "You see, Grace lost her job when Evelyn died, and it sounds like the poor woman is between a rock—"

"Can you put a point on this for me like yesterday? I've got this stuffed shirt wearing a bow tie fit for a clown show waiting." Steve's tone sounded exasperated.

"Hang on. I'm getting to the point of Mickey's sharing. Chester's tough-type creditors are after him for not paying. He's a collector of Netsuke and overextended himself in a big way by purchasing the figures. So much so that he asked Grace for money, and she agreed. Here it is, Tanner. This guy's motive might have been to do away with Evelyn and stop having to pay her hush money for more than having his TA write his books. His back was against the wall. Desperation makes for hasty decisions and actions." Page stared at Steve.

"Duly noted, Sherlocka." Steve inclined his dark head. His eyes softened on Page. "Anything else you forgot to tell me?"

"Actually, yes. Bring your own bottle of antacids to dinner."

Steve groaned and returned to the interrogation.

"Pardon the interruption, Mr. Tickle." Steve pulled out the chair next to the author and sat.

Chester glanced at his watch. "Can we wrap this up? The inn serves dinner promptly at six."

"Don't worry about missing dinner. We can order a tray for you. Unfortunately, your potential cellmate has a history of food snatching. He's a big boy with a big appetite." Andre snickered.

Page chuckled, thinking Andre was playing his role to perfection.

"Whatever is he going on about?" Chester wore his affront well.

"Detective Lyon is merely assuring you there's no need to worry about your dinner. Let's get back to your motive for sending that statue crashing down on Ms. Potts." Steve held up his hand to stop Chester from responding. "I've got the floor. This is the place where you keep your mouth shut and listen. You're in debt. Your passion for owning collectibles you can't afford caught up with you. Evelyn was an alligator you had to keep feeding pounds to or risk losing your job and publishing contract. You're flat broke. You let another person write your book while you claimed the glory. That puts you in a bad way, Mr. Tickle." Steve paused a tick. "I'd sure hate to be wearing your bow tie."

Page burst out laughing as she watched Chester touch his tie and cough.

"You're our number one suspect possessing a powerful motive to solve your problems once and for all. Well, except for the need for immediate cash. That's still hanging out there." Steve paced the room.

Page knew he was ready to deliver a zinger.

"My finances are settled, and none of your concern." Chester pulled his shoulders back.

Steve came to face him and bent over the table. "Your finances have improved five hundred pounds, but I doubt they're settled, Mr. Tickle. You pressed Ms. Culpepper for money in exchange for promising her a job. I understand she caved and wired the money to your account."

"How could you possibly know—Grace wouldn't have divulged something so personal." Chester shuffled in his chair.

"My sources aren't your concern. I'm three minutes from charging you with causing Ms. Potts's death." Steve's knuckles rapped the table. He resumed his walk.

Page waited for Steve to deliver the final surprise.

"I've told you repeatedly that I had nothing to do with her death. I know you've tried to create a motive using my financial problems, but it's weak. It's laughable." Chester adjusted his suspenders. "I've nothing to hide."

Steve pivoted and stood over Chester. He arched a brow in a sardonic inquiry. "Is that a fact?"

Chester glared back. "That's a fact."

Steve signaled Andre.

Page watched Andre leave the room, return in seconds, and discreetly pass something to Steve.

"Nothing to hide? I'm calling you a liar, Mr. Tickle." Steve laid the evidence bag in front of Chester. "You hid your handkerchief in the statue garden's hedge." Steve looked over at Andre. "Don't you think this is something to hide, Detective Lyon?"

"I certainly do." Andre nodded.

Chester stared at the handkerchief. "It's not mine."

Steve ignored Tickle's denial and continued, "Our crime lab is checking to confirm this is Ms. Potts's blood, but we feel pretty confident it'll be a match." Steve pulled out the chair and sat down. Looking at Chester at eye level, he said, "You're lousy at hiding anything, Mr. Tickle."

"I'm telling you again that isn't mine." Chester swiped

at the perspiration above his lip.

"Strike one, Chester." Page watched Steve deftly set things in motion.

"Of course it's your handkerchief." Steve flipped the bag over and pointed. "See those initials? C.T.? That's you."

Chester rubbed his forehead. Within seconds, his expression changed, and color returned to his face. He tilted his head in a cocky manner. "Want me to help you out? That handkerchief belongs to one of the guests staying at the inn. Her name is Chatty Tapper. C. T. same as what's on the handkerchief. That's hers. You detectives need a refresher course on solving a case. I write mysteries and know a thing or two."

Page felt surprised and amused that Chester managed a fast comeback. She didn't have to wait long for Steve's reaction. "Strike two coming up," she said aloud.

"I beg to differ. We happen to feel pretty confident in our detecting abilities." Steve gave a quick nod. "But I will give you credit. Coming up with matching initials to a guest was some fast thinking, Mr. Tickle."

"I've heard enough. I'm leaving." Chester tried to rise from the chair.

Andre's strong hand helped him get re-situated with a thud. "You're going to hurt Detective Tanner's feelings trying to cut out on our little soiree before he's finished." Andre returned to the door to act as a deterrent to Chester's leaving. "Please continue, Detective. Mr. Tickle is anxious to hear more."

"I can speak for myself." Chester remained in his chair and glared at Steve. "Finish whatever you have to say. I'm done with you amateurs." His hands shoved the evidence bag toward the detective.

"Bad move, Chester. Never poke the snake," mumbled

Page.

Steve moved the handkerchief closer to Chester. "You're missing a couple of key facts, which I'm obliged to share. Number one, Chatty didn't have a relationship with Evelyn. The only connection she had to the deceased was that they were both guests at Three Fables. There's no motive."

"You don't know that for sure." Chester's huffiness was deflating.

"I do know that for sure, which brings me to the second fact you're missing. "Chatty's last name isn't Tapper. It's Tanner. Does that have a familiar ring?"

"No, why should it? I don't know this Chatty person." Chester affected a bored expression.

"Ah, but I do. Chatty is my aunt. Her last name is Tanner and not Tapper." Steve unclipped his name badge and shoved it under Chester's nose.

"That old bird is your aunt?" Chester did a series of gulps.

"She is. And I take offense when anyone disparages my Aunt Chatty and tries to hang someone's death on her. It riles me right up." Steve adjusted the badge on his belt and made eye contact with Andre.

"I...I didn't—" Chester's words died in his mouth.

"Strike three. You're out." Page nodded.

"Detective Lyon, book Mr. Tickle on suspicion. Make sure his roommate is Big Cletus, and they dine together."

"You're making a big mistake. I didn't harm Evelyn." Chester held on to his chair seat when Andre tried to lift his arm. "Let me explain. I admit it's my handkerchief. Okay?"

Steve motioned to Andre to stand down.

"This is your final chance to convince me." Steve stood over Chester. "Now," he voiced with impatience.

Chester inhaled. "I didn't tell you the truth about

meandering around the gardens that afternoon. The credit goons had called my cell phone and threatened to meet my plane and take me for a ride. I've heard about those rides, and I needed to walk around and try to figure out options. In the distance, I heard angry voices from the statue garden." Chester touched his temple. "I was in my poxy hell. I had no desire to join in someone else's. I ignored them."

"Go on, Mr. Tickle." Steve typed notes.

"Maybe two or three minutes later came the sound of what I now know was the statue falling on Evelyn. Then there was just silence. Nothing. So, I walked over and opened the gate. That's when I saw Evelyn lying there with blood all around her head. I felt for a pulse in her neck, but she was gone." Chester pulled out an identical ivory handkerchief and wiped his eyes.

Steve and Andre exchanged looks but said nothing.

"I wiped the blood off my hands with my handkerchief, only to realize I needed to get rid of it fast. I heard more voices heading towards the garden. I'm pretty sure it was that snoop that followed you around and her red-haired friend."

"You dapper dummy. I'm no snoop," Page said to the mirror.

"What was your next move?" asked Steve.

"I had to get rid of the handkerchief fast in case those two spotted me. I shoved it in the hedge and hurried inside the inn. I'm surprised you found it. I should have gone back for it. My mistake." Chester folded his handkerchief. He gave a nervous laugh and pointed to it. "Seems I'm not as sharp as I used to be." His hoity accent changed.

"I'd agree with that statement." Steve handed Andre the evidence bag. "So, you left Evelyn and went inside the inn."

"Yeah, it wasn't like there was anything I could do for

her. And the last thing I needed was someone hanging her death on me. The others already knew I hated Evelyn and had threatened her. Though I swear, they were just words. They're my tools of the trade, or at least they were until I hit writer's block. Words don't kill. They only hurt the emotions."

Page considered what he said. She disagreed. Words could kill in unseen ways. Chester wasn't guilty of anything but being a coward and weak. One question remained, and she waited for Steve to ask.

"Mr. Tickle, for some reason that defies the evidence I have against you, I'm inclined to believe you didn't do this. You omitted what I need to know most. If I'm to let you return to the inn tonight and not spend an overnighter with Cletus, I need another answer. Think long and hard about lying to me again."

Chester nodded. "I won't lie again. I've no reason to now. What's the question?"

"Do you know who was arguing with Evelyn?" Steve leaned closer to the man's face.

"I wish I did. I was too far away. I didn't know it was Evelyn until I found her. I can tell you it sounded like a woman's voice. It wasn't Leo. I'm sure. It had to be Ruby, Grace, or Fiona. That's all I know. I swear it, Detective." Chester's voice broke. "Please, may I go back to Three Fables?"

Steve stood up. "On one condition. You call us if you see or hear anything involving this case. Anything at all, no matter how inconsequential it may seem. Can I trust you to deliver on this?"

"Does it include those ghosts' doing things to me and the others?" Chester's expression told Steve he was serious. "That inn is ripe with apparitions. Tomorrow's plane can't take me home fast enough." Chester's fingers touched his toupee.

"Perhaps Mr. Tickle would prefer Cletus's company tonight to the inn's," said Andre, keeping a straight face.

"No, I don't think Mr. Cletus would appreciate my finer qualities. I'll take my chances with those I can't see." Chester looked to Andre for permission. "May I rise?"

Andre gave an affirmative nod and opened the door to the officer waiting in the hall. "Please drive Mr. Tickle back to Three Fables."

Steve waited for Chester to exit before returning to Page. "Back to square one. I'd hoped we'd have this case locked up tonight."

"Me too. I agree, Chester didn't do the deed. At least we've whittled it down to three suspects unless you want to toss Chatty into the mix. She didn't think much of Evelyn," teased Page.

"Don't you start on my Aunt Chatty. You saw how it went for Tickle." Steve tugged on Page's hair. "Let's get out of here. I'll walk you to your pride and joy."

"My British SUV is a fine piece of kit. Remember that fact, Detective."

"I will as long as you remember that you owe me a cuddle, assuming we survive Betsy's Tex-Mex Monday meal." Steve stopped by the duty officer on their way out. "I'm on call tonight. Don't hesitate to bother me, especially around dinner time."

"Sir?" The uniformed officer looked confused.

"Private joke, Pete." Steve held the door for Page.

"Right, sir. I think I understand."

Page passed Pete and gave him a thumbs up. She heard him muttering Steve's instructions to himself.

Steve inhaled deeply. "Ah, the salt air. I'd love for us to have Carpe Diem out this evening, but alas."

"We'll go out as soon as the case is solved. Yes?" Page

got into the driver's seat.

"We will. Listen, I'm going to grab a quick shower and have a visit with Aunt Chatty. I'll make it to dinner by seven. Okay?" Steve leaned down and surprised Page with a quick kiss.

It was enough to wake up her pulse. "Sure." She'd copy Betsy's hot-flash ritual and flick the AC on high going home, but for a different reason.

CHAPTER 29

Page entered Hibiscus as the aroma of cumin and some unknown spices hit her nose with a pow. The sound of rattling pans and dishes propelled her to discover what karma had in store.

"Hi, there. Come chop for me." Betsy set the colander of mixed peppers on the counter next to the cutting board. "And I'm anxious to hear how things went with Chester. Update me before you go change."

Page spared some time to detail Chester's takedown and supposed innocence.

"He's not the one." Betsy tore lettuce for a salad with additional verve.

"Nope, but we're getting closer to who is by process of elimination."

"If you say so. I won't deny feeling disappointed that we don't have our whodunit," said Betsy. "We must soldier on."

"And so, we shall," replied Page.

"Hurry and change. I need your chopping skills pronto."

"Okay, I'm your sous chef in two shakes." Page entered her bedroom and pulled a pair of jeans and a crisp, white blouse from her closet. "On second thought, white and Betsy's meals never go well together." She exchanged the white top for a navy knit. "You're the safe choice." Glancing in the mirror, she canceled the frown with a smile.

"Want gloves?" asked Betsy, lifting a lid on a pot of

rice.

"Gloves?" Page peered at the assorted hot peppers on the cutting board.

"For one of the peppers. It's super hot and can—"

"Why you insist on choosing something that can burn the skin is beyond my comprehension. Which one is the culprit?" Page stared at assorted colors of green and red peppers.

"That one." Betsy pointed. She grabbed a spoon and tasted something from a saucepan. "Perfecto."

Page lifted the trouble-making pepper with a paper towel and stepped on the garbage can pedal. "Adios, amigo."

Betsy spun around. "Did you just toss my pepper in the garbage? I needed it for my—"

"I did, and I know three people who don't need it on their plate." Page ignored Betsy's shocked expression. "Face it. Our palates are not as advanced as yours."

"But my pepper was the jolt the recipe needed." Betsy pouted.

The cuckoo bird came out to distract her.

"That hateful bird." Betsy glared at the clock as the door knock sounded. "That's Andre. Hurry and get the other peppers chopped for my burrito topping."

"Yes, chef." Page stole a fast peek at what was on the stove and in the oven. Betsy put everything into her cooking. Page silently vowed to find a compliment to give her cousin over dinner. She felt grateful for having Betsy in her life and for the happiness they'd found at Shell Isle. And when the inklings came, Page knew she could have no better partner by her side.

"Hi, Page. Something sure smells like a fiesta in here." Andre came into the kitchen.

Betsy wiped her brow. "Come sample my Peppercorn

Honey Cornbread."

Andre studied the cornbread coming from the oven. "Make it a small sample. I don't want to ruin my appetite. May I have some of this reviving nectar?" He pointed to the glass pitcher.

"Help yourself." Page winked, knowing Andre needed a cold chaser.

"Thanks." Andre poured a glass of raspberry lemonade. "Okay, I'm ready."

Betsy placed a chunk of cornbread in his mouth. "Now savor those flavors and the one I added to jazz up the recipe," instructed Betsy.

Andre chewed and sipped. Surprise washed over his face. "Why, Betsy Ross, this is the best cornbread I've ever tasted."

Page came over to where they stood by the pan. "Really?" She cut a small piece and plopped it in her mouth. "Wow! I've never tasted any cornbread like this. It's delicious."

"Yeah?" Betsy tossed her head and preened. "What do you like about it?"

Page took a second bite before replying. "The texture is smooth and not crumbly. And the flavor is all buttery, sweet, and with just the right kick." She turned to Betsy. "Outstanding, Bets. I want at least two pieces." Page licked her fingers.

"My Tex-Mex Monday Fiesta is off to a rousing start. Let me have those peppers to finish off my rice dish. You two take the pitcher of lemonade and glasses to the table."

"I've got the pitcher." Andre disappeared onto the porch. "Hey, Barnacle is standing outside the screen door. What's his fate?"

"Let him in," said both women in unison.

Betsy stared up at the cuckoo. "It's gone seven, and

where is Dreamboat? My dinner is ready for the table."

"He should arrive any minute," answered Page. "Want me to get Barnacle his beef bone?"

"Yeah, he can't sit at the table tonight. Andre has his place." Betsy switched the stove burners off and grabbed her oven mitt. "I'm serving now."

The door chimed, and Steve let himself in. "I smell a —"

"Delicious dinner," finished Page, coming to greet him. She whispered in his ear. "Go for the cornbread."

"Are you sure?" Steve cocked an eyebrow.

"Yep." Page motioned him to the porch.

"Hi, everyone." Steve spied Barnacle in the hammock. "At least my dog arrives promptly, invite or no invite." Steve ruffled his ears. "Good looking bone you got there, but I think Page and Betsy want you on the floor with it." Steve dragged the dog off the hammock before sitting at the table.

Betsy placed a ceramic bowl next to Andre. "Let's fiesta, Betsy style. We've got Buckin' Burritos here." Betsy pointed at the sheet pan. "Olé Rice, Salsa Salad, and Page's new favorite Peppercorn Honey Cornbread. Dig in, everyone."

"I think Tex-Mex Monday may need to become a tradition," said Page, activating her vow to give Betsy more compliments.

Andre, with a mouthful of rice, nodded enthusiastically.

A surprised Steve took his first tentative bite of the burrito. "Whoa. This thing does have a buck to it."

Page kicked him under the table and frowned.

"But it's the perfect amount of buck," said Steve, clearing his throat and grabbing his glass of lemonade. "Pass the cornbread, Page."

For the next half hour, the four tucked into Betsy's fixings, avoiding any conversation about the case. They discussed Shell Isle announcing the construction of a second marina. Steve lamented how boat-slip rental spaces seldom became available. Residents had voiced the need, and the town's commissioners listened and voted for the funds to construct it.

Pushing away from the table, Steve rose. "How about we all top this fine fiesta with a gelato and a competitive game of miniature golf at Rolfe's? My treat. Any takers?"

"I like the way you think, Dreamboat. Be warned. I'm going for the large pistachio." Betsy gathered the plates.

"Would you lose the Dreamboat already, Bets?" Page avoided Steve's devilish smirk and stacked the glasses on the tray to take to the kitchen.

"Hey, I like that you think of me as a dreamboat," teased Steve, handing Andre the empty bowls.

Andre tapped Betsy's arm. "I wouldn't mind being thought of as someone's dreamboat."

Page groaned and left the three laughing as she wore her flushed face to the kitchen.

"I'll be right back. I need to take Barn home." Steve opened the screen door and whistled his dog outside.

The three made fast work of loading the dishwasher before leaving for a fun outing. "Who's driving?" asked Betsy.

"Since it was my idea, I'll drive us," replied Steve from the front door. "Come on."

***

Rolfe's defined fun with its quirky theme of colorful sea life figures that beckoned golf balls to try and score par on the challenging course. Page and Steve had a knack for entertaining other players as they argued over who snuck their ball closer to the cup or slipped in an extra stroke when the other was not looking. Their competing nature scored more points than their balls.

Before the night's game began, Page and Steve lived up

to their reputations. They each grabbed for the same ball. War broke out as their words and hands tried to claim ownership.

"I always have green," said Page, trying to remove the ball from Steve's closed fist.

"That may be, but I'm tired of you commandeering the winning color. Tonight, I mean to triumph. My ego is in the basement after losing the last two games." Steve placed the ball on the carpeted mat.

Betsy snatched it before Page could act. "Enough, you two. I'm playing green tonight to complement my pistachio gelato. And I'm up first. Step aside."

"Do you dare invite anything green back into your life? Remember those close encounters today with green, Irish whipped cream and batter." Page wagged a finger in her cousin's direction.

Betsy hesitated, staring at the ball.

"Ignore them, Betsy. Cleave to that green orb. Your destiny is to become my winning partner," chimed Andre.

"We're doomed to lose, thanks to your stealing my ball." Page bopped Steve on the arm.

***

The lighthearted mood followed the four back to Hibiscus and lasted until Steve got called to the station. He disconnected with a regretful-sounding sigh. He pulled Page aside. "No cuddle for us due to another vacation home break-in."

Page looped both arms around Steve's neck and stood on her tiptoes. "I understand. It's really okay." She kissed his chin.

"It's not okay with me, but it's my job. Listen, I need to ask a big favor. But first, I'll butter you up with some happy news." His expression softened as his eyes gazed at Page.

"What's the butter? What kind of favor? Your favors

are unpredictable." Page stepped back, sizing him up. "Well?"

"When I visited Aunt Chatty tonight, Rake pulled me to the side. He confessed he'd repaired Althea's foundation to surprise Alice. I think he's sweet on her."

"Hmm, no ghostly doings there? That's good news for Alice, and one mystery is solved. I think Rake is a great guy. Maybe something will come of that." Page nodded. "I'm buttered up. Now, what's the favor?"

"It's Aunt Chatty. I feel guilty doing so little with her. Is there any chance you could invite her for a short visit tomorrow? She loves being ensconced in a beach chair and reading her historical romance." Steve hesitated. "I know you have Honey Bees to run, so if it's inconvenient, I understand."

Page's fingers touched his lips. "I'm happy to invite Chatty to Hibiscus. It's fine. I'm scheduled to work on the accounts tomorrow, which I do from home. I'll ring her first thing in the morning and settle her in a lounger by ten o'clock. I'll even make tuna sandwiches for lunch. How's that?"

"I owe you, Page, but then I seem to keep a debt tally running," Steve spoke thoughtfully, never taking his eyes off Page.

"That you do, Tanner. You can easily repay this one. When I solve the case, I want a full day out on Carpe Diem. No interruptions by Andre, Koch, or the lawbreakers. Just you, me, and Carpe. Deal?" Page nodded to Betsy, waving her inside.

"Deal. I'm ignoring your bait about you being the one to solve the case." Steve reached for Page's hand and kissed it. "I see your duenna beckons. Night, Sherlocka."

A resolute Page marched up the steps. She pledged to solve the case the next day and show her detective what this Sherlocka could do. All she needed was the final inkling and nudge.

CHAPTER 30

Another Tuesday was set in motion as Page surveyed the beach activity from her screen porch. Gazing at the few stray clouds parked over the horizon informed her the sun would rule the day.

She'd made it a point to rise early to post Honey Bees's monthly sales on the computer spreadsheet and pay their bills. "Another ten minutes should tidy the shop's accounts, and then I'm having my kind of breakfast," Page said to the computer screen.

She congratulated herself on finishing a bowl of oatmeal and a second cup of coffee before Betsy appeared. Her cousin's out-of-tune humming signaled the day was officially open for business.

"Morning; I slept like a baby." Betsy eyed the coffee.

"Good for you," replied Page. "A nice restful—"

"No. Not good for me. Babies sleep two to three hours, and that's all I logged." Betsy pulled a mug from the cabinet.

"Ah, sorry to hear it. Maybe you can get to bed earlier tonight."

"Maybe." Betsy shrugged. "I did enjoy a splendid shower using our newest honey soap." Betsy fluffed her still-damp hair. "It's so moisturizing."

"I'm happy to know your morning meets expectations." Page strolled to the coffee maker. She poured cream into her cup and took a sip. She could tell something else was preying on her cousin's mind.

Betsy placed her mug under the coffee dispenser and

chose a vanilla dark roast. "Page?"

Here it comes, thought Page. "Yes? Go ahead. Spill it, but not the coffee."

Betsy's eyes sparkled with excitement. "I just had a surprise call from my neighbor. You know the guy who is over the moon at how my bungalow renovation turned out." Betsy drank from her mug. "Can we chat on the porch? I want to float my simply divine idea by you."

Page nodded, letting her worry follow Betsy to their chairs.

"Are you in a good mood?" asked Betsy.

"Reasonably, considering I haven't solved this case. What are you up to now?" Page saw Barnacle at the screen door. She went to let him inside.

"Why must he get in my hammock?" Betsy eyed the spaniel.

Page blew out a breath of exasperation. "Because it's comfy. Are you going to tell me the latest bee to land in your bonnet?"

"Yeah, don't get chapped. I need you receptive." Betsy pulled a thread loose from her lavender crop pants. "Albert wants to buy my bungalow for his sister so she can relocate to Shell Isle. Having her next door allows them to look after each other as they age. His offer is generous, and I'd make a tidy profit."

"Hold the fort. Where would you move with this tidy profit? Don't you need to find another place?" Page appreciated Betsy's desire to make a nice jingle, but she needed a home.

Betsy sipped more of her coffee before replying. "Just give a listen. Since I clearly have a real knack for restoring beach bungalows, I'm considering doing another one. I can parlay my money earned on this one into the next property."

"But—" Page tried to get a word in.

Betsy lifted her hand. "Not yet. You need to hear my entire plan. If I could do one flip a year or so, my coffers would be ever so happy. And I'd get to use another of my many talents to provide a cute home for someone. And before you say anything about Honey Bees and me, I can easily ramrod my subcontractors and manage things while working, just like before. Now, what do you think of my brilliant idea?"

Page started to shake her head, but hesitated. Betsy's enthusiasm was contagious. Her cousin needed new projects to stave off boredom. And having her content and living in Shell Isle mattered. Page swallowed her objection. "I can see how doing another restoration would feel rewarding in many ways. I have one question, Bets. Assuming you find a property, where would you live while doing this next rehab?"

"Oh, that's the best part of my scheme. I will move back to Hibiscus and see that you eat properly. We'll have scads of time for fun and frolic and not feel lonely at night." Betsy clapped her hands together. "What do you think? I know. I've outdone myself again."

Page gulped air. Did she want Betsy to reside at Hibiscus again? Were her nights that lonely? Page's mind scattered questions for her to ponder before replying. "You've come up with this plan pretty doggone fast, Bets."

"I'm good at seeing opportunities to meet needs. By the way, I want to do some things to enhance my bedroom and bathroom here. Of course, I'd pay for it all. And I'm definitely finding that cuckoo a new home. Aunt Tilly will have to deal with it her way." Betsy released a loud laugh and looked upward. "Hear that, Tilly?"

Page shook her head and laughed. "Hush. Don't bother our aunt. I admit that I do like parts of this proposal. So, you want to live at Hibiscus while you oversee the next project.

You'll move into that property until you find a buyer at your price and repeat this process if everything aligns again. Is that right?"

"You got it, toots. Then, after maybe three flips, I can settle into a place and not carry a mortgage. What's not to love? Right?" Betsy finished her coffee and stood to let Barnacle outside.

Page grew thoughtful, processing more of their exchange. "Okay, I'll agree to the next renovation plan, but with one caveat. We need to negotiate the cooking arrangements. You must keep all the hot peppers off my plate."

Betsy shoved her hand out. "Deal. What else?"

"We take turns cooking dinner. It's not fair for you to—"

"Fine. I'll see that you get three Best Betsy dinners each week. And I insist on paying all utilities." Betsy pushed her hand toward Page for an encore. "Deal?"

"Deal." Page rose, dazed by what had transpired and what she'd agreed to. And for some unfathomable reason, she felt glad that Betsy wasn't leaving.

"I'm texting Albert right now that I accept his offer. Wait until I tell Ina our big news." The renovator extraordinaire pulled her cell phone from a pocket. "We must wait to celebrate our new arrangement until we solve this mysterious death hanging over us."

"I agree." Page followed Betsy to the kitchen.

"May this case get a wrap soon." Betsy's eyes narrowed as she focused on Page. "What's happening? Are you receiving an inkling?"

Page nodded and waited for the flushing sensation to pass and the message to enter her mind. "To answer your question, this inkling tells me we need to act."

"What kind of act are you planning? You're already

scheduled off, but do I need to ask Ina and Daisy to cover for me?" Betsy added three teaspoons of sugar to her coffee and shrugged. "My only vice. Talk to me."

"No, you should open Honey Bees and bake your Tuesday menu with Ina. I'll call you if anything changes. I got up early to do the account postings so I could invite Chatty for a beach day." Page glanced at the clock.

Betsy placed two cake doughnuts on a plate. "Have you called her?"

"No, I think I'll ring Chatty now. She's probably up."

Betsy's laughter rang out. "Here comes Barnacle again. You'd better make the call from the den. He's making his loud whine because Dreamboat left him. I don't know why Steve bothers having a fence. Barn digs his way out most every day." Betsy opened the screen door.

"He loves people and hates being left. Please give him a biscuit. There's a new box in the pantry. Back in a jiffy." Page closed the den's door and dialed Chatty's cell phone.

"Good morning. Chatty here," she answered.

"Good morning to you. It's Page. I hope that I didn't ring you too early."

"Not at all. I rise before the birds in case I need to roust them." Chatty gave a little chuckle. "What a pleasant surprise to hear from you."

"I called to ask if you'd like a little beach excursion. I thought I'd make tuna sandwiches for a picnic lunch, and we could enjoy relaxing by the water."

"Why, Page, what a delightful invitation. I would love to visit you and your charming cottage. Are you sure you have time for this? I know Honey Bees demands your attention."

"Tuesdays are my day to work from home, so it's perfect. Shall I swing by Three Fables in an hour?"

"Perfect. I shall look forward to seeing you very soon."

Chatty grew quiet for a moment. "Page, just so you know, I told my nephew last evening he has excellent taste in lady friends. Your invitation proves this true. I must dash to get ready." Chatty disconnected.

Page returned to the porch to see Betsy and Barnacle swinging at a crazy speed in the hammock, each trying to own it. "I leave you for a couple of minutes and return to an epic battle for king or queen of my hammock. I thought you were going to the shop."

"I am, but I decided to worry." Betsy failed to stop the hammock's wild swings. "Barn, get off me. Stop licking my face!" hollered Betsy, unable to sit upright.

Laughing and wishing she had witnesses to the scene, Page extended her hand. "Grab hold."

Barnacle toppled out as Betsy vacated the hammock.

"I don't know why I persist in wanting to lay in that Venus flytrap." Betsy tugged her blouse down. "Great. Here comes a hot flash. Where's my fan?"

Page reached for a floral one left on the table. "You've got these things scattered all over the cottage."

"Never mind that. I've been out here worrying. Things are amping up. These authors are flying out soon. We both know that time has turned against us. It's now or never." Betsy sighed.

"Trust me. I'm feeling the pressure." Page touched her temple, hoping a migraine wouldn't interfere with her day.

"I can see the worry on your face, too. Did you reach Chatty?" Betsy spread the fan and put it to work.

"I did. We're all set. I need to do a few more things for Honey Bees before I leave to pick her up."

Betsy frowned. "Page?"

"Yes? Do you want to fret longer?"

"I do, and I'm really good at it. I've had years of

practice being your sleuthing partner." Betsy attempted to make a happy face. "Are you sure I shouldn't tag along to Three Fables? You did have an inkling this morning." She swallowed. "Inklings spell action."

"Let's hope we'll get some action. I've got this, but you're on call." Page leaned in to hug Betsy. "Thank you for your willingness to help."

"I've known my role since we were kids and your gift first presented. You took after Aunt Tilly, being all intuitive." Betsy tossed the fan back to the table. "Okay, I'd better wear my baking apron. You stay aware and safe."

"I will. Now scoot. Make sure you save me one of today's special apple turnovers." Page pulled out the suspect board and headed toward the den. Moments later, she heard the front door close, and silence returned to the cottage.

Page studied the board before she had to leave for Three Fables. Nothing stood out to link Fiona or Grace to Evelyn's death. Ruby still held first place. She hoped that some missing puzzle pieces would fall into place once Steve received the all-important reports on the button and cell phone today. But the earlier inkling had nothing to do with those reports. Something else was about to unfold.

Walking to the window, she noticed foreboding dark clouds forming. Their edges were tinged a grim shade of grey and moving in to blot the sun. An urgent nudge to leave for Three Fables propelled her back a step.

Grabbing her keys and handbag, Page rushed toward whatever awaited.

CHAPTER 31

James greeted Page as she entered Three Fables. "Good morning. Are you here to see Alice? She's in the dining room serving breakfast."

Page walked over to where he was seated behind the check-in desk. "I've come to take Chatty for an outing, but I'm early. It's good to see you recovered from your bout with an oyster. I hope your sister is well."

Surprise flashed briefly across James's face. "News moves around here fast. We're both fine. Thank you. Shall I ring Ms. Tanner's room?"

"No, I think I'll go say hello to Alice. When Chatty comes downstairs, would you mind telling her I'm in the dining room?" Page gave an impish smile. "I may try and snag one of Alice's cinnamon rolls."

James nodded dismissively to Page and answered the ringing phone.

The nudge returned but with less intensity. It felt like a subtle reminder to remain observant. Page strolled down the hallway, allowing herself time to study the oil paintings along the gallery wall. It was as if she'd stepped through the wardrobe to author C.S. Lewis's *Narnia* to another era. Each ornately framed painting depicted a younger Three Fables. The trees weren't as tall, but the gardens were resplendent with flowers. A gazebo existed in the exact location, but in a different style than the present one.

Page continued her study as she turned the corner and noticed the painting scenes changed to the inn's interior. One depicted a grand gala in the parlor that captured her interest. Women dressed in pastel gowns arranged themselves with elegance in settees and chairs, while the men appeared to vie for their affection. Three couples held each other in a waltz pose as a trio of musicians performed. A melancholy feeling washed over Page, envying their simpler ways of socializing. No computer or cell phone screens to intrude on a day. She halted, hearing two women's voices coming from the library. Perhaps the inkling was tied to the conversation. Seeing no one about, Page drew closer and eavesdropped.

"Fiona, I've been waiting for the opportunity to talk to you alone. Can you give me a moment?"

"If you insist, Grace. I merely slipped into the library to return a book. What is it you wish to discuss?"

"Could we sit?" Grace's meek tone made it difficult for Page to hear her.

"Okay, I'm seated. Make it snappy because I'm famished and want breakfast before Chester devours the rolls."

"I'll make it brief. I bring you two matters of some importance to me. First, I know you have authors bothering you constantly to read their work. Since you know me, I'm hoping you wouldn't mind reading the first twenty pages of my manuscript. I printed them for you."

Page heard paper rustling and assumed Grace had passed it to Fiona.

"I'm not looking to represent new unpublished clients, Grace. You'd need to go through the proper submission requirements with whatever you've written." Fiona's tone flirted with harshness.

"I understand the process, but might you give my work a bit of a peek today? It would mean so much to me. I'm not without talent as a writer. Evelyn liked my writing and promised to ask you to review my manuscript, but she never seemed to get around to it."

"Maybe because she didn't think your writing was elevated enough to ask me. Honestly, Grace, I represent only authors with exceptional writing abilities, like your past employer. As I already stated, my publisher has no interest in signing authors lacking a stellar portfolio of work. Let's say no more about this."

Grace's voice came up a notch. "Wait. I know some things about Evelyn, beginning with the fact that she'd already signed with another publisher. She possessed not an ounce of loyalty to anyone, including me."

"Tell me something I didn't already know," replied Fiona. "I couldn't stand the woman but tolerated her baser behaviors because she made us money."

"You're sadly misinformed. Evelyn didn't make you money. I did. I wrote for her." Grace grew silent.

"What? Don't make me laugh. You expect me to buy you're involved somehow in writing Evelyn's bestselling books. I have no interest in this charade. Nor am I interested in reading what I'm sure is your ridiculous drivel on a page."

Fiona's tone of disdain fueled Grace's next words. "I can see why Evelyn chose to go elsewhere with our next book. I'll take my ridiculous novel back. The day will come when you'll soon eat your words spoken to me."

Page felt sorry for timid Grace, who had likely rehearsed the request countless times only to get an unkind rejection. She heard what sounded like sniffing.

Fiona's voice chilled even further. "Come back to me when you have a backbone and are a seasoned writer."

"Ms. Salt, I could have saved your job with this novel, but you're too self-absorbed to see it. All's the pity. Clearly, you're no better than Evelyn."

Page silently applauded Grace for finding her gumption.

Hearing footsteps approaching the door, Page hurried toward the dining room and felt another inkling. She glanced at an antique, walnut grandfather clock, showing she had only a few minutes to discover its meaning before Chatty appeared.

Page entered the dining room and waved to Alice, who was pouring tea for Ruby. The buffet had attracted Chester with his plate overflowing with pastries and bacon.

Fiona's voice broke the silence as she walked over and took a plate from the stack. She delivered a dour expression. "Good morning, my nefarious soon-to-be ex-authors. Congratulations on your success in ruining my retreat at this ghost-ridden inn. I'm counting the hours until I can bid you farewell."

Page watched in shock as the heavy silver tongs from the pastry platter fell on Fiona's sandaled foot.

"Ouch! Who did this?" The editor looked over her shoulder and saw no one. She reached down to rub her foot. "Am I bleeding?" Fiona asked Chester as he passed, wearing a smirk.

"One could only hope." Chester moved to an empty seat at the dining table next to Ruby. "You angered one of our unseen friends with your insult to the inn."

Page wondered if Althea and Julian had a hand in this mishap. Either way, score one for Three Fables. Page stepped to the beverage station, where a subdued Alice poured orange juice into a glass.

Alice leaned closer and whispered to Page, "I think that was Althea's doing. I smelled lilacs." She handed Page the glass. "Their shuttle can't take these people away fast enough."

"I agree. Thanks for a serving of the sunshine vitamin." Page sipped. "I'm waiting on Chatty to come downstairs. Steve asked me to invite her to the beach today."

"I know she's quite enthusiastic about the outing. Chatty came to the kitchen bright and early. I put her to work icing the cinnamon rolls. We've become fast friends. Now, *she's* one I don't want to leave."

"I'm so glad you've both bonded. And I heard Rake did an unexpected kindness for you and Althea by repairing the base. I like that guy a lot." Page's lips formed a smile.

"Yes, he did. At least one mystery was solved. I find myself drawing on his kindness and company more and more." Alice's cheeks blushed.

Page felt genuine joy for her new friend. "See? Things are already looking up for you. More good things are coming. I know it."

"I'm sure you're right." Alice's eyes surveyed her guests. "Everyone seems settled with their breakfast and behaving for the moment. Excuse me while I check on some things. Please help yourself to my fresh rolls. If I see Chatty, I'll tell her you're here."

"Thank you." Page reached for a cornflower-blue napkin and lifted a cinnamon roll from the platter. She'd taken her first bite when a somber-faced Grace entered the room and approached the buffet. "Good morning." Page added a dose of cheerfulness to her greeting.

Grace turned to face Page. "I think not."

"Aren't we in a mood?" Ruby came alongside. She reached in front of Grace for a slice of bacon, showing more rudeness.

Page gazed in shock as the answer to who harmed Evelyn stared back. The inkling had rewarded her in spades. Time was of the essence to act.

CHAPTER 32

Trying to appear calm and nonchalant to the four now seated around the dining table, Page excused herself. She hurried toward the reception area.

"Ma'am, I let Ms. Tanner know you were here. She went to the kitchen to ask Alice a question. I'm sure she'll return to reception soon," said James.

"Thanks. I'll dash to the kitchen. I need to speak to them both anyway." Page's mind whirled, knowing what she must do.

"Hello, dear Page. I was coming to find you." Chatty raised her beach bag. "As you can see, I'm fully prepared for our beach outing. Alice, why don't you slip away and join us?"

The innkeeper placed the clean baking sheet on the rack to drain. "How I'd love that. Maybe another day soon."

"Absolutely, Alice." Page tried to appear relaxed despite her pulse pounding. "Chatty, I'm sorry, but we must reschedule the beach fun. Something important has come up. I'll return in a couple of hours and explain."

"Gracious. I hope nothing serious," said Chatty.

Page didn't answer but turned to face Alice. "I need you to do something."

"Of course. Page, you seem quite flustered. How can I help?" asked Alice.

"I need you to keep your guests here. Under no circumstances let them leave. Get Rake to help if there's a problem." Page waited.

"I shouldn't have a problem. They're spending the morning packing. Since their visit here has been so upsetting, I have a photographer coming to snap souvenir photos of them in the garden. It's my gift to them."

"How kind of you, Alice," said Chatty.

"That will work perfectly." Page's expression turned serious. "Just one more thing before I leave. Please call my cell if anything or anyone behaves or says something of concern."

Chatty nodded in agreement. "Even though we're at a loss about what's happening, you may rely on us doing our part. Right, Alice?"

"Yes. We're up for this. Chatty and I make a team like you and that hilarious Betsy." Alice made shooing motions. "Go. We'll expect your return in a couple of hours."

"Do hurry back. I'm quite engaged in this next adventure," said Chatty. "It gets one's constitution revved up."

"That's one way to view this." Page waved and hurried out the kitchen's side door. Once in her SUV, she dialed Betsy.

"Hi. Now isn't a good time. I've got the doughnuts in the fryer, and Ina's sprinkling the powdered sugar on the gingerbread for me to slice."

"Stop talking and listen. I need you to bake the honey cake." Page blew out a pent-up breath.

"What? Bake the cake now? Are you telling me you know whodunit to Evelyn? How do you know?" Betsy lowered her voice. "You need me to leave for the cottage now to bake the cake?"

"If not sooner. Tell Ina and Daisy you're going. I'm on my way home. Hurry." Page disconnected and released another breath. Her logical mind took over planning.

***

Betsy stirred the honey cake's batter while babbling. "I

can't believe this. If you'd told me this morning, we'd know who — is that your cell phone?"

Page hurried to the porch and answered, "Hi, it's Page."

"It's Chatty. You told us to call if we heard anything concerning. I'm not sure if this counts, but you can decide."

"What's happened?"

Betsy motioned for Page to put the phone on speaker.

"I overheard a conversation that caused my worry antenna to rise. Hang on. I need to close my door. Ears are everywhere." Chatty returned. "Are you there, Page?"

"Yes. Tell me, please."

"I'm quite surprised as I thought Mara and James were delightful young people."

"But?"

"But they were talking to their grandfather on speaker and unaware I was nearby. It seems he has them spying on Alice for some unknown reason. That has me bothered. I can't imagine why this man's interested, but he railed at them for not getting financial information on her. I mean, we know our Alice has money issues. Three Fables has drained her with unexpected expenses." Chatty grew quiet.

"Thanks for letting me know. I agree. Something is up with these two. For now, you and Alice enjoy the rockers on the front porch and keep an eye peeled for anyone who wants to leave. Maybe invite Rake to join you and act as a deterrent."

Chatty sighed. "Whatever you think best."

"I think that's best. Betsy and I will return to the inn by noon. Everything's going to turn out fine. I promise." Page hung up and turned to Betsy.

"Well?" Betsy returned to her batter.

"I can't believe I'm about to say this. We need a second enchanted honey cake."

"You want me to make two?" Betsy's brow furrowed, showing her confusion. "We've never needed two cakes before."

"We do today and fast. I know. Let's split the batter into two pans. It'll save time," said Page.

"Good thinking." Betsy pulled out another cake pan. "Two honey cakes going to the same place, no less. This day is one humdinger." Betsy placed the pans in the oven and turned to Page. "Now what?"

"While they bake, we'll orchestrate our plan of action."

Betsy untied her apron. "Talk to me while I change into my free-flowing muumuu. It's better suited for a takedown."

Page followed Betsy to her bedroom, catching herself again thinking of it as Betsy's. To her surprise, she still didn't mind the idea. Page sat on the edge of the bed. "Okay, pay attention. Here's how we'll serve the two magical honey cakes. Tell me if you agree."

"First, how about the chartreuse dress complementing my hair color?" Betsy held up the dress.

"Perfect. I won't have any trouble finding you." Page's ribbing served to keep things light.

Betsy huffed. "Well, I like this one. Where are you going?"

"I'm going to change my top. I have icing drops from eating one of Alice's cinnamon rolls. Let's keep talking. I can hear you." Page opened a drawer and pulled out a red tie-dyed top.

"Which honey cake gets served first?" hollered Betsy.

"Evelyn's because we're dealing with someone facing a charge of at least manslaughter. Whatever Mara and James are up to is nothing compared to this crime."

"Right," said Betsy, stretching out the word. "I guess I'm stuck calling Detective Dreamboat and getting him all riled as usual."

"Yep." Page nodded, anticipating Steve's reaction. She was going to best him again by solving this case. Applying a fresh application of mascara and lipstick, Page went to find Betsy.

"Look out the window. Everything is going our way. Dreamboat's off duty now. I see him outside washing his vehicle. That means he can get to the inn super speedy, although I'm not sure where he'll put his pistola. He's wearing swim trunks." Betsy grabbed her fan. "He sure knows how to develop a muscle."

"No time for gawking." Page stole a peek at Steve. Sighing, she forced her attention on what she had left to do. "Sing out when the cakes are ready to roll. I'll be in the den finalizing my plan of action."

CHAPTER 33

Page entered Three Fables, with Betsy tagging behind and carrying the two honey cakes. All seemed unusually subdued and quiet. "Hi, James. We're back bearing two special cakes. Is Alice about?"

Betsy placed both cakes on the reception counter and glanced around. "Where is everyone?"

James stared at the cakes before answering. "Alice is in the office. The other guests are scattered about doing their thing before departing." He eyed the cakes again. "Pardon me. I'll tap on the door and tell Alice you're here."

Page and Betsy exchanged knowing looks.

Betsy slipped outside to make the call. She returned, signaling Page with a nod.

Alice appeared. "Hello, ladies. Sorry for making you wait. James has been my lookout while I had to handle a minor problem in the office. I see two delectable looking cakes came along with you. Shall we go to the kitchen?"

"Good idea. We can prepare the cakes to serve." Page followed Alice.

"They're still warm from the oven," said Betsy, trailing behind.

Page closed the kitchen's double doors and turned to Alice. "I need a knife and napkins. Betsy will explain what's about to happen."

"Prepare yourself," warned Betsy. "What I'm going to share with you is almost as strange as having Althea and Julian in residence."

"I'm bracing myself for more of the unexplained. Whatever are you two about?" Alice handed Page a stack of napkins and a cake knife. "Please take extra care."

"She's protected. Don't worry." Betsy ate a crumb off the second cake's plate.

"Alice, tell me where the guests are right now?" Page waited.

"Let me call Chatty. She's been monitoring them for you." Alice pulled the phone from her pants pocket. "Chatty, could you come to the kitchen right away? Page and Betsy have arrived."

Page looked at Betsy. The concern over what was coming showed on her cousin's face.

A breathless Chatty rushed in the door. "I'm here. Ready for my next assignment."

"Where can I find the guests?" Page grabbed a tray and placed the cake, knife, and napkins on it.

"Let's see." Chatty held up her index finger. "Fiona is in the library making calls. Ruby and Chester are on the veranda playing backgammon and arguing, of course. And I just saw Grace walking toward the gazebo carrying a notebook."

Alice jumped in. "I have Mara polishing trays in the dining room. James, as you already know, is at the front desk. Rake is outside fertilizing the fruit trees." Alice touched her throat with a trembling hand. "And Chatty and I stand before you. That's everyone."

"Thank you both. Betsy will detail what's happening and what you need to do." Page lifted the tray. "Showtime."

Betsy moved closer to Page. "Remember, let the enchanted honey cake do the work. Don't you dare try—"

"I won't, Bets. Explain what's happening to the ladies and go greet you know who." Page headed toward the person whose hand caused Evelyn Potts's death. She felt the comforting presence around her as she walked. Her inkling gift and the magical honey cake's ability to have the person eating it speak the truth ensured the case would soon become a memory.

Taking a deep inhale, Page closed the distance. "Good afternoon, Grace. Isn't it a lovely day to visit the gardens?"

Grace glanced up from writing. "Yes. You're a friend of Alice's and the one who found Evelyn."

"Yes." Page stepped inside the gazebo. "I thought you might enjoy a slice of our enchanted honey cake. It's like nothing you've ever experienced. We brought two to serve today." Page placed the tray on the small table before Grace.

Leaning over to look at the cake, Grace spoke timidly. "It does look quite scrummy. How thoughtful of you to trouble yourself to bring me the first slice."

Page forced a smile to keep things pleasant. "It was no trouble. I wanted to visit the gardens anyway, and here you are. I left my cousin inside with the other cake." Page passed the slice. "Enjoy."

Grace took her first bite.

"The secret to this cake's enchanting ways is the special honey." Page watched as Grace devoured the slice.

"I've never tasted anything like this. I can't quite describe the flavor. Might I have another?" Grace held up her napkin.

"Of course." Page cut another piece. "Here you go. I always enjoy the mellow feeling that comes from eating the honey cake. Not the sugar rush you get from most desserts."

"Now that you mention it, I do feel rather relaxed. I haven't been myself these last days." Grace gazed toward the statue garden.

Page sat down next to her. "That's understandable. You've been through so much. Evelyn's death—"

"Evelyn's death should be celebrated. She was a wicked woman. She has always been wicked." Grace's voice edged louder.

Page had set the hook. She'd allow the cake's enchantment to unfold. Her eyes glanced around the hedge, and seeing no sign of Steve, she crafted her words to stall time. "You know, Grace, I've met my share of wicked people. It's hard when you work for someone like Evelyn and give your all each day to help them succeed."

Grace ate the last few crumbs. "I did give Evelyn my everything. You're right. And she never thanked me. Not once."

Page caught Steve's appearance behind the hedge. He gave her a familiar look. The lecture would come later. Page waited for his signal that everything was in place for her to proceed. "That must have made you feel quite angry." Page placed another slice of cake on Grace's napkin.

"Quite. You know I write fiction. Evelyn promised to have Fiona read my story while we were here."

"Only she lied and let you down again. I bet you felt used by Evelyn." Page was leading Grace to break emotionally with the cake's help.

"Used? You have no idea what I did for her." Grace's voice cracked with emotion. "I wrote her books and let her bask in the glory of fame and adoration. I did her bidding every single day. And I grew tired of it all. The whole charade. Evelyn made unkept promises to me."

"What? Are you saying Evelyn didn't write her novels?" Page pretended she didn't know. Grace fit the personality type of someone deprived of affection by others her whole life. "You're the gifted author who wrote the Potts bestsellers?"

"Just so. Evelyn might have devised a story idea, but

that was the extent of her contribution. And that dreadful Fiona wouldn't even give my manuscript a glance today. She's making a grand mistake by refusing to believe I'm Evelyn's ghost writer." Grace took a tiny bite.

Page softened her tone. "Grace, what made you give Evelyn so much of yourself and your talents? Did she pay you well, or was it something else?"

"Pay me well? Hardly a farthing some months did I get. Why? You want to know why I devoted myself to her?" Tears welled up in Grace's eyes. "Because she was my sister. My only family."

"Grace, I'm so sorry. It must have hurt terribly to have your sister treat you so—"

"Shabbily. Oh, it hurt, and my anger and resentment grew over these many years. I loathed her. My own sister." Grace snatched a napkin from the tray and wiped the tears.

The cake's powers were short-lived. Page knew she needed to wrap things quickly. "I can see how your anger might boil over during some discussion where Evelyn acted especially hateful. You'd suffered enough." Page carefully steered the conversation toward the eventful day. "Did something happen while you've been here?"

Grace studied Page. "You know it did." Her face took on the look of someone else. A sinister gleam found Grace's eyes.

"Would you like to tell me what happened? It might free you to let it out."

"Free me? I did that for myself the other day. I freed myself from having to spend another day in service to my evil sister." Grace released a sob. "She promised to have Fiona read my novel. I wanted my career as a writer. I'd waited long enough. But then Evelyn said unspeakable horrid things to me. She went too far." Grace rose.

"You were in the statue garden when your sister said those things. I'm sure you'd reached your absolute limit. What happened, Grace?"

"How do you know I was in the statue garden?" Grace's demeanor changed. Her defenses were returning. "How do you know?"

Page pointed. "Your shirt is missing a button. The same button I found clutched in your sister's hand where I found her lying in a pool of blood." Page saw Steve, Koch, and Andre move into sight.

"Maybe you didn't plan to kill her. Maybe your anger at that moment caused you to push the statue on her. After so many years of verbal abuse by Evelyn, you lost control of your emotions. Is that what happened, Grace?"

"You were there. Weren't you? You heard her say those dreadful things to me. You heard her fire me on the spot when I told her I would tell Fiona the truth. I wrote those books. I deserve the royalties. And now, I'm going to get it all once the truth comes out that I wrote them. Soon, I won't have to fret over money. Soon my books will be in every London bookshop." Grace looked at the cake with confusion and back to Page. "Don't you see? Everything worked out. I solved my problem. I even have a new job to add legitimacy to my work."

Page nodded, seeing the three detectives circling the gazebo.

Grace continued. "You understand. You won't tell anyone. It'll be our secret." She paused. Her face lit with happiness. "Besides, I'm leaving soon." Grace reached for her notebook.

Page rose, putting distance between them. "I'm truly sorry to hear how your life has unfolded and your choices brought you to this place. But your sister died from your hand. And you know that action has consequences that you must face. Because you trusted me to confess what you've done to, I will make a promise to you."

Steve approached the gazebo steps and placed handcuffs on a dazed Grace while Koch and Andre waited.

"What's the promise?" whispered the returning meek-sounding Grace.

"I promise to have your laptop delivered to you wherever you're going. Perhaps you'd like to keep writing stories, and this time they'll get published as Grace Culpepper."

"You'd do that for me? It won't become another unkept promise?" Grace pulled her arms away from Steve.

"It's a promise that I'll keep. You need to go with Detective Tanner." Page nodded to Steve as she watched Grace being escorted away. Another cake awaited delivery.

CHAPTER 34

Betsy caught up with Page as she walked across the inn's lawn. "Dreamboat let me hide behind the hedges. I heard every word. You're amazing, Page Wright."

"Your honey cake ain't bad either," said Page, trying to interject some lightness after the draining experience with Grace. "I need something to drink before I confront Mara and James."

"Since our trolley is still here, I left Alice and Chatty preparing a soothing chamomile tea and finger sandwiches for everyone. You've earned first dibs." Betsy draped her arm around Page.

"That's the kind of reviving I crave. Walk faster. The sooner we get this next mystery solved with James and Mara, the sooner we return to living our Shell Isle dream." Page held the door for Betsy to pass into the kitchen.

Chatty and Alice came scurrying toward Page.

"Are you okay?" asked Alice.

"I'm fine." Page went to the sink and rinsed her hands.

"I'm so sorry I involved you both in all of this. Betsy filled us in on the horrid details. I never suspected Grace as being capable of murdering her boss."

Chatty handed Page a cup of steaming tea.

"Thanks. Actually, Evelyn was her sister, which makes it even worse." Page sipped the tea.

"My heavens. Evelyn was Grace's sister." Chatty made a tsk sound.

Betsy took a sandwich from the trolley. "It's all

dreadful, and we're not done." She tilted her head toward the waiting honey cake.

Page set her cup on the counter. "She's right. It's time to serve Mara and James and find out what's behind their showing up at Three Fables to snoop." Page glanced at Alice. "Can you invite them to tea and cake on the veranda? I'm heading out there now."

"I still can't believe they're here to cause me more distress." Alice hurried away.

"Should one of us be present?" asked Chatty.

"Page flies solo, but we can listen. Break a leg, Sherlocka." Betsy handed Page the tray.

"Okay, act two starts now," said Page.

Betsy motioned. "Follow me, Chatty. We'll sneak around the side entrance."

Page waited on the veranda for James and Mara to join her. She hadn't devised a discovery plan. Instead, she would let the powers-that-be guide her. Waving to Rake as he set a soaking hose in the nearby flowerbed, Page wondered again if Althea and Julian liked his presence. They must, judging by his family's history of tending the grounds and the perpetual smile on the gardener's face. Or perhaps it had more to do with Three Fables' owner. The thought filled Page with gladness. And that glad face greeted Mara and James as they entered the veranda.

"Isn't it a beautiful afternoon? I'm looking forward to summer beach days here at Shell Isle. Please, won't you join me?" Page indicated the two empty chairs.

Taking their seats, Mara spoke first. "Alice said you wanted to speak to us."

Page nodded. "I also thought we might enjoy this enchanting honey cake my cousin baked. You must have a slice." Page didn't wait for a reply but moved the two plates in front of the brother and sister. "Enjoy."

"Aren't you having any?" asked James, taking his first bite. "Hey, this is good. You should try some."

"I confess needing to lose a few pounds, but maybe a small morsel wouldn't hurt." Page winked and cut a bite-sized piece. "Mara? Do you like it?"

Mara studied the cake on her fork. "The flavor is curious. I can't figure out what I'm tasting. She ate another bite and chewed thoughtfully. "The sweetness of the honey is present, but something else almost familiar...." Mara shrugged and forked another mouthful.

"Dang, if this cake isn't taking my headache away. May I have another?" James held up his empty plate to Page.

"Of course. Have as much as you like, both of you." Page slipped a second piece onto Mara's plate. She sensed the cake's secret gift was taking effect. "So, tell me. How do you like Shell Isle?"

"It's growing on me. I've discovered fishing, and I hope to get a surfboard soon. That would be super cool." James's eyes sparked. "Ya know. I could become one of the surfer dudes of Shell."

"My next-door neighbor surfs. He's amazing on his board. Maybe I could ask him to guide you in buying a board and offer some tips on surfing. Would you like that?" Page took the opportunity to build trust and friendship.

"Yeah, sure." James glanced at Mara. "You haven't answered. How do you like Shell?" He turned back to Page. "She met a guy the other night at the pier. He asked her out."

"Shut up, James. I didn't accept." Mara took a bite of the second piece. "I'm feeling a bit worn from working so hard at Three Fables. There's a lot that needs to be done running the inn. Anyway, I like what little I've seen of the town. I noticed many interesting people around, not to mention the two ghosts living with us." Mara's smile reflected a prettiness Page had missed before.

"I'm glad to know you like Shell. It's an eclectic town, as you will come to see if you stay." Page cast her hook with the next question and hoped the cake would hook two fish. "What brought you here?"

"Our grandfather," replied James. "He gave us a job to do."

"And it was a job we couldn't decline without serious consequences to our allowances." Mara sat back in her chair.

"That sounds troubling." Page hesitated, gauging their body language. "So, you decided to do the job?"

James held up his hand to his sister to let him speak. "We tried and failed to do one part of the assignment. Now, he's flying here tomorrow to take over."

"Yeah, and we don't know if he'll follow through with cutting off our allowance. It's not fair." Mara exhaled loudly.

Page kept her grin inside, seeing their immaturity, which was probably fostered by a too-generous grandfather. "James, what is there for your grandfather to take over? I'm afraid I don't understand. Maybe I can help if you explain."

Mara shook her head at her brother. "We can't say more." Mara started to rise.

Page knew she'd have to shift from interrogator to intimidator if she was going to succeed in finding out what these two young people were doing at Three Fables. "Mara, I need you to stay seated. The three of us need to shoot straight with each other."

"What do you mean? We don't know you," answered Mara with an insolent tone.

"No, you don't. And I don't know you. That's what we're about to resolve." Page fixed her no-nonsense gaze on Mara until she sat down.

"Thank you." Page leaned forward. "I'll go first. I know you were planning to snoop in Alice's office. I'd like to find out why you're interested in the inn's financials, which are none of your business. Looking at her private accounts can and will land you in hot water. The detectives outside won't mind talking to you if I give them the nod." Page let her words penetrate the two shocked faces staring back at her.

"We haven't done anything wrong," said James.

Page held her anger inside. "But you have done wrong. Dishonesty is wrong. Pretending to be someone needing a job is wrong. Alice is a kind and forgiving person. Whatever you're up to, she might forgive you if you tell the truth."

"We can't discuss why our grandfather sent us here. Please." Mara teared up.

"Listen to me. I don't care about your grandfather. I care about my friend trying to make a go of this inn. She doesn't need two twenty-somethings showing up and causing her more worry." Page employed Steve's tactic and smacked the table.

Mara jumped in reaction.

"Tell me the truth now, or I promise I'll call Detective Tanner here to get the answers. You choose—him or me. And by the way, he can charge you with something. I can't and won't." Page could only hope that eating the honey cake would cause them to spill the truth.

"Let me tell her." James sat up straighter in his chair.

With a resigned face, Mara folded her arms. "Okay."

"Our grandfather wants to know what kind of person Alice is and her financial situation. He sent us to Shell Isle when he saw she posted two help-wanted ads with instructions that we nail the jobs. We've been reporting back to him everything we could find out about Alice."

"Everything," repeated Mara. "But we haven't told

him about the ghosts. We like Alice, and we don't want to cause her harm."

"Yeah, Mara's telling you the truth. We do like her a lot. We even like her ghosts and how they messed with those authors. Those people were so extra."

"Extra?" Page's amusement surfaced.

"You know, over the top. That's the group we've dealt with since we got the jobs." Mara rolled her eyes. "We'll be glad when they leave today."

"I think we can all agree on that. But you're not telling me why your grandfather is interested in Alice's affairs. Where does he live?"

"He's in New England. You see, our grandfather has tremendous wealth. He's used to people trying to take advantage of him and get to his money all the time." James snuck another piece of cake over to his plate.

"Okay. The guy is rich. I'm still wondering why he's got you tracking Alice. That's the one answer I need, and we're likely done here." Page stood. "Listen. I'm sympathetic to the fact that I'm asking you to break a confidence. But remember what I said? It's me or the detective." Page moved toward the inn's door. "Last chance."

James pushed the plate to the side. "Okay. I'll tell you." He paused, looking at his sister. "Alice is our grandfather's lost daughter. He only recently found out about her existence. We were sent here to get to know Alice and find out things before he decides whether to contact her."

"Yeah, she's our Aunt Alice," said Mara. "And we care about her. We think she's wonderful. All we have is a grandfather, and having an aunt like Alice is super great."

The happy surprise of hearing Alice had family washed over Page. "This is one amazing story if it's true."

"It's one hundred percent true," said James.

Page nodded, accepting. "Okay. I believe you. I'm relieved you both care about Alice and mean her no harm. I think we're done here." Page shook both their hands. "Thank you. I hope everything works out. I really do."

"It will. Grandfather will adore Alice. I know it," said Mara.

James nodded. "We'll see to it. We're sorry to have caused so much worry."

Alice came rushing out after hearing their admission, tears streaming down her cheeks. She grabbed James and Mara and pulled them into a hug.

Page slipped away and found Betsy blubbering behind the door, and Chatty holding a box of tissues.

"It's all so wonderful for Alice. You wait. When this grandfather gets a load of Three Fables' potential, he'll open his checkbook." Betsy grabbed a fresh tissue.

Chatty's eyes danced. "If he doesn't, I will. I've decided to rent her cottage on the back of the property and make Shell Isle my new home."

"How wonderful!" Page turned to Betsy. "Finally, the inklings deliver us a happy ending."

A strong breeze whisked white rose petals inside the room. They fluttered down, landing in the women's hair.

"Sorry, Althea and Julian. Thank you, too," said Page.

Steve appeared. "Ladies, please excuse us." He steered Page toward the inn's parking area.

A breathless Page stopped walking and planted her feet. "Where are we going, Detective Tanner?"

Steve pulled Page closer. His eyes twinkled. "If you recall, you owe me a cuddle, and I owe you another lecture on taking over my case and risking harm to yourself. I've got Carpe Diem waiting for us. Are you my first mate?"

Page stood on tiptoe and kissed her dreamboat. "I

believe I can get on board with that plan. Let's seize what's left of this day."

ABOUT THE AUTHOR

As an author, Tonya's moved by the effect humor and narratives have on readers. That observation illuminates why her stories often convey messages inviting personal exploration. She is enthusiastic about crafting stories with beguiling characters, adding dashes of snappy humor and engaging dialogue that leaves her fingerprint on each page.

When Tonya relocated to the mountains, she found fresh writing ideas waiting. From her favorite porch chair gazing at a tranquil lake, the nudge to scribe her first novel came calling. From her beach chair, she got the idea for a cozy series, Shell Isle Mysteries. Tonya confesses new respect for a chair's ability to motivate her to write. She chases her writing joy from the mountains to the seashore.

The Shell Isle Mystery Series introduces four novels: *Baubles to Die For, Red, White, and Boom, Murder by Numbers,* and *Teatime Trouble.* The characters of Page and Betsy keep chattering to Tonya, so expect future stories in this collection.

Tonya's other books include *Old Mountain Cassie: The*

Three Lessons, A Secret Gift, and *Welcome to Charm.*

    Her book *Venetian Rhapsody* represents an exciting collaboration with award-winning composer David Bazo. Words and music present an unforgettable immersive experience in a book and a companion soundtrack album. Find the album at: David Bazo – Sitio Oficial | Autor, Intérprete & Productor.

    Tonya Penrose's fiction and nonfiction stories are published in numerous anthologies, e-magazines, local press, and literary magazines. She's a member of Poets and Writers. Tonya Penrose is her fiction pen name.

Visit:
Website: http://www.tonyawrites.com
X: @TonyaWrites
Instagram: @TonyaPenroseWrites
Threads.net @TonyaPenroseWrites

BETSY'S RECIPES

Sure Fire Tacos
1-pound ground sirloin
1 onion diced
1 package of spicy taco mix
1 ghost pepper chopped
1-2 chopped tomatoes
1 bunch of arugula
1 16 oz. package of shredded Mexican cheese
1 jar of extra spicey salsa
Corn taco shells warmed

Sauté ground beef in a cast-iron skillet. Add the onion, garlic, and taco seasoning mix and water. Stir.
Choose a lovely ceramic platter and arrange the fixins on it.
Present with a smile and a loud "Ta-dah."
Serves 4.

NOTE: Page insisted I tell you to omit the ghost pepper. Ignore her. I chose the special pepper to honor Althea and Julian. I want them to like me.

Betsy's Fiesta Rice
1 C. Basmati rice
1 ¾ C water
½ C white cooking wine
1 can fire-roasted tomatoes
1 chicken bouillon cube
1 t. salt
2 t. cayenne pepper (optional)

1 onion chopped
1 bell pepper chopped
1-2 T chili powder
2 T parsley
1-2 T organic butter or olive oil

Bring water to a boil. Add all the ingredients. Give a good stir. Cover and simmer for 23 minutes or until done. Serve in a bright-colored bowl. Bring to the table with a proud "Olé" Serves 4-6.

Betsy's Sensational Salad

2-3 heads of radicchio
1 head of endive
1 ripe mango
½ cup pistachio nuts
¼ cup Spanish olives (Page said to tell you to omit.)

Rinse lettuce and place in a salad bowl. Chop the mango into small pieces. Add to lettuce. Drizzle the dressing and toss. Sprinkle nuts on top.

Dressing:
¼ cup white vinegar
2 t. Dijon mustard
2 t. orange marmalade
¼ cup olive oil
Salt and pepper to taste
Combine all the ingredients, adding the oil last.
Get ready for compliments.

Spicer Cookie
3 cups all-purpose flour
¾ cup organic butter softened
¾ cup brown sugar
1 t baking soda
1/3 cup dark molasses (Choose a quality brand and not blackstrap.)
1 egg from a happy hen
1 t pure vanilla extract
1 t rum extract. (Trust me here.)
¼ t kosher salt
¼ t cloves
1-2 t ginger
1 t cinnamon
1 t cayenne pepper (That makes them Spicer Cookies. Page insists I tell you to omit this.)
White sugar for rolling the cookies.

Note: Let the egg and butter be at room temperature.
Combine all the dry ingredients in a mixing bowl. In another bowl and using a mixer, combine butter and brown sugar beating at a medium speed until fluffy. Fold in the other liquid ingredients mixing as you go. Next, slowly, and I do mean slowly, add the dry ingredients to the mixing bowl, beating at the lowest speed. Be careful you don't overmix.

Now, cover the bowl with plastic wrap and place it in the fridge for a few hours. Go do something fun.
Preheat the oven to 350 degrees.

Roll the dough into small balls no more than an inch, roll in the sugar, and lay them on a cookie sheet lined with parchment paper. Sometimes I spray the paper with cooking spray.

Bake for 12 minutes or until the cookie edge browns but the center is soft. You'll know. Let them cool. Serves 6-8…maybe. *I like to serve a dish of coffee ice cream with the cookies. It helps cool the throat from the Spicers.*

Slam Bam Ham Hash
1-2 cups chunked honey-baked ham
1 cup cooked Yukon gold potatoes
1 sweet onion coarsely chopped
¼ t garlic powder
3 t red pepper flakes. (Again, Page says nay.)
Fresh ground pepper
Dash of kosher salt
1 egg
1/3 cup of plain fine breadcrumbs
4 T organic unsalted butter

Mince everything except the crumbs in a food processor. Shape into six or eight cakes. Dip them into the breadcrumbs. You can chill them for a bit if you want. Fry the cakes in a coated skillet until brown and smelling delish.

Tip: I mix a cup of plain full-fat organic Greek yogurt with fresh dill and serve it as a side. Page and the guys appreciate the cooling effect.

Dippity Dagger
2 cups organic sour cream
2 T dried Dagger pepper flakes
1/3 cup roasted eggplant chopped into small pieces

1 yellow pepper roasted and chopped into small pieces
Hefty splashes of Worcestershire sauce
1 t fresh chives
½ t cumin

Combine all the ingredients in a fancy bowl. Chill for an hour
or so. Serve with blue corn tortilla chips.
Disclaimer: Page felt the Dagger for three days. Consider a
healthy dash of cayenne as a substitute for weak constitutions.

Sassy Sausage Surprise
1 pound of high-quality hot ground breakfast sausage
1 T red pepper flakes
1 cup yellow grits
1 cup grilled fresh pineapple sprinkled with black pepper
1 jalapeño pepper for each plate
½ stick of organic salted butter

Add the extra flakes to the sausage mixture and shape them
into patties. Fry the sausage in a skillet.
Make the grits according to directions but be prepared to keep
adding water while they cook. Stir in a half stick of organic
butter at the end and heat through.

Serve the grits in a colorful individual ceramic bowl. Top with
sausage patties. Dress the side of the bowl with pineapple and
sliced jalapeños.
*Note: I'm not divulging my secret pepper that Page says is a gift for
you not to know.*

Bets Best Brownies
1 can of low-sodium black beans
2 T almond butter
1/3 cup carob powder
10-12 Medjool dates
1 t pure vanilla extract
½ t cinnamon
1 T ground chia seeds
1-2 t cayenne pepper (optional says you know who.)
1/3 cup chopped pecans
1/3 cup sweetened carob chips (optional)

Combine the beans, extract, dates, and almond butter in a high-powered blender or a food processor. Mix until well blended. Add the carob powder, cinnamon, cayenne, and seeds. Blend again until combined.

Spray an 8x8 pan with baking spray. Spread the mixture evenly into pan.
Preheat oven to 200 degrees. Bake for 30 minutes or till set.
Cut into squares. Serve warm. Top with a few fresh berries.

Betsy's Peppercorn Cornbread
1 cup yellow cornmeal
1 cup all-purpose flour
1 T baking powder
¼ cup sugar
1 T mixed crushed peppercorns
2 eggs at room temperature, beaten a bit
¾-1 cup organic heavy whipping cream
¼ cup canola or corn oil
1/3 cup wildflower honey or your honey choice

Combine the dry ingredients in a bowl and blend well. Make a crater in the center of the mix. Add the wet ingredients and stir. Pour batter into an oiled 9x9 baking pan.

Bake in a 400-degree oven for 25 minutes or until your toothpick comes out clean.
Cut into squares and serve with organic butter pats that are softened.
Compliments come after the first bite.

Betsy's Enchanted Honey Cake
Betsy agreed to share the basic honey cake recipe but confessed that what makes her cake enchanted is the special kind of honey she uses. That is her secret ingredient, and she won't divulge the source of this amazing nectar. It seems our Betsy can keep her yap shut when it comes to creating magic for garnering a confession and closing a murder case.

3 2/3 cups all-purpose flour
1 t baking soda
½ t Celtic salt
1 T baking powder
1 cup quality vegetable oil
1 cup of the honey bee's magical nectar
1 ½ cups organic sugar
½ cup dark brown sugar
3 large organic eggs from happy hens
½ cup orange juice
2-3 T Kentucky Bourbon (*optional*)
¾ t vanilla extract (*Don't dare use imitation extract.*)
1 cup coffee freshly brewed (*I prefer a dark French roast.*)

Set the oven to 345 degrees. (*I find most ovens run hot.*)
Spray a 9x13 pan liberally with butter-flavored baking spray.
(*Page likes a Bundt pan, but I don't. Too finicky to get my cake out.*)

Mix the flour, salt, soda, and powder in a rainbow-colored
ceramic bowl (No eyebrow-raising. You are making magic
here.) In a separate bowl, combine the oil, ¾ cup of the honey
nectar, sugars, eggs, coffee, vanilla, and juice. Mix. Add the
wet mixture to the dry until everyone looks married nicely.
Pour the magic into the pan. Drizzle in a lovely pattern the
remaining nectar atop the batter. Bake until done. I start
testing with a toothpick after 30 minutes.

Let the enchanted honey cake cool before removing it from
the pan.

*I drizzle more nectar on top, but that's just me helping Page solve
our latest caper.*